BRICK SHAKESPEARE

BRICK SHAKESPEARE

THE TRAGEDIES—HAMLET, MACBETH, ROMEO AND JULIET, AND JULIUS CAESAR

AS TOLD AND ILLUSTRATED BY
JOHN McCANN, MONICA SWEENEY,
AND BECKY THOMAS

Skyhorse Publishing

Editor's Note: The text that was used in this book is from http://shakespeare.mit.edu. *Hamlet* and *Macbeth* were edited against *Four Tragedies*, edited by David Bevington and David Scott Kastan, published by Bantam Dell as a Bantam Classic edition. *Julius Caesar* was also edited against a Bantam Classic edition of *Julius Caesar*, edited by David Bevington and David Scott Kastan.

Skyhorse Publishing books may be purchased in bulk at special discounts for sales promotion, corporate gifts, fundraising, or educational purposes. Special editions can also be created to specifications. For details, contact the Special Sales Department, Skyhorse Publishing, 307 West 36th Street, 11th Floor, New York, NY 10018 or info@skyhorsepublishing.com.

www.skyhorsepublishing.com

10 9 8 7 6 5 4 3 2 1

Library of Congress Cataloging-in-Publication Data is available on file.

ISBN: 978-62636-303-8

ACKNOWLEDGMENTS

We would like to extend our biggest thank-yous to Kelsie Besaw, our wonderful editor; to Bill Wolfsthal and Tony Lyons, who gave us this tremendous opportunity; and to everyone at Skyhorse who worked tirelessly to bring this book to market. To Holly Schmidt and Allan Penn, who have continuously mentored us and have been confident that we can handle any project. And to our loving families, who probably stepped on a lot of LEGO bricks over the years.

Introduction

William Shakespeare is the world's most known and loved playwright. Almost four hundred years after his life and death, his plays are still widely read and viewed by theater goers, avid readers, students, and film buffs alike. While the world these plays were written for has substantially changed, the characters, their stories, and their most famous lines continue to influence and inspire contemporary arts and culture.

Shakespeare's works, being theatrical, lend themselves well to visual representation. With a little imagination and *a lot* of LEGO Bricks, we have taken these classic stories, previously relegated to the page, screen, and stage, and made them into something new!

Due to the length of Shakespeare's works, each play is modestly abridged. We carefully combed through every line and handpicked the scenes that would be the most interesting in brick form and would maintain the integrity of Shakespeare's original dramatic arc. This fun spin on Shakespeare's four best-known tragedies presents the included scenes just as he wrote them, along with extra narrative descriptions to fill you in on what we have left out.

Whether you are new to Shakespeare or an old friend, we now present The Bard in brick.

Contents

Hamlet

There has never been an author so prolific as William Shakespeare and never a work so ubiquitous as Hamlet. The play shadows the grief and vengeance of the Prince of Denmark, whose Uncle Claudius has murdered his father, usurped the throne, and taken the former king's widow as his new queen. Likely first performed in or around 1600 and published into the First Quarto in 1603, Hamlet is one of the most adapted works of all time and continues to permeate modern storytelling through its use of powerful plot devices and transcendent characterization.

As a departure from traditional dramatic works its senior, *Hamlet* uses soliloquies as existential portals to the characters' thoughts and motives, rather than through dramatic action. Particularly true for the play's namesake, this spotlight on characterization gives the story infinite layering, from how it parallels Hamlet's true madness against his feigned madness to how it uses metafictional ploys through *The Mousetrap* to draw out Claudius's guilt. Hamlet is both a tortured victim of his father's murder as well as a reluctant instrument of revenge. He spends much of the play toiling over whether to take action against his fratricidal uncle or himself, which causes a slow undoing of his own tether to sanity.

While *Hamlet* caused a shift in dramatic perspective through its introspective characters, the Elizabethan audience was simultaneously coping with its own dramatic shift within the powers of the Church. Not unlike other Shakespearean plays, *Hamlet* intertwines both Catholic doctrine and Protestant, specifically when focusing on the Ghost of King Hamlet and the death of Ophelia. Although Denmark and Shakespeare's audience were historically Protestant, the subtle lacing of Catholic allusions suggests the remaining ties to the Catholic Church, if not in outward affiliation, then in lingering culture. Resultantly, Shakespeare's audience would have empathized with Hamlet's internal struggles with depression and guilt, establishing the play as a dark look into their own philosophical ambivalence.

Hamlet tracks the gloom of a forlorn Prince as he looks death in the face as both a victim and a vigilante. Hamlet's conflicts bridge worldly misfortune and existential woe through deep character development, clever plot devices, and the subtle weaving of religious significance. Just as it was when it first hit the stage, *Hamlet* remains a powerful play in its raw humanity, marking it as infinitely adaptable to modern theater, literature, and media.

Dramatis Personae

GHOST of King Hamlet, the former King of Denmark

CLAUDIUS, King of Denmark, the former King's brother

GERTRUDE, Queen of Denmark, widow of the former King and now wife of Claudius

HAMLET, Prince of Denmark, son of the late King and of Queen Gertrude

HORATIO, Hamlet's friend and fellow student

POLONIUS, councillor to the King

LAERTES, Polonius's son

OPHELIA, Polonius's daughter

FORTINBRAS, Prince of Norway

MARCELLUS, a soldier on watch

OSRIC, a member of the Danish Court

PROLOGUE

PLAYER KING

PLAYER QUEEN

LUCIANUS

PRIEST

FIRST AMBASSADOR from England

Not Pictured

REYNALDO, Polonius's servant
VOLTIMAND
CORNELIUS
ROSENCRANTZ
GUILDENSTERN
A GENTLEMAN
A LORD
BERNARDO
FRANCISCO
CAPTAIN in Fortinbras's army
Two MESSENGERS
FIRST SAILOR
Two CLOWNS, a gravedigger and his companion

Lords, Soldiers, Attendants, Guards, other Players, Followers of Laertes, other Sailor
another Ambassador or Ambassadors from England

ACT I. Scene II (64–159).

As the play opens, a shivering night watchman of the castle is relieved of his duties, while three others come on to the scene. Hamlet's closest friend, Horatio, and the guards Marcellus and Barnardo, huddle together in anticipation of a recent phenomenon—the late night haunting of the newly deceased King Hamlet. Just as they begin to murmur of the dead king—as the clock strikes one and the North Star has aligned just so in the sky—the ghost of King Hamlet appears. Dressed in full armor, rather than the clothing in which he died, the ghost appears to the men as a dreadful omen of things to come. They speculate that the ghost's armor, as well as a recent spike in Danish military activity, could only mean one thing—that the son of the conquered King Fortinbras of Norway is sure to come knocking at Denmark's door. Horatio and the guardsmen watch the ghost and, when he abruptly leaves, decide that they should soon tell Hamlet, King Hamlet's son, of this late-night anomaly.

KING CLAUDIUS
But now, my cousin Hamlet, and my son—

HAMLET
A little more than kin, and less than kind.

KING CLAUDIUS
How is it that the clouds still hang on you?
HAMLET
Not so, my lord. I am too much in the sun.

QUEEN GERTRUDE
Good Hamlet, cast thy nighted color off,
And let thine eye look like a friend on Denmark.
Do not for ever with thy vailèd lids
Seek for thy noble father in the dust.
Thou know'st 'tis common, all that lives must die,
Passing through nature to eternity.
HAMLET
Ay, madam, it is common.
QUEEN GERTRUDE
If it be,
Why seems it so particular with thee?

HAMLET
Seems, madam? Nay, it is. I know not "seems."
'Tis not alone my inky cloak, good mother,
Nor customary suits of solemn black,
Nor windy suspiration of forced breath,
No, nor the fruitful river in the eye,
Nor the dejected havior of the visage,
Together with all forms, moods, shapes of grief,
That can denote me truly. These indeed seem,
For they are actions that a man might play.
But I have that within which passes show;
These but the trappings and the suits of woe.

KING CLAUDIUS
'Tis sweet and commendable in your nature, Hamlet,
To give these mourning duties to your father.
But you must know your father lost a father,
That father lost, lost his, and the survivor bound
In filial obligation for some term
To do obsequious sorrow. But to persever
In obstinate condolement is a course
Of impious stubbornness. 'Tis unmanly grief.
It shows a will most incorrect to heaven,
A heart unfortified, a mind impatient,
An understanding simple and unschooled.

KING CLAUDIUS (cont.)
For what we know must be and is as common
As any the most vulgar thing to sense,
Why should we in our peevish opposition
Take it to heart? Fie, 'tis a fault to heaven,
A fault against the dead, a fault to nature,
To reason most absurd, whose common theme
Is death of fathers, and who still hath cried,
From the first corpse till he that died today,
"This must be so." We pray you, throw to earth
This unprevailing woe and think of us
As of a father; for let the world take note,
You are the most immediate to our throne,
And with no less nobility of love
Than that which dearest father bears his son

KING CLAUDIUS (cont.)
Do I impart toward you. For your intent
In going back to school in Wittenberg,
It is most retrograde to our desire,
And we beseech you bend you to remain
Here in the cheer and comfort of our eye,
Our chiefest courtier, cousin, and our son.

QUEEN GERTRUDE
Let not thy mother lose her prayers, Hamlet.
I pray thee, stay with us, go not to Wittenberg.
HAMLET
I shall in all my best obey you, madam.

KING CLAUDIUS
Why, 'tis a loving and a fair reply.
Be as ourself in Denmark. Madam, come.
This gentle and unforced accord of Hamlet
Sits smiling to my heart, in grace whereof
No jocund health that Denmark drinks today
But the great cannon to the clouds shall tell,
And the King's rouse the heavens shall bruit again,
Respeaking earthly thunder. Come away.

HAMLET
O, that this too too solid flesh would melt,
Thaw, and resolve itself into a dew!
Or that the Everlasting had not fixed
His canon 'gainst self-slaughter!

HAMLET (cont.)
O God! God!
How weary, stale, flat and unprofitable
Seem to me all the uses of this world!
Fie on't, ah fie! 'Tis an unweeded garden
That grows to seed. Things rank and gross in nature
Possess it merely. That it should come to this!
But two months dead—nay, not so much, not two.
So excellent a king, that was to this
Hyperion to a satyr, so loving to my mother
That he might not beteem the winds of heaven
Visit her face too roughly. Heaven and earth,
Must I remember? Why, she would hang on him
As if increase of appetite had grown
By what it fed on, and yet within a month—

ACT I. Scene IV (39–91).

As the sorrowful Hamlet toils over the loss of his father and his mother's unseemly new marriage, Horatio, Marcellus, and Barnardo happen upon him. Careful not to cause too much of a stir, Horatio explains the irksome sightings of King Hamlet's ghost. Hamlet decides he should join them that evening to see the ghost for himself.

Meanwhile, Laertes is preparing to leave Elsinore and warns his sister, Ophelia, of the difficulties of courting royalty. While Hamlet may be fond of her now, Laertes insists that his affections will stray for larger responsibilities, and that she should be diligent in not getting into any questionable circumstances that could tarnish her good name. Their father, Polonius, comes in and gives Laertes a long-winded farewell, which sprouts the famous line, "This above all: to thine own self be true" (I.iii.78). While Polonius is known for being a bit of a rambling, self-important fool, he occasionally stumbles onto little gems of wisdom. He continues in the same vein as Laertes and tells Ophelia not to get too involved with Hamlet and to be wary of his advances.

HAMLET
Angels and ministers of grace defend us!
Be thou a spirit of health or goblin damned,
Bring with thee airs from heaven or blasts from hell,
Be thy intents wicked or charitable,
Thou com'st in such a questionable shape
That I will speak to thee. I'll call thee Hamlet,
King, father, royal Dane.

HAMLET (cont.)
O, answer me!
Let me not burst in ignorance, but tell
Why thy canonized bones, hearsèd in death,
Have burst their cerements; why the sepulchre
Wherein we saw thee quietly inurned
Hath oped his ponderous and marble jaws
To cast thee up again. What may this mean,
That thou, dead corpse, again in complete steel,
Revisits thus the glimpses of the moon,
Making night hideous, and we fools of nature
So horridly to shake our disposition
With thoughts beyond the reaches of our souls?
Say, why is this? Wherefore? What should we do?

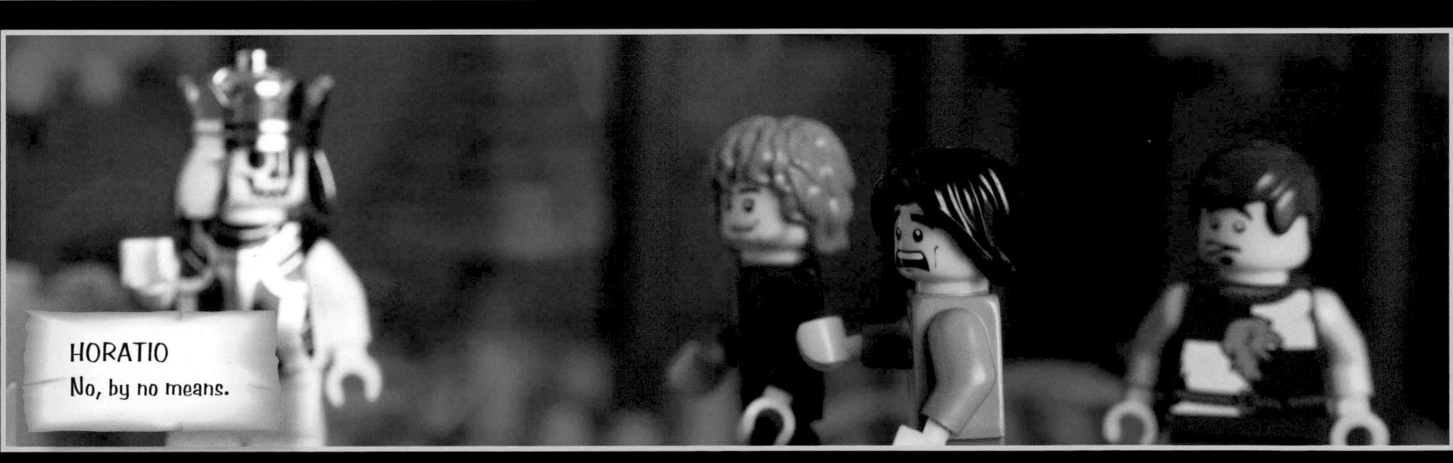

HAMLET
It will not speak. Then I will follow it.
HORATIO
Do not, my lord!

HAMLET
Why, what should be the fear?
I do not set my life in a pin's fee,
And for my soul, what can it do to that,
Being a thing immortal as itself?
It waves me forth again. I'll follow it.

HORATIO
What if it tempt you toward the flood, my lord,
Or to the dreadful summit of the cliff
That beetles o'er his base into the sea,
And there assume some other horrible form
Which might deprive your sovereignty of reason
And draw you into madness? Think of it.
The very place puts toys of desperation,
Without more motive, into every brain
That looks so many fathoms to the sea
And hears it roar beneath.

HAMLET
It wafts me still.—Go on, I'll follow thee.
MARCELLUS
You shall not go, my lord.
HAMLET
Hold off your hands!
HORATIO
Be ruled. You shall not go.

HAMLET
My fate cries out,
And makes each petty artery in this body
As hardy as the Nemean lion's nerve.
Still am I called. Unhand me, gentlemen.
By heaven, I'll make a ghost of him that lets me!
I say, away!—Go on, I'll follow thee.

HORATIO
He waxes desperate with imagination.
MARCELLUS
Let's follow. 'Tis not fit thus to obey him.

HORATIO
Have after. To what issue will this come?
MARCELLUS
Something is rotten in the state of Denmark.

HORATIO
Heaven will direct it.
MARCELLUS
Nay, let's follow him.

ACT I. Scene V (1–113).

HAMLET
Where wilt thou lead me? Speak. I'll go no further.

GHOST
Mark me.
HAMLET
I will.

GHOST
My hour is almost come,
When I to sulf'rous and tormenting flames
Must render up myself.

HAMLET
Alas, poor ghost!

GHOST
Pity me not, but lend thy serious hearing
To what I shall unfold.
HAMLET
Speak. I am bound to hear.

GHOST
So art thou to revenge, when thou
shalt hear.
HAMLET
What?

GHOST (cont.)
But that I am forbid
To tell the secrets of my prison house,
I could a tale unfold whose lightest word
Would harrow up thy soul, freeze thy young blood,
Make thy two eyes like stars start from their spheres,
Thy knotted and combinèd locks to part,
And each particular hair to stand on end
Like quills upon the fretful porpentine.
But this eternal blazon must not be
To ears of flesh and blood. List, list, O, list!
If thou didst ever thy dear father love—

HAMLET
O God!
GHOST
Revenge his foul and most unnatural
murder.
HAMLET
Murder?

GHOST
Murder most foul, as in the best it is,
But this most foul, strange, and unnatural.
HAMLET
Haste me to know't, that I, with wings as swift
As meditation or the thoughts of love,
May sweep to my revenge.

GHOST
I find thee apt;
And duller shouldst thou be than the fat weed
That roots itself in ease on Lethe wharf,
Wouldst thou not stir in this. Now, Hamlet, hear.
'Tis given out that, sleeping in my orchard,
A serpent stung me. So the whole ear of Denmark
Is by a forgèd process of my death
Rankly abused. But know, thou noble youth,
The serpent that did sting thy father's life
Now wears his crown.

HAMLET
O, my prophetic soul! My uncle!
GHOST
Ay, that incestuous, that adulterate beast,
With witchcraft of his wit, with traitorous gifts—
O, wicked wit and gifts, that have the power
So to seduce!—won to his shameful lust
The will of my most seeming-virtuous queen.
O, Hamlet, what a falling off was there!
From me, whose love was of that dignity
That it went hand in hand even with the vow
I made to her in marriage, and to decline
Upon a wretch whose natural gifts were poor
To those of mine!
But virtue, as it never will be moved,
Though lewdness court it in a shape of heaven,
So lust, though to a radiant angel linked,
Will sate itself in a celestial bed,
And prey on garbage.

GHOST (cont.)
But soft, methinks I scent the morning air.
Brief let me be. Sleeping within my orchard,
My custom always of the afternoon,
Upon my secure hour thy uncle stole,
With juice of cursèd hebona in a vial,
And in the porches of my ears did pour
The leperous distilment, whose effect
Holds such an enmity with blood of man

GHOST (cont.)
Thus was I, sleeping, by a brother's hand
Of life, of crown, of queen at once dispatched,
Cut off even in the blossoms of my sin,
Unhouseled, disappointed, unaneled,
No reck'ning made, but sent to my account
With all my imperfections on my head.

GHOST (cont.)
O, horrible! O, horrible, most horrible!
If thou hast nature in thee, bear it not.
Let not the royal bed of Denmark be
A couch for luxury and damnèd incest.
But, howsomever thou pursues this act,
Taint not thy mind, nor let thy soul contrive
Against thy mother aught. Leave her to heaven
And to those thorns that in her bosom lodge,
To prick and sting her. Fare thee well at once.

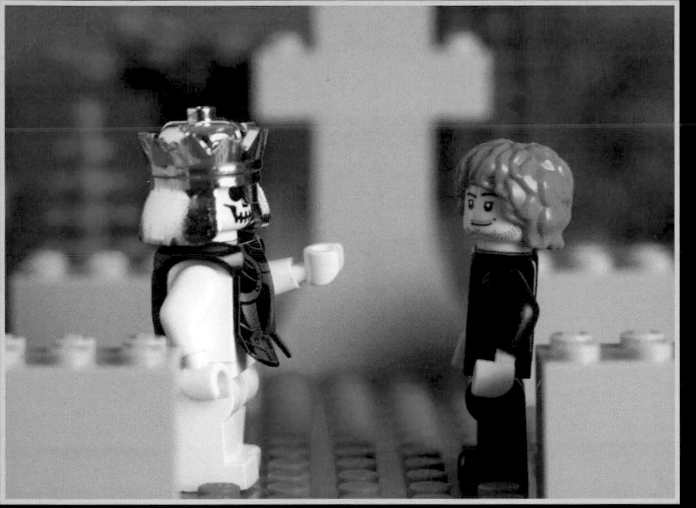

GHOST (cont.)
The glowworm shows the matin to be near,
And 'gins to pale his uneffectual fire.
Adieu, adieu, adieu! Remember me.

HAMLET
O all you host of heaven! O earth! What else?
And shall I couple hell? O, fie! Hold, hold, my heart,
And you, my sinews, grow not instant old,
But bear me stiffly up. Remember thee?
Ay, thou poor ghost, while memory holds a seat
In this distracted globe. Remember thee?

HAMLET (cont.)
Yea, from the table of my memory
I'll wipe away all trivial fond records,
All saws of books, all forms, all pressures past
That youth and observation copied there,
And thy commandment all alone shall live
Within the book and volume of my brain,
Unmixed with baser matter. Yes, by heaven!
O, most pernicious woman!
O, villain, villain, smiling, damnèd villain!
My tables—meet it is I set it down
That one may smile, and smile, and be a villain.
At least I'm sure it may be so in Denmark.

HAMLET (cont.)
So, uncle, there you are. Now to my word:
It is "Adieu, adieu! Remember me."
I have sworn't.

ACT II. Scene II (85–170).

Horatio and Marcellus catch up with Hamlet to make sure that the mysterious ghost has not led him to an untimely demise. Hamlet assures them that he is okay but insists that they keep the ghost and his message to themselves until Hamlet can figure out what to do with what he knows. Now that Hamlet has reason to suspect that Claudius is responsible for King Hamlet's death, he must decide how to best avenge his father without drawing suspicion.

Back at the castle, Polonius is concocting a scheme to catch his son, Laertes, in a scandal. He orders Reynaldo to go to Paris and discretely ask around to see if Laertes has been up to any unwholesome activities. Polonius is proving himself to be a meddler in his own right, foreshadowing some of his efforts to come in the royal household. Ophelia enters, frazzled by an interaction she has just had with Hamlet. She mistakes his white pallor and somewhat unhinged demeanor from seeing the ghost of his father as a lovesick reaction to her rejection. Polonius and Ophelia surmise that Hamlet is so forlorn about Ophelia that he is slowly going mad, and Polonius insists that they tell Claudius.

King Claudius calls Rosencrantz and Guildenstern to his court to ask them for a favor. He is disturbed by Hamlet's odd behavior and requests that the two men spy on Hamlet to find the root of the problem before it grows into a much larger one. Queen Gertrude agrees, though her concern is a motherly one, rather than that of a paranoid king. Ambassadors from Norway interrupt their discussion, bringing news that they have foiled their own Prince Fortinbras's war preparations against Denmark. His ailing uncle was able to convince Fortinbras to change his plans and has sent a letter to Claudius asking that the Norwegian soldiers be allowed to travel through his country to head to Poland instead. In the meantime, Polonius is standing in wait, excitedly preparing to tell Claudius and Gertrude his analysis of Hamlet's heartbreak and subsequent maddened behavior.

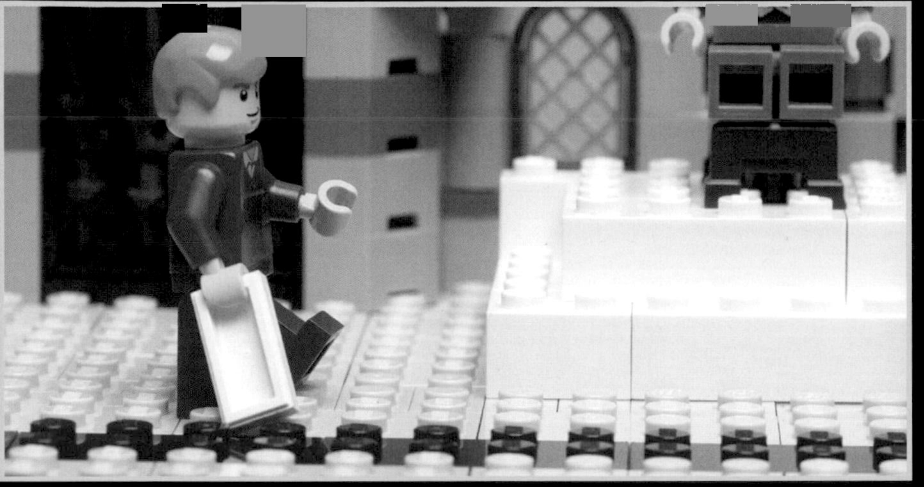
LORD POLONIUS
This business is well ended.
My liege, and madam, to expostulate
What majesty should be, what duty is,
Why day is day, night night, and time is time,
Were nothing but to waste night, day, and time.
Therefore, since brevity is the soul of wit,
And tediousness the limbs and outward flourishes,
I will be brief. Your noble son is mad.
Mad call I it, for, to define true madness,
What is't but to be nothing else but mad?
But let that go.

QUEEN GERTRUDE
More matter, with less art.

LORD POLONIUS
Madam, I swear I use no art at all.
That he is mad, 'tis true; 'tis true 'tis pity,
And pity 'tis 'tis true—a foolish figure,
But farewell it, for I will use no art.
Mad let us grant him, then, and now remains
That we find out the cause of this effect,
Or rather say, the cause of this defect,
For this effect defective comes by cause.
Thus it remains, and the remainder thus.
Perpend.
I have a daughter—have while she is mine—
Who, in her duty and obedience, mark,
Hath given me this. Now gather and surmise.

LORD POLONIUS (cont.)
"To the celestial and my soul's
idol, the most beautified Ophelia,"—
That's an ill phrase, a vile phrase; "beautified" is a
vile phrase. But you shall hear. Thus:
"In her excellent white bosom, these, etc."

QUEEN GERTRUDE
Came this from Hamlet to her?

LORD POLONIUS
Good madam, stay awhile, I will be faithful.
"Doubt thou the stars are fire,
Doubt that the sun doth move,
Doubt truth to be a liar,
But never doubt I love.
O dear Ophelia, I am ill at these numbers. I have not art to reckon my groans. But that I love thee best, O most best, believe it. Adieu.
Thine evermore most dear lady, whilst this machine is to him, Hamlet."
This in obedience hath my daughter shown me,
And, more above, hath his solicitings,
As they fell out by time, by means, and place,
All given to mine ear.

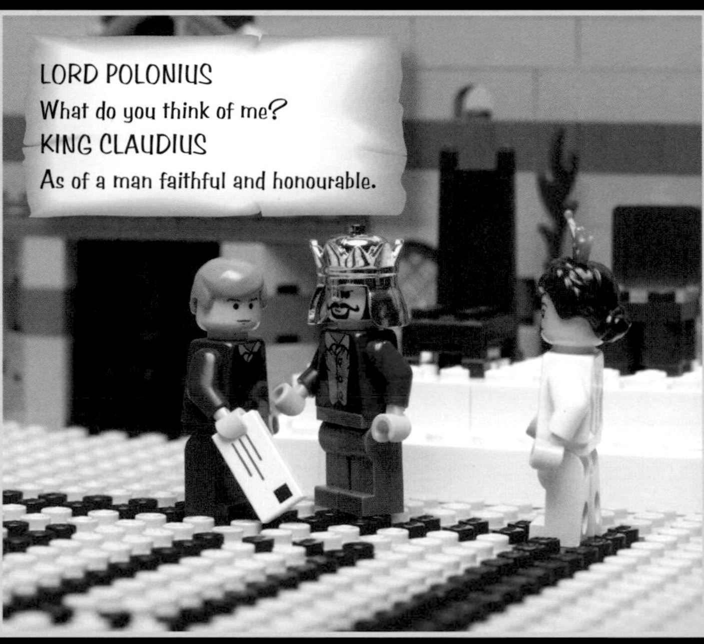

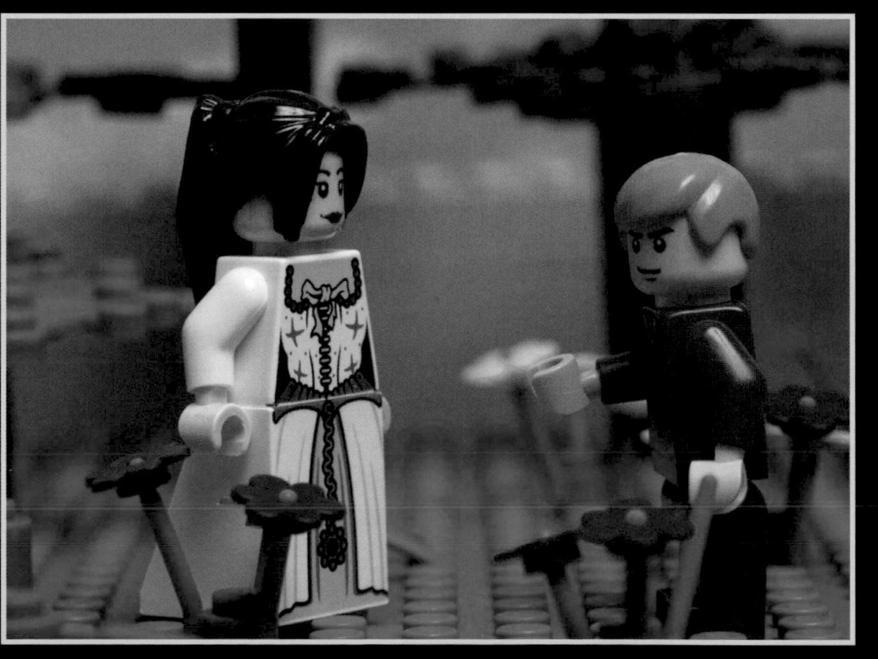

LORD POLONIUS
I would fain prove so. But what might you think,
When I had seen this hot love on the wing—
As I perceived it, I must tell you that,
Before my daughter told me—what might you,
Or my dear Majesty your queen here, think,
If I had played the desk or table book,
Or given my heart a winking, mute and dumb,
Or looked upon this love with idle sight?
What might you think? No, I went round to work,
And my young mistress thus I did bespeak:
"Lord Hamlet is a prince out of thy star;
This must not be." And then I prescripts gave her,
That she should lock herself from his resort,
Admit no messengers, receive no tokens.
Which done, she took the fruits of my advice;

LORD POLONIUS (cont.)
And he, repelled—a short tale to make—
Fell into a sadness, then into a fast,
Thence to a watch, thence into a weakness,
Thence to a lightness, and by this declension
Into the madness wherein now he raves,
And all we mourn for.

KING CLAUDIUS
Do you think 'tis this?
QUEEN GERTRUDE
It may be, very like.

LORD POLONIUS
Hath there been such a time—I'd fain know that—
That I have positively said "'Tis so,"
When it proved otherwise?
KING CLAUDIUS
Not that I know.

KING CLAUDIUS
How may we try it further?
LORD POLONIUS
You know, sometimes he walks four hours together
Here in the lobby.
QUEEN GERTRUDE
So he does indeed.

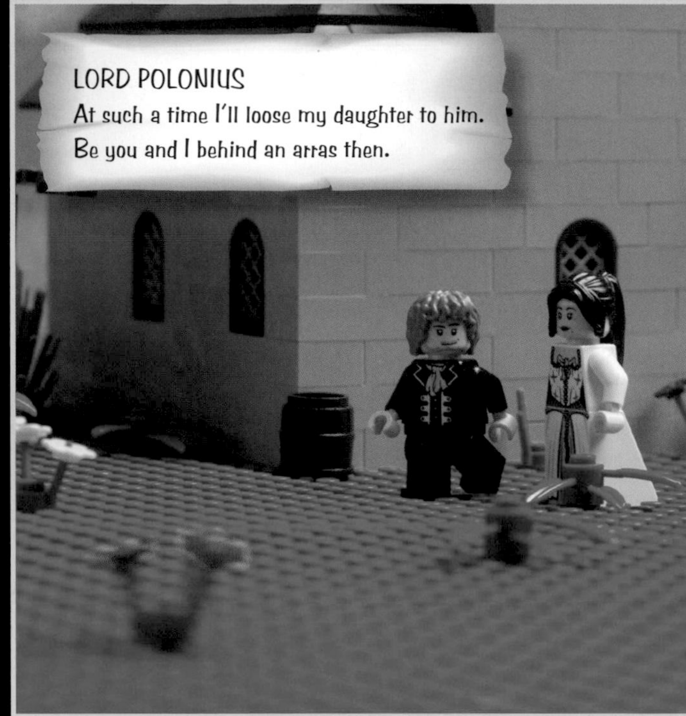
LORD POLONIUS
At such a time I'll loose my daughter to him.
Be you and I behind an arras then.

LORD POLONIUS (cont.)
Mark the encounter. If he love her not
And be not from his reason fall'n thereon,
Let me be no assistant for a state,
But keep a farm and carters.
KING CLAUDIUS
We will try it.

VENI, VIDI, VICI
QUEEN GERTRUDE
But, look, where sadly the poor wretch comes reading.

LORD POLONIUS
Away, I do beseech you both, away.
I'll board him presently. O, give me leave.

H

Polonius ventures out to find Hamlet and, coming upon him, tries to test his wits. Hamlet, rather slyly, plays into Polonius's suspicions and comes off as completely detached from reality. Polonius is now certain that Hamlet has gone mad because of his daughter, Ophelia, while Hamlet sees Polonius as being a bore and a waste of time.

Rosencrantz and Guildenstern, also under the direction of Claudius, come into the scene to talk with Hamlet. As his friends, Rosencrantz and Guildenstern do a poor job of hiding their motivations for coming to speak to Hamlet. Hamlet quickly unveils this but decides to use it to his advantage by gathering information. Polonius and various play actors come into the scene, as there will be a performance shown to the King, Queen, and their entourage the following day. Hamlet devises to have the actors perform *The Murder of Gonzago,* which will mirror the death of Hamlet's father and elicit Claudius's guilty conscience. Hamlet expects for the pivotal scene in the play to completely unseat Claudius's resolve that his crime has gone undiscovered.

Rosencrantz and Guildenstern report back to Claudius that they approached Hamlet, who had been civil but danced around their questions. Polonius mentions the play, and Claudius and Gertrude seem excited that Hamlet was so eager for them to join him for the performance. Claudius asks Gertrude to leave, indicating that he and Polonius plan to spy on Hamlet. They convince Ophelia to sit reading in the open in the hopes that Hamlet will pass by and they will be able to gain insight into his feelings for her when they interact. As Claudius and Polonius hide, Hamlet approaches the group, unaware of anyone's presence.

HAMLET
To be, or not to be, that is the question:
Whether 'tis nobler in the mind to suffer
The slings and arrows of outrageous fortune,
Or to take arms against a sea of troubles
And by opposing end them. To die, to sleep—
No more—and by a sleep to say we end
The heartache and the thousand natural shocks
That flesh is heir to. 'Tis a consummation
Devoutly to be wished.

HAMLET (cont.)
To die, to sleep;
To sleep, perchance to dream. Ay, there's the rub,
For in that sleep of death what dreams may come,
When we have shuffled off this mortal coil,
Must give us pause. There's the respect
That makes calamity of so long life.
For who would bear the whips and scorns of time,
Th'oppressor's wrong, the proud man's contumely,
The pangs of disprized love, the law's delay,
The insolence of office, and the spurns
That patient merit of th'unworthy takes,
When he himself might his quietus make
With a bare bodkin?

HAMLET (cont.)
Who would fardels bear,
To grunt and sweat under a weary life,
But that the dread of something after death,
The undiscovered country from whose bourn
No traveller returns, puzzles the will,
And makes us rather bear those ills we have
Than fly to others that we know not of?
Thus conscience does make cowards of us all;

HAMLET (cont.)
And thus the native hue of resolution
Is sicklied o'er with the pale cast of thought,
And enterprises of great pitch and moment
With this regard their currents turn awry
And lose the name of action.

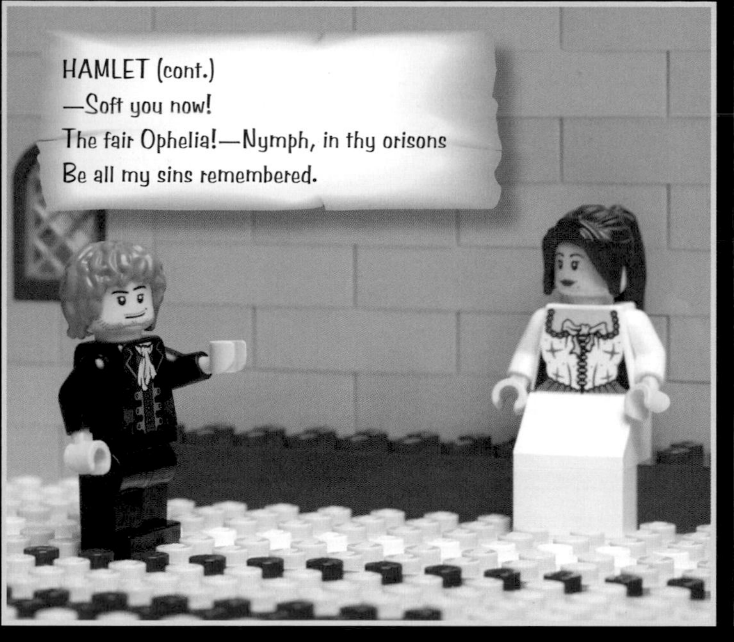

OPHELIA
My honoured lord, you know right well you did,
And with them words of so sweet breath composed
As made the things more rich. Their perfume lost,
Take these again, for to the noble mind
Rich gifts wax poor when givers prove unkind.
There, my lord.
HAMLET
Ha, ha! Are you honest?
OPHELIA
My lord?

HAMLET
Are you fair?
OPHELIA
What means Your Lordship?

HAMLET
That if you be honest and fair, your honesty should admit no discourse to your beauty.
OPHELIA
Could beauty, my lord, have better commerce than with honesty?

HAMLET
Ay, truly; for the power of beauty will sooner transform honesty from what it is to a bawd than the force of honesty can translate beauty into his likeness. This was sometime a paradox, but now the time gives it proof. I did love you once.

HAMLET
Get thee to a nunnery. Why wouldst thou be a breeder of sinners? I am myself indifferent honest, but yet I could accuse me of such things that it were better my mother had not borne me: I am very proud, revengeful, ambitious, with more offences at my beck than I have thoughts to put them in, imagination to give them shape, or time to act them in.

HAMLET (cont.)
What should such fellows as I do crawling between earth and heaven? We are arrant knaves, all; believe none of us. Go thy ways to a nunnery.

OPHELIA
O, help him, you sweet heavens!
HAMLET
If thou dost marry, I'll give thee this plague for thy dowry: be thou as chaste as ice, as pure as snow, thou shalt not escape calumny. Get thee to a nunnery, farewell. Or, if thou wilt needs marry, marry a fool, for wise men know well enough what monsters you make of them. To a nunnery, go, and quickly too. Farewell.
OPHELIA
Heavenly powers, restore him!

HAMLET
I have heard of your paintings too, well enough. God hath given you one face, and you make yourselves another. You jig, you amble, and you lisp, you nickname God's creatures, and make your wantonness your ignorance. Go to, I'll no more on't; it hath made me mad. I say we will have no more marriage. Those that are married already—all but one—shall live. The rest shall keep as they are. To a nunnery, go.

OPHELIA
O, what a noble mind is here o'erthrown!
The courtier's, soldier's, scholar's, eye, tongue, sword,
Th'expectancy and rose of the fair state,
The glass of fashion and the mould of form,
Th'observed of all observers, quite, quite down!
And I, of ladies most deject and wretched,
That sucked the honey of his music vows,
Now see that noble and most sovereign reason
Like sweet bells jangled out of tune and harsh;
That unmatched form and feature of blown youth
Blasted with ecstasy. O, woe is me,
T'have seen what I have seen, see what I see!

KING CLAUDIUS
Love? His affections do not that way tend;
Nor what he spake, though it lacked form a little,
Was not like madness. There's something in
his soul
O'er which his melancholy sits on brood,
And I do doubt the hatch and the disclose
Will be some danger; which for to prevent,
I have in quick determination
Thus set it down: he shall with speed to England,
For the demand of our neglected tribute.
Haply the seas and countries different
With variable objects shall expel
This something-settled matter in his heart,
Whereon his brains still beating puts him thus
From fashion of himself. What think you on't?

LORD POLONIUS
It shall do well. But yet do I believe
The origin and commencement of his grief
Sprung from neglected love.—How now, Ophelia?
You need not tell us what Lord Hamlet said;
We heard it all.—My lord, do as you please,
But, if you hold it fit, after the play
Let his queen-mother all alone entreat him
To show his grief. Let her be round with him;
And I'll be placed, so please you, in the ear
Of all their conference. If she find him not,
To England send him, or confine him where
Your wisdom best shall think.

Act III. Scene II (89–2[illegible]3).

Hamlet helps the play actors prepare for the coming performance, emphatically asking the actors not to overact their lines or run away with the play. Polonius, Rosencrantz, and Guildenstern enter the scene and give word that Claudius and Gertrude will be attending the play. Horatio and Hamlet then come together for a private discussion, during which Hamlet explains his motivations for selecting this particular play. He urges Horatio to pay attention to Claudius's reactions to parts of the play, which will prove him culpable for the murder of the dead king.

HAMLET
They are coming to the play. I must be idle.
Get you a place.

KING CLAUDIUS
How fares our cousin Hamlet?
HAMLET
Excellent, i'faith, of the chameleon's dish: I eat
the air, promise-crammed. You cannot feed capons so.

KING CLAUDIUS
I have nothing with this answer, Hamlet. These
words are not mine.
HAMLET
No, nor mine now.

HAMLET (cont.)
My lord, you played once i'th'university, you say?
LORD POLONIUS
That did I, my lord, and was accounted a
good actor.
HAMLET
What did you enact?

LORD POLONIUS
I did enact Julius Caesar. I was killed i'th'
Capitol; Brutus killed me.
HAMLET
It was a brute part of him to kill so capital a
calf there.

HAMLET (cont.)
—Be the players ready?
ROSENCRANTZ
Ay, my lord. They stay upon your patience.

QUEEN GERTRUDE
Come hither, my dear Hamlet, sit by me.

HAMLET
No, good mother, here's metal more attractive.

LORD POLONIUS
Oho, do you mark that?

HAMLET
Lady, shall I lie in your lap?

OPHELIA
No, my lord.
HAMLET
I mean, my head upon your lap?

OPHELIA
Ay, my lord.
HAMLET
Do you think I meant country matters?

OPHELIA
I think nothing, my lord.
HAMLET
That's a fair thought to lie between maids' legs.

OPHELIA
What is, my lord?
HAMLET
Nothing.
OPHELIA
You are merry, my lord.
HAMLET
Who, I?
OPHELIA
Ay, my lord.

HAMLET
O, God, your only jig maker. What should a man do but be merry? For look you how cheerfully my mother looks, and my father died within 's two hours.
OPHELIA
Nay, 'tis twice two months, my lord.

HAMLET
So long? Nay then, let the devil wear black, for I'll have a suit of sables. O heavens! Die two months ago, and not forgotten yet? Then there's hope a great man's memory may outlive his life half a year. But, by'r Lady, 'a must build churches, then, or else shall 'a suffer not thinking on, with the hobbyhorse, whose epitaph is "For oh, for oh, the hobbyhorse is forgot."

OPHELIA
What means this, my lord?
HAMLET
Marry, this' miching mallico; it means mischief.
OPHELIA
Belike this show imports the argument of the play.

HAMLET
We shall know by this fellow. The players cannot keep counsel; they'll tell all.
OPHELIA
Will 'a tell us what this show meant?
HAMLET
Ay, or any show that you'll show him. Be
not you ashamed to show, he'll not shame to tell you what it means.
OPHELIA
You are naught, you are naught. I'll mark the play.

HAMLET
Is this a prologue, or the posy of a ring?
OPHELIA
'Tis brief, my lord.
HAMLET
As woman's love.

PLAYER KING
Full thirty times hath Phoebus' cart gone round
Neptune's salt wash and Tellus' orbèd ground,
And thirty dozen moons with borrowed sheen
About the world have times twelve thirties been,
Since love our hearts and Hymen did our hands
Unite commutual in most sacred bands.
PLAYER QUEEN
So many journeys may the sun and moon
Make us again count o'er ere love be done!
But, woe is me, you are so sick of late,
So far from cheer and from your former state,
That I distrust you. Yet, though I distrust,
Discomfort you, my lord, it nothing must.
For women's fear and love holds quantity;
In neither aught, or in extremity.
Now, what my love is, proof hath made you know,
And as my love is sized, my fear is so.
Where love is great, the littlest doubts are fear;
Where little fears grow great, great love grows there.

PLAYER KING
Faith, I must leave thee, love, and shortly too;
My operant powers their functions leave to do.
And thou shalt live in this fair world behind,
Honoured, beloved; and haply one as kind
For husband shalt thou—
PLAYER QUEEN
O, confound the rest!
Such love must needs be treason in my breast.
In second husband let me be accurst!
None wed the second but who killed the first.

PLAYER QUEEN
The instances that second marriage move
Are base respects of thrift, but none of love.
A second time I kill my husband dead
When second husband kisses me in bed.
Player King
I do believe you think what now you speak,
But what we do determine oft we break.
Purpose is but the slave to memory,
Of violent birth, but poor validity,
Which now, like fruit unripe, sticks on the tree,
But fall, unshaken when they mellow be.
Most necessary 'tis that we forget
To pay ourselves what to ourselves is debt.
What to ourselves in passion we propose,
The passion ending, doth the purpose lose.
The violence of either grief or joy
Their own enactures with themselves destroy.
Where joy most revels, grief doth most lament;
Grief joys, joy grieves, on slender accident.
This world is not for aye, nor 'tis not strange
That even our loves should with our fortunes change;
For 'tis a question left us yet to prove,
Whether love lead fortune, or else fortune love.
The great man down, you mark his favourite flies;
The poor advanced makes friends of enemies.

PLAYER KING (cont.)
And hitherto doth love on fortune tend;
For who not needs shall never lack a friend,
And who in want a hollow friend doth try,
Directly seasons him his enemy.
But, orderly to end where I begun,
Our wills and fates do so contrary run
That our devices still are overthrown;
Our thoughts are ours, their ends none of our own.
So think thou wilt no second husband wed,
But die thy thoughts when thy first lord is dead.

PLAYER QUEEN
Nor earth to me give food, nor heaven light,
Sport and repose lock from me day and night,
To desperation turn my trust and hope,
An anchor's cheer in prison be my scope!
Each opposite that blanks the face of joy
Meet what I would have well and it destroy!
Both here and hence pursue me lasting strife
If, once a widow, ever I be wife!

HAMLET
Madam, how like you this play?
QUEEN GERTRUDE
The lady protests too much, methinks.
HAMLET
O, but she'll keep her word.

KING CLAUDIUS
Have you heard the argument? Is there no offence in't?
HAMLET
No, no, they do but jest, poison in jest. No offence i'th' world.
KING CLAUDIUS
What do you call the play?

HAMLET
The Mousetrap. Marry, how? Tropically.
This play is the image of a murder done in Vienna. Gonzago is the Duke's name, his wife, Baptista. You shall see anon. 'Tis a knavish piece of work, but what of that? Your Majesty, and we that have free souls, it touches us not. Let the galled jade wince, our withers are unwrung.

OPHELIA
You are as good as a chorus, my lord.
HAMLET
I could interpret between you and your love, if I could see the puppets dallying.
OPHELIA
You are keen, my lord, you are keen.

HAMLET
It would cost you a groaning to take off my edge.
OPHELIA
Still better, and worse.
HAMLET
So you mis-take your husbands.—Begin, murderer; pox, leave thy damnable faces, and begin. Come, the croaking raven doth bellow for revenge.

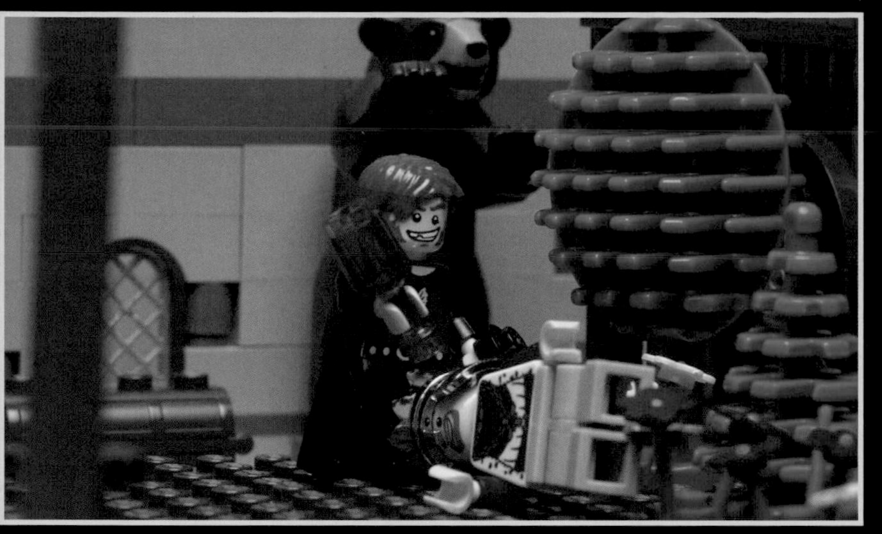

LUCIANUS
Thoughts black, hands apt, drugs fit, and time agreeing,
Confederate season, else no creature seeing,
Thou mixture rank, of midnight weeds collected,
With Hecate's ban thrice blasted, thrice infected,
Thy natural magic and dire property,
On wholesome life usurp immediately.

HAMLET
'A poisons him i'th' garden for his estate. His name's Gonzago. The story is extant, and written in very choice Italian. You shall see anon how the murderer gets the love of Gonzago's wife.

OPHELIA
The King rises.
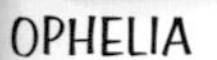
HAMLET
What, frighted with false fire?

HAMLET
"Why, let the stricken deer go weep,
The hart ungallèd play.
For some must watch, while some must sleep;
Thus runs the world away."
Would not this, sir, and a forest of feathers—if the rest of my fortunes turn Turk with me—with two Provincial roses on my razed shoes, get me a fellowship in a cry of players?
HORATIO
Half a share.

HAMLET
A whole one, I.
"For thou dost know, O Damon dear,
This realm dismantled was
Of Jove himself, and now reigns here
A very, very—pajock."
HORATIO
You might have rhymed.
HAMLET
O good Horatio, I'll take the ghost's word for a thousand pound. Didst perceive?

HORATIO
Very well, my lord.
HAMLET
Upon the talk of the poisoning?
HORATIO
I did very well note him.

HAMLET
Aha! Come, some music! Come, the recorders!
"For if the king like not the comedy,
Why then, belike, he likes it not, perdy."
Come, some music.

ACT III. Scene III (36–98).

H

The Mousetrap has just ended, and Rosencrantz and Guildenstern approach Hamlet. They are disturbed by the events and explain that Claudius has cloistered himself in his room in anger from the play. Rosencrantz passes on a message that Gertrude would like to speak to Hamlet in her bedchamber because she, too, is upset. Hamlet agrees, though he is visibly scatterbrained and suspicious. Hamlet asks Guildenstern to play a tune on the recorder, who insists that he does not have the talent for it. Hamlet uses this to say that if Guildenstern cannot even play the recorder, then he and Rosencrantz should not have tried to play Hamlet for a fool, either.

Polonius joins the group and reminds Hamlet that his mother would like to see him. When Hamlet prepares himself to go meet with her, he makes a pact with himself that he will "speak daggers to her but use none" (III.ii.395). While she is knitted tightly into the death of Hamlet's father, she does not deserve his vengeance.

Away in King Claudius's chamber, the King decides that Hamlet is too much of a threat and that he should be sent away to England with Rosencrantz and Guildenstern to mind him. Polonius comes in and tells Claudius that he will help by spying on Gertrude and Hamlet while they meet.

KING CLAUDIUS
O, my offence is rank! It smells to heaven.
It hath the primal eldest curse upon't,
A brother's murder. Pray can I not,
Though inclination be as sharp as will;
My stronger guilt defeats my strong intent,
And like a man to double business bound
I stand in pause where I shall first begin,
And both neglect. What if this cursèd hand
Were thicker than itself with brother's blood,
Is there not rain enough in the sweet heavens
To wash it white as snow? Whereto serves mercy
But to confront the visage of offence?
And what's in prayer but this twofold force,
To be forestallèd ere we come to fall,
Or pardoned being down?

KING CLAUDIUS (cont.)
Then I'll look up.
My fault is past. But, O, what form of prayer
Can serve my turn? "Forgive me my foul murder"?
That cannot be, since I am still possessed
Of those effects for which I did the murder:
My crown, mine own ambition, and my queen.
May one be pardoned and retain th' offence?
In the corrupted currents of this world
Offence's gilded hand may shove by justice,
And oft 'tis seen the wicked prize itself
Buys out the law. But 'tis not so above.
There is no shuffling, there the action lies
In his true nature, and we ourselves compelled,
Even to the teeth and forehead of our faults,
To give in evidence. What then? What rests?

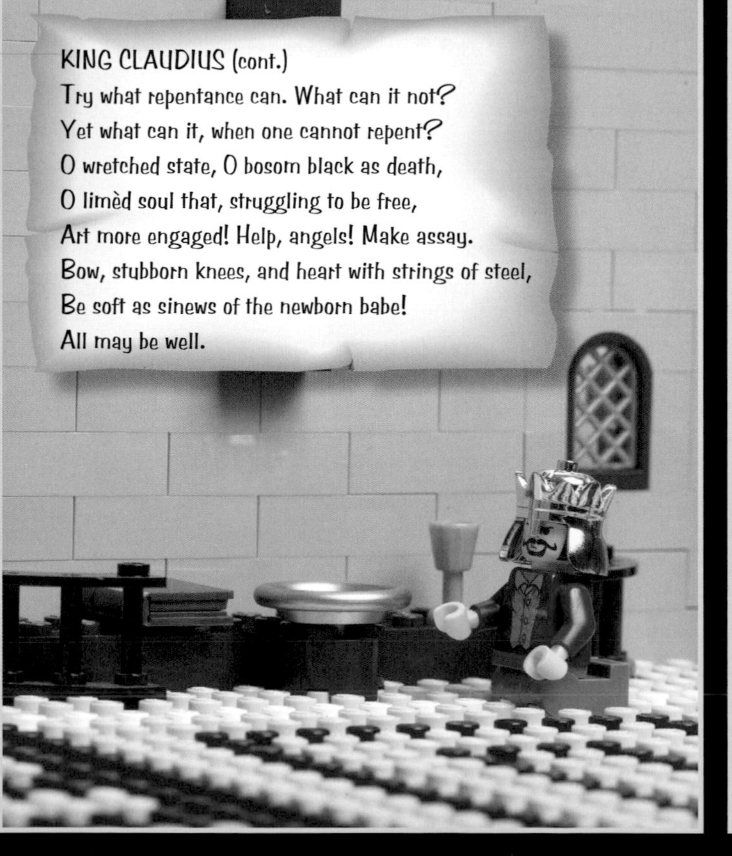

HAMLET (cont.)
But in our circumstance and course of thought
'Tis heavy with him. And am I then revenged,
To take him in the purging of his soul,
When he is fit and seasoned for his passage?
No!
Up, sword, and know thou a more horrid hent.

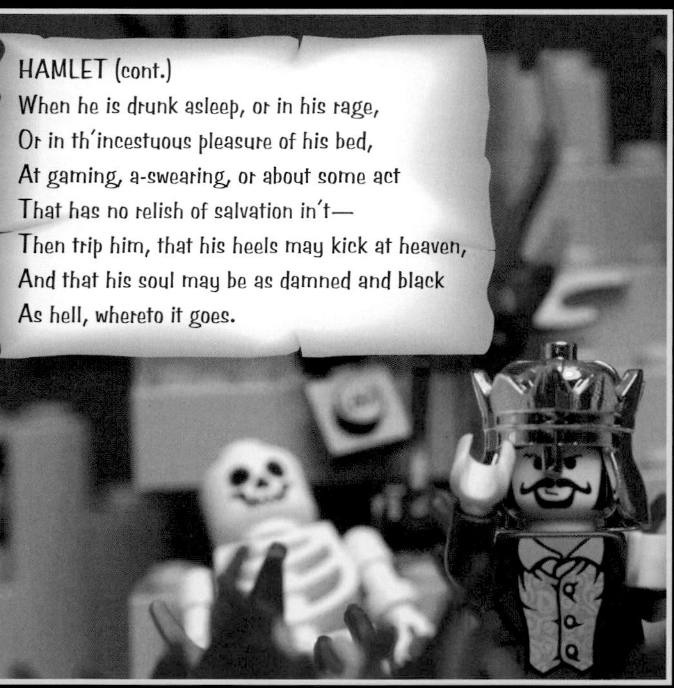

ACT III. Scene IV (10–105).

QUEEN GERTRUDE
Hamlet, thou hast thy father much offended.
HAMLET
Mother, you have my father much offended.

QUEEN GERTRUDE
Come, come, you answer with an idle tongue.
HAMLET
Go, go, you question with a wicked tongue.
QUEEN GERTRUDE
Why, how now, Hamlet!

HAMLET
What's the matter now?
QUEEN GERTRUDE
Have you forgot me?

HAMLET
No, by the rood, not so:
You are the Queen, your husband's brother's wife,
And—would it were not so!—you are my mother.
QUEEN GERTRUDE
Nay, then, I'll set those to you that can speak.
HAMLET
Come, come, and sit you down; you shall not budge.
You go not till I set you up a glass
Where you may see the inmost part of you.

HAMLET
How now? A rat? Dead for a ducat, dead!

LORD POLONIUS
O, I am slain!

QUEEN GERTRUDE
O, me, what hast thou done?
HAMLET
Nay, I know not. Is it the king?

QUEEN GERTRUDE
O, what a rash and bloody deed is this!

HAMLET
A bloody deed—almost as bad, good mother,
As kill a king, and marry with his brother.

QUEEN GERTRUDE
As kill a king!
HAMLET
Ay, lady, it was my word.

HAMLET (cont.)
Thou wretched, rash, intruding fool, farewell!
I took thee for thy better. Take thy fortune.
Thou find'st to be too busy is some danger.—
Leave wringing of your hands. Peace, sit you down,
And let me wring your heart, for so I shall,
If it be made of penetrable stuff,
If damnèd custom have not brazed it so
That it be proof and bulwark against sense.

QUEEN GERTRUDE
What have I done, that thou darest wag thy tongue
In noise so rude against me?

HAMLET
Such an act
That blurs the grace and blush of modesty,
Calls virtue hypocrite, takes off the rose
From the fair forehead of an innocent love
And sets a blister there, makes marriage vows
As false as dicers' oaths. O, such a deed
As from the body of contraction plucks
The very soul, and sweet religion makes
A rhapsody of words. Heaven's face doth glow
O'er this solidity and compound mass
With tristful visage, as against the doom,
Is thought-sick at the act.

HAMLET
Look here upon this picture, and on this,
The counterfeit presentment of two brothers.
See what a grace was seated on this brow:
Hyperion's curls, the front of Jove himself,
An eye like Mars to threaten and command,
A station like the herald Mercury
New-lighted on a heaven-kissing hill—
A combination and a form indeed
Where every god did seem to set his seal
To give the world assurance of a man.
This was your husband. Look you now what follows:
Here is your husband, like a mildewed ear,
Blasting his wholesome brother. Have you eyes?
Could you on this fair mountain leave to feed
And batten on this moor? Ha, have you eyes?

HAMLET (cont.)
You cannot call it love, for at your age
The heyday in the blood is tame, it's humble,
And waits upon the judgment, and what judgment
Would step from this to this? Sense, sure, you have,
Else could you not have motion but sure that sense
Is apoplexed, for madness would not err,
Nor sense to ecstasy was ne'er so thralled,
But it reserved some quantity of choice
To serve in such a difference. What devil was't
That thus hath cozened you at hoodman-blind?
Eyes without feeling, feeling without sight,
Ears without hands or eyes, smelling sans all,
Or but a sickly part of one true sense
Could not so mope. O shame, where is thy blush?
Rebellious hell,
If thou canst mutine in a matron's bones,
To flaming youth let virtue be as wax
And melt in her own fire. Proclaim no shame
When the compulsive ardour gives the charge,
Since frost itself as actively doth burn,
And reason panders will.

QUEEN GERTRUDE
O, Hamlet, speak no more!
Thou turn'st mine eyes into my very soul,
And there I see such black and grainèd spots
As will not leave their tinct.

HAMLET
Nay, but to live
In the rank sweat of an enseamèd bed,
Stewed in corruption, honeying and making love
Over the nasty sty!

QUEEN GERTRUDE
O, speak to me no more!
These words like daggers enter in mine ears.
No more, sweet Hamlet!

HAMLET
A murderer and a villain,
A slave that is not twentieth part the tithe
Of your precedent lord, a vice of kings,
A cutpurse of the empire and the rule,
That from a shelf the precious diadem stole
And put it in his pocket!

QUEEN GERTRUDE
No more!

ACT IV. Scene VII (108–195).

While Hamlet and Gertrude continue to bicker in her bedchamber, the ghost of Hamlet's father appears. Hamlet speaks to him, which frightens Gertrude and solidifies her fears that he has gone insane. Hamlet condemns Gertrude for her relationship with Claudius, telling her to stop sleeping with him, lest she continue to be marred by Claudius's wrongdoings. He apologizes for having accidentally killed Polonius and takes the body away with him.

Gertrude reports to Claudius that Hamlet has gone completely mad, and she explains the inadvertent death of Polonius. Claudius instructs Rosencrantz and Guildenstern to go find Hamlet and to bring Polonius's body to the chapel. They soon find Hamlet, who has just disposed of the body in a secret location. Hamlet is brought back to the king, who asks him repeatedly where he has hidden Polonius's corpse. Hamlet offers him vague riddles, so Claudius has attendants search the castle. Claudius refuses to waste any more time and sends Hamlet to England.

As Hamlet is leaving, Prince Fortinbras of Norway comes to the castle to ask Claudius if his troops can pass through Denmark on their way to Poland. Hamlet witnesses the frivolity of the battle Fortinbras is creating, and analyzes the role of wealthy leaders with little to do but start wars.

Meanwhile, Gertrude and Ophelia are talking and it becomes clear that Ophelia has gone crazy. She rattles off nonsensical things and recites poems, all of which Gertrude and Claudius take to mean that she is heartsick over Hamlet and unhinged by her father's death. A messenger comes in and tells Gertrude and Claudius that Laertes, the son of Polonius and sister of Ophelia, is organizing a revolt. Laertes vows to avenge his father's death, saying that having not done so already is enough to bastardize him as a son. Claudius insists that he is not the one responsible for Polonius's death, and tells Laertes that vengeance is fine, as long as he directs his anger where it is due. Ophelia enters the scene and wistfully begins handing out flowers to the king, queen, and her brother, each of which symbolizes a larger character flaw. She recites more poetry in a singsong voice, and while she comes off as insane, the words she speaks carry a grain of truth.

Horatio receives a letter from Hamlet, who had been on his way to England but was taken by pirates. He urges Horatio to pass on several letters to the king, and to return to Hamlet with the messenger as soon as he can. Rosencrantz and Guildenstern are still on their way to England.

Laertes and Claudius discuss revenge on Hamlet. Claudius tells Laertes that although he had the opportunity, he did not kill Hamlet because he did not want to offend his wife or his country, both of whom hold Hamlet in good graces. Claudius receives the letters from Hamlet. The letter is a warning to Claudius that he is returning to Denmark and wishes to speak with him. Claudius and Laertes decide that it will be the perfect opportunity to plot Hamlet's death.

KING CLAUDIUS
Laertes, was your father dear to you?
Or are you like the painting of a sorrow,
A face without a heart?
LAERTES
Why ask you this?
KING CLAUDIUS
Not that I think you did not love your father,
But that I know love is begun by time,
And that I see, in passages of proof,
Time qualifies the spark and fire of it.
There lives within the very flame of love
A kind of wick or snuff that will abate it,
And nothing is at a like goodness still,
For goodness, growing to a pleurisy,
Dies in his own too much. That we would do,
We should do when we would; for this "would" changes
And hath abatements and delays as many
As there are tongues, are hands, are accidents,
And then this "should" is like a spendthrift sigh,
That hurts by easing. But, to the quick o'th'ulcer:
Hamlet comes back. What would you undertake
To show yourself in deed your father's son
More than in words?

KING CLAUDIUS
No place, indeed, should murder sanctuarize;
Revenge should have no bounds. But, good Laertes,
Will you do this, keep close within your chamber.
Hamlet returned shall know you are come home.
We'll put on those shall praise your excellence
And set a double varnish on the fame
The Frenchman gave you, bring you in fine together,
And wager on your heads.

KING CLAUDIUS (cont.)
He, being remiss,
Most generous, and free from all contriving,
Will not peruse the foils, so that with ease,
Or with a little shuffling, you may choose
A sword unbated, and in a pass of practise
Requite him for your father.

LAERTES
I will do't,
And for that purpose I'll anoint my sword.
I bought an unction of a mountebank
So mortal that, but dip a knife in it,
Where it draws blood no cataplasm so rare,
Collected from all simples that have virtue
Under the moon, can save the thing from death
That is but scratched withal. I'll touch my point
With this contagion, that if I gall him slightly,
It may be death.

KING CLAUDIUS
Let's further think of this,
Weigh what convenience both of time and means
May fit us to our shape. If this should fail,
And that our drift look through our bad performance,
'Twere better not assayed. Therefore this project
Should have a back or second, that might hold
If this did blast in proof. Soft, let me see.
We'll make a solemn wager on your cunnings—
I ha 't!
When in your motion you are hot and dry—
As make your bouts more violent to that end—

QUEEN GERTRUDE
There is a willow grows askant the brook,
That shows his hoar leaves in the glassy stream;
Therewith fantastic garlands did she make
Of crowflowers, nettles, daisies, and long purples,
That liberal shepherds give a grosser name,
But our cold maids do dead men's fingers call them.
There on the pendent boughs her crownet weeds
Clamb'ring to hang, an envious sliver broke,
When down her weedy trophies and herself
Fell in the weeping brook. Her clothes spread wide,
And mermaidlike awhile they bore her up,
Which time she chanted snatches of old lauds,
As one incapable of her own distress,
Or like a creature native and endued
Unto that element.

QUEEN GERTRUDE (cont.)
But long it could not be
Till that her garments, heavy with their drink,
Pulled the poor wretch from her melodious lay
To muddy death.

LAERTES
Alas, then she is drowned?
QUEEN GERTRUDE
Drowned, drowned.
LAERTES
Too much of water hast thou, poor Ophelia,
And therefore I forbid my tears. But yet
It is our trick; nature her custom holds,
Let shame say what it will. When these are gone,
The woman will be out. Adieu, my lord.
I have a speech of fire that fain would blaze,
But that this folly douts it.

KING CLAUDIUS
Let's follow, Gertrude.
How much I had to do to calm his rage!
Now fear I this will give it start again;
Therefore let's follow.

ACT V. Scene I (197–302).

Outside the castle, the gravediggers are preparing for Ophelia's funeral. They discuss the oddity that Ophelia is being given a Christian funeral, as many signs point to her having drowned herself. The gravediggers continue to chatter and sing as they dig the grave, when Hamlet and Horatio happen upon them. Before they make themselves known, they watch the gravediggers toss around a skull and jovially sing their tunes. Hamlet approaches the man standing in the grave, asking whose it is. After a tug-of-war of puns, the gravedigger explains that the grave is for a woman who has just died, and Hamlet is still unaware of Ophelia's death.

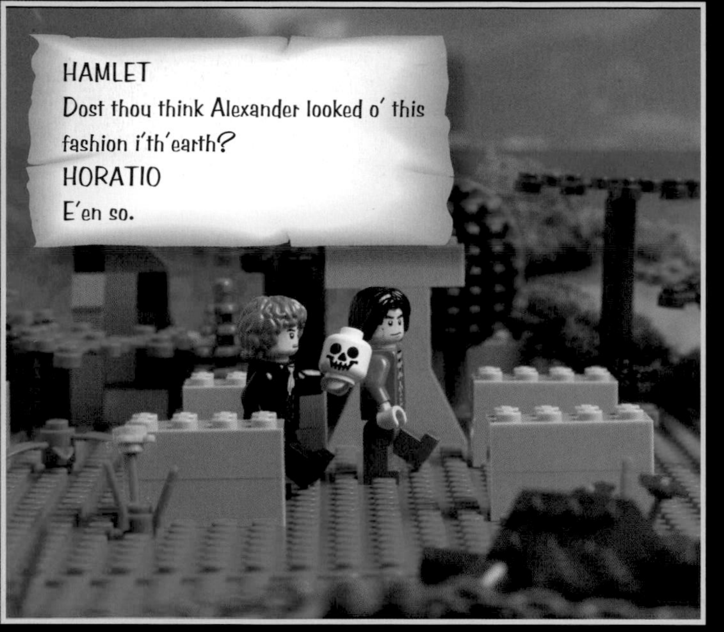

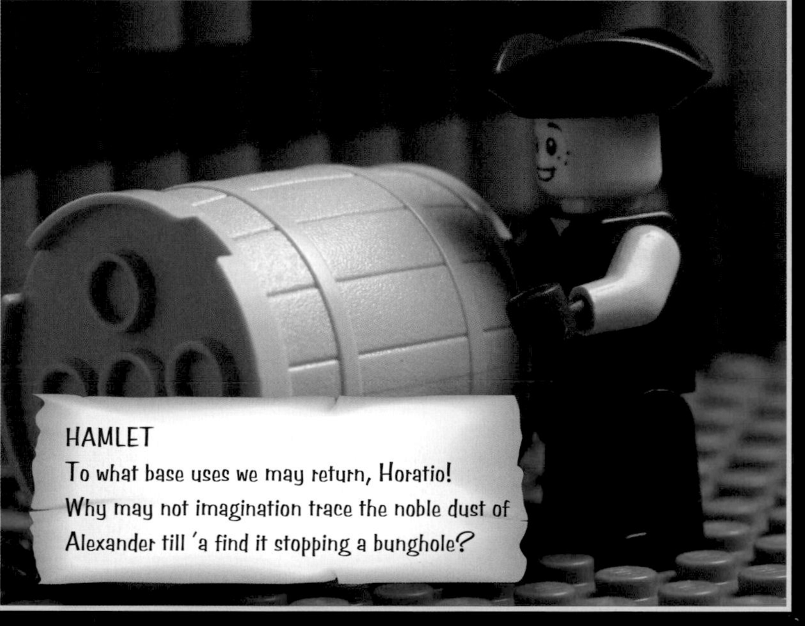

HAMLET
No, faith, not a jot; but to follow him thither
with modesty enough, and likelihood to lead it. As
thus: Alexander died, Alexander was buried,
Alexander returneth to dust, the dust is earth, of earth
we make loam, and why of that loam whereto he was
converted might they not stop a beer barrel?
Imperious Caesar, dead and turned to clay,
Might stop a hole to keep the wind away.
O, that that earth which kept the world in awe
Should patch a wall t'expel the winter's flaw!

HAMLET (cont.)
But soft, but soft awhile! Here comes the King,
The Queen, the courtiers. Who is this they follow?
And with such maimèd rites? This doth betoken
The corpse they follow did with desperate hand
Fordo its own life. 'Twas of some estate.
Couch we awhile and mark.

LAERTES
What ceremony else?
HAMLET
That is Laertes, a very noble youth. Mark.
LAERTES
What ceremony else?

FIRST PRIEST
Her obsequies have been as far enlarged
As we have warranty. Her death was doubtful,
And but that great command o'ersways the order
She should in ground unsanctified have lodged
Till the last trumpet. For charitable prayers,
Shards, flints and pebbles should be thrown on her.
Yet here she is allowed her virgin crants,
Her maiden strewments, and the bringing home
Of bell and burial.

LAERTES
Must there no more be done?
FIRST PRIEST
No more be done.
We should profane the service of the dead
To sing a requiem and such rest to her
As to peace-parted souls.

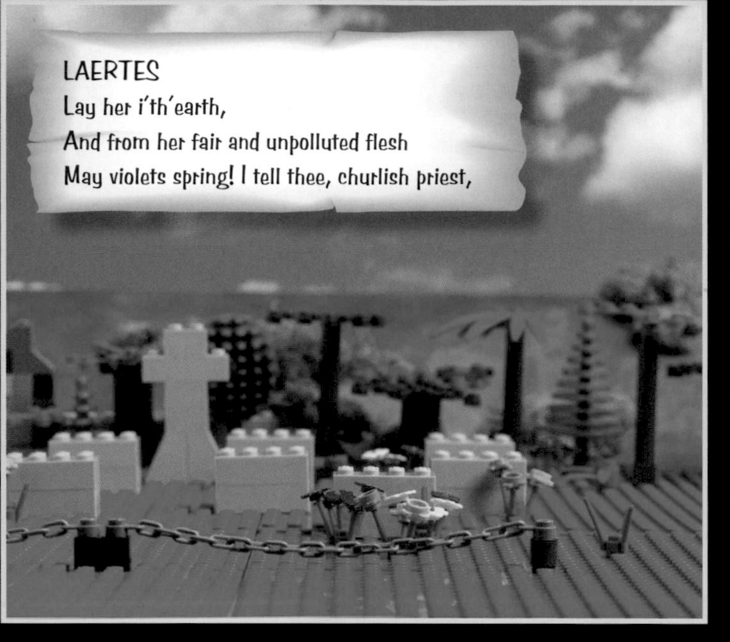

QUEEN GERTRUDE
Sweets to the sweet! Farewell.
I hoped thou shouldst have been my Hamlet's wife.
I thought thy bride-bed to have decked, sweet maid,
And not t' have strewed thy grave.

LAERTES
O, treble woe
Fall ten times treble on that cursèd head,
Whose wicked deed thy most ingenious sense
Deprived thee of! Hold off the earth awhile,
Till I have caught her once more in mine arms.
Now pile your dust upon the quick and dead,
Till of this flat a mountain you have made
T' o'ertop old Pelion, or the skyish head
Of blue Olympus.

HAMLET
What is he whose grief
Bears such an emphasis, whose phrase of sorrow
Conjures the wandering stars and makes them stand

HAMLET (cont.)
Like wonder-wounded hearers? This is I,
Hamlet the Dane.

HAMLET
Thou pray'st not well.
I prithee, take thy fingers from my throat,
For though I am not splenitive and rash,
Yet have I something in me dangerous,
Which let thy wisdom fear. Hold off thy hand.

HAMLET
Why, I will fight with him upon this theme
Until my eyelids will no longer wag.
QUEEN GERTRUDE
O, my son, what theme?
HAMLET
I loved Ophelia. Forty thousand brothers
Could not with all their quantity of love
Make up my sum. What wilt thou do for her?

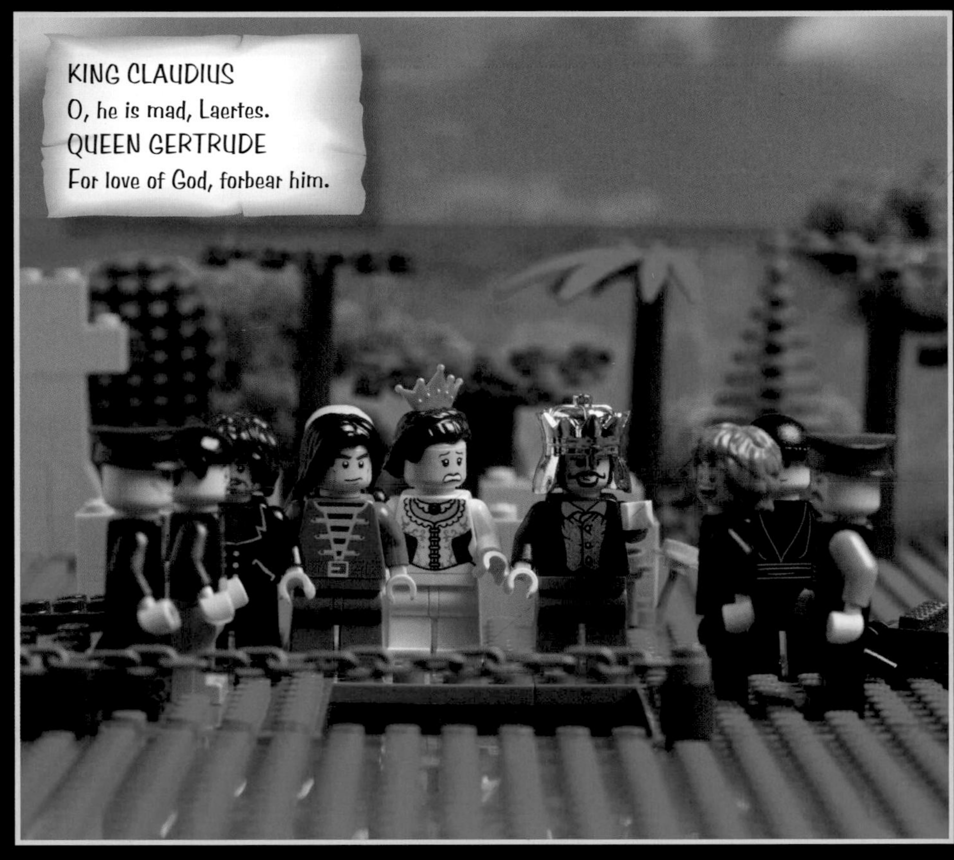

HAMLET
'Swounds, show me what thou'lt do.
Woo't weep? Woo't fight? Woo't fast?
Woo't tear thyself?
Woo't drink up eisel? Eat a crocodile?
I'll do't. Dost thou come here to whine?
To outface me with leaping in her grave?
Be buried quick with her, and so will I.
And if thou prate of mountains, let them throw
Millions of acres on us, till our ground,
Singeing his pate against the burning zone,
Make Ossa like a wart! Nay, an thou'lt mouth,
I'll rant as well as thou.

KING CLAUDIUS
I pray you, good Horatio, wait upon him.
Strengthen your patience in our last night's speech;
We'll put the matter to the present push.—
Good Gertrude, set some watch over your son.—
This grave shall have a living monument.
An hour of quiet shortly shall we see;
Till then, in patience our proceeding be.

ACT V. Scene II (207–405).

Hamlet tells Horatio that when he was on his way to England with Rosencrantz and Guildenstern, he was able to sneak off and read Claudius's instructions on what to do with Hamlet once they arrived in England. Claudius had decreed that Hamlet be executed with a dull axe. He goes on to say that he was able to forge new documents that altered the instructions with flowery, diplomatic ideas about strengthening relations between the two countries, and that the two messengers, Rosencrantz and Guildenstern, should be killed on the spot. Hamlet decides that they are collateral damage for having interfered with such powerful people. Hamlet laments his scuffle with Laertes at Ophelia's funeral, noting that he thinks highly of him, but felt he was being too ostentatious. Moments later, Osric, a courtier, approaches the men and informs Hamlet that Laertes has challenged him to a fencing match.

HORATIO
You will lose, my lord.
HAMLET
I do not think so. Since he went into France, I have been in continual practice; I shall win at the odds. But thou wouldst not think how ill all's here about my heart; but it is no matter.
HORATIO
Nay, good my lord—

HAMLET
Not a whit, we defy augury. There is special providence in the fall of a sparrow. If it be now, 'tis not to come; if it be not to come, it will be now; if it be not now, yet it will come. The readiness is all. Since no man of aught he leaves knows, what is't to leave betimes? Let be.

KING CLAUDIUS
Come, Hamlet, come and take this hand from me.
HAMLET
Give me your pardon, sir. I have done you wrong,
But pardon't as you are a gentleman.
This presence knows,
And you must needs have heard, how I am punished
With a sore distraction. What I have done
That might your nature, honour, and exception
Roughly awake, I here proclaim was madness.
Was't Hamlet wronged Laertes? Never Hamlet.
If Hamlet from himself be ta'en away,
And when he's not himself does wrong Laertes,
Then Hamlet does it not, Hamlet denies it.
Who does it, then? His madness. If't be so,
Hamlet is of the faction that is wronged;
His madness is poor Hamlet's enemy.

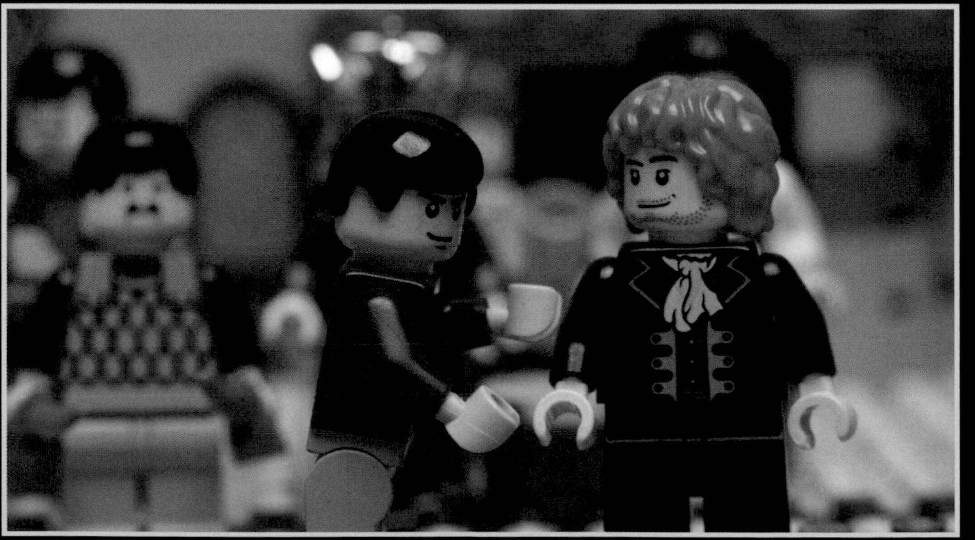

LAERTES
I am satisfied in nature,
Whose motive in this case should stir me most
To my revenge. But in my terms of honour
I stand aloof, and will no reconcilement
Till by some elder masters of known honour
I have a voice and precedent of peace
To keep my name ungored. But till that time
I do receive your offered love like love,
And will not wrong it.

HAMLET
I embrace it freely,
And will this brother's wager frankly play.—
Give us the foils. Come on.
LAERTES
Come, one for me.
HAMLET
I'll be your foil, Laertes. In mine ignorance
Your skill shall, like a star i'th' darkest night,
Stick fiery off indeed.

LAERTES
You mock me, sir.
HAMLET
No, by this hand.
KING CLAUDIUS
Give them the foils, young Osric. Cousin Hamlet,
You know the wager?
HAMLET
Very well, my lord
Your grace hath laid the odds o'th' weaker side.
KING CLAUDIUS
I do not fear it; I have seen you both.
But since he is bettered, we have therefore odds.

LAERTES
This is too heavy. Let me see another.
HAMLET
This likes me well. These foils have all a length?
OSRIC
Ay, my good lord.

KING CLAUDIUS
Set me the stoops of wine upon that table.
If Hamlet give the first or second hit,
Or quit in answer of the third exchange,
Let all the battlements their ordnance fire.
The King shall drink to Hamlet's better breath,
And in the cup an union shall he throw
Richer than that which four successive kings
In Denmark's crown have worn. Give me the cups,
And let the kettle to the trumpet speak,
The trumpet to the cannoneer without,
The cannons to the heavens, the heavens to earth,
"Now the King dunks to Hamlet." Come, begin.
And you, the judges, bear a wary eye.

HAMLET
Come on, sir.
LAERTES
Come, my lord.

HAMLET
One.

LAERTES
No.
HAMLET
Judgment.
OSRIC
A hit, a very palpable hit.
LAERTES
Well, again.

KING CLAUDIUS
Stay, give me drink. Hamlet, this pearl is thine.
Here's to thy health. Give him the cup.

HAMLET
I'll play this bout first. Set it by awhile.
Come.

HAMLET (cont.)
Another hit; what say you?
LAERTES
A touch, a touch, I do confess't.

KING CLAUDIUS
Our son shall win.
QUEEN GERTRUDE
He's fat and scant of breath.
Here, Hamlet, take my napkin, rub thy brows.
The Queen carouses to thy fortune, Hamlet.

HAMLET
Good madam!
KING CLAUDIUS
Gertrude, do not drink.
QUEEN GERTRUDE
I will, my lord, I pray you pardon me.

HAMLET
Come, for the third, Laertes. You do but dally.
I pray you, pass with your best violence;
I am afeard you make a wanton of me.
LAERTES
Say you so? Come on.
OSRIC
Nothing neither way.

OSRIC
Look to the Queen there, ho!
HORATIO
They bleed on both sides. How is it, my lord?
OSRIC
How is't, Laertes?

LAERTES
It is here, Hamlet. Hamlet, thou art slain.
No med'cine in the world can do thee good;
In thee there is not half an hour's life.
The treacherous instrument is in thy hand,
Unbated and envenomed. The foul practise
Hath turned itself on me. Lo, here I lie,
Never to rise again. Thy mother's poisoned.
I can no more. The King, the King's to blame.

HAMLET
The point envenomed too? Then, venom, to thy work.
ALL
Treason! Treason!

KING CLAUDIUS
O, yet defend me, friends. I am but hurt.
HAMLET
Here, thou incestuous, murderous, damnèd Dane,
Drink off this potion. Is thy union here?
Follow my mother.

LAERTES
He is justly served.
It is a poison tempered by himself.
Exchange forgiveness with me, noble Hamlet.
Mine and my father's death come not upon thee,
Nor thine on me!

HAMLET
Heaven make thee free of it! I follow thee.
I am dead, Horatio. Wretched Queen, adieu!
You that look pale and tremble at this chance,
That are but mutes or audience to this act,
Had I but time—as this fell sergeant, Death,
Is strict in his arrest—O, I could tell you—
But let it be. Horatio, I am dead;
Thou livest. Report me and my cause aright
To the unsatisfied.

HAMLET
As thou'rt a man,
Give me the cup! Let go! By heaven, I'll ha 't.
O, God, Horatio, what a wounded name,
Things standing thus unknown, shall I leave behind me!
If thou didst ever hold me in thy heart,
Absent thee from felicity awhile,
And in this harsh world draw thy breath in pain
To tell my story.

HAMLET (cont.)
What warlike noise is this?
OSRIC
Young Fortinbras, with conquest come from Poland,
To th'ambassadors of England gives
This warlike volley.

HAMLET
O, I die, Horatio!
The potent poison quite o'ercrows my spirit.
I cannot live to hear the news from England,
But I do prophesy th'election lights
On Fortinbras. He has my dying voice.
So tell him, with th'occurrents, more and less
Which have solicited. The rest is silence.

HORATIO
Now cracks a noble heart. Good night sweet prince,
And flights of angels sing thee to thy rest!
Why does the drum come hither?

PRINCE FORTINBRAS
Where is this sight?
HORATIO
What is it you would see?
If aught of woe or wonder, cease your search.
PRINCE FORTINBRAS
This quarry cries on havoc. O proud death,
What feast is toward in thine eternal cell,
That thou so many princes at a shot
So bloodily hast struck?

FIRST AMBASSADOR
The sight is dismal,
And our affairs from England come too late.
The ears are senseless that should give us hearing,
To tell him his commandment is fulfilled,
That Rosencrantz and Guildenstern are dead.
Where should we have our thanks?

HORATIO
Not from his mouth,
Had it th'ability of life to thank you.
He never gave commandment for their death.
But since, so jump upon this bloody question,
You from the Polack wars and you from England
Are here arrived, give order that these bodies
High on a stage be placèd to the view,
And let me speak to th' yet unknowing world
How these things came about. So shall you hear
Of carnal, bloody, and unnatural acts,
Of accidental judgments, casual slaughters,
Of deaths put on by cunning and forced cause,
And, in this upshot, purposes mistook
Fall'n on the inventors' heads. All this can I
Truly deliver.

PRINCE FORTINBRAS
Let us haste to hear it,
And call the noblest to the audience.
For me, with sorrow I embrace my fortune.
I have some rights of memory in this kingdom,
Which now to claim my vantage doth invite me.
HORATIO
Of that I shall have also cause to speak,
And from his mouth whose voice will draw on more.
But let this same be presently performed,
Even while men's minds are wild, lest more mischance
On plots and errors happen.
PRINCE FORTINBRAS
Let four captains
Bear Hamlet, like a soldier, to the stage,
For he was likely, had he been put on,
To have proved most royal; and for his passage,
The soldiers' music and the rites of war
Speak loudly for him.
Take up the bodies. Such a sight as this
Becomes the field, but here shows much amiss.
Go bid the soldiers shoot.

Macbeth

The tale of *Macbeth* is one of the most powerful of William Shakespeare's tragedies, and one which delves into the most cavernous parts of the human psyche. Written in the early years of the 1600s and later published in folio form in 1623, *Macbeth* follows the corrosion of a Scottish leader's conscience and sanity after he is given a prophecy of royal ascension.

The characterization of Macbeth and his wife's psychoses carry much of the play's arc, but such a play would not be quintessentially Shakespearean without a heavy-handed dose of word play. The three witches who leave prescient breadcrumbs that feed Macbeth's greed throughout the play allow Macbeth to lean heavily on the words that make up their divinations. This leads to several moments of literary quibble, in which Macbeth becomes overconfident in the witches' prophecies of his infallibility but is denied such protection in subtle twists of linguistic meaning.

With the prophetic knowledge offered by the witches, Macbeth quickly transforms from a noble and brave Scottish thane into a regicidal usurper, whose all-consuming guilt leads to even more madness and destruction. Often cited as the darkest of William Shakespeare's plays, *Macbeth* presents a unique scope into the lives of the powerful and what happens when their greed is left to fester.

Dramatis Personae

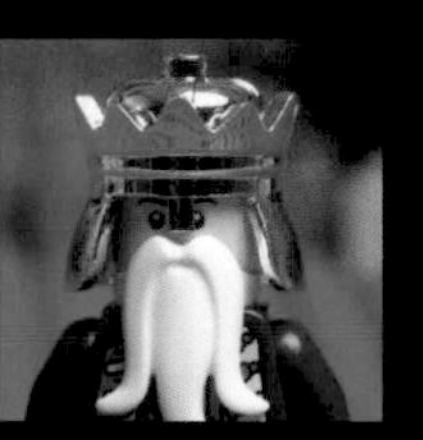
DUNCAN, King of Scotland

MALCOLM, son of Duncan

DONALBAIN, son of Duncan

MACBETH, Thane of Glamis, later of Cawdor, later King of Scotland

LADY MACBETH

BANQUO, a thane of Scotland

FLEANCE, Banquo's son

MACDUFF, Thane of Fife

LADY MACDUFF

SON of Macduff and Lady Macduff

LENNOX, thane and nobleman of Scotland

ROSS, thane and nobleman of Scotland

ANGUS, thane and nobleman of Scotland

SIWARD, Earl of Northumberland

YOUNG SIWARD, Siward's son

DOCTOR

GENTLEWOMAN attending Lady Macbeth

PORTER

FIRST MURDERER

SECOND MURDERER

THIRD MURDEERER

MESSENGER

FIRST WITCH

SECOND WITCH

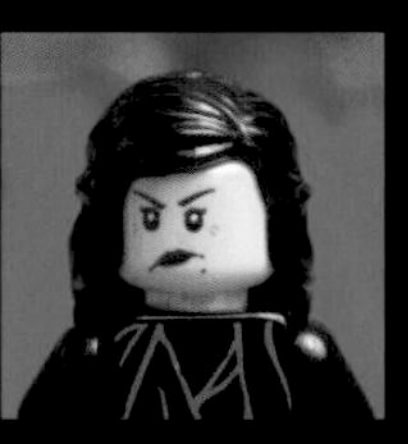
THIRD WITCH

HECATE

FIRST APPARITION

SECOND APPARITION

THIRD APPARITION

Not Pictured

MENTEITH, thane and nobleman of Scotland
CAITHNESS, thane and nobleman of Scotland
SEYTON, an officer attending Macbeth
Another LORD
CAPTAIN serving Duncan

OLD MAN
SERVANT to Macbeth
SERVANT to Lady Macbeth

Lords, Gentlemen, Officers, Soldiers, Murderers, and Attendants

ACT I. Scene I (1–12).

FIRST WITCH
When shall we three meet again
In thunder, lightning, or in rain?
SECOND WITCH
When the hurlyburly's done,
When the battle's lost and won.

FIRST WITCH
I come, Grimalkin!

SECOND WITCH
Paddock calls.
THIRD WITCH
Anon.

ALL
Fair is foul, and foul is fair:
Hover through the fog and filthy air.

ACT I. Scene II (1–70).

DUNCAN
What bloody man is that? He can report,
As seemeth by his plight, of the revolt
The newest state.

SERGEANT (cont.)
As two spent swimmers that do cling together
And choke their art. The merciless Macdonwald—
Worthy to be a rebel, for to that
The multiplying villanies of nature
Do swarm upon him—from the Western Isles
Of kerns and gallowglasses is supplied;
And Fortune, on his damnèd quarrel smiling,
Showed like a rebel's whore. But all's too weak:

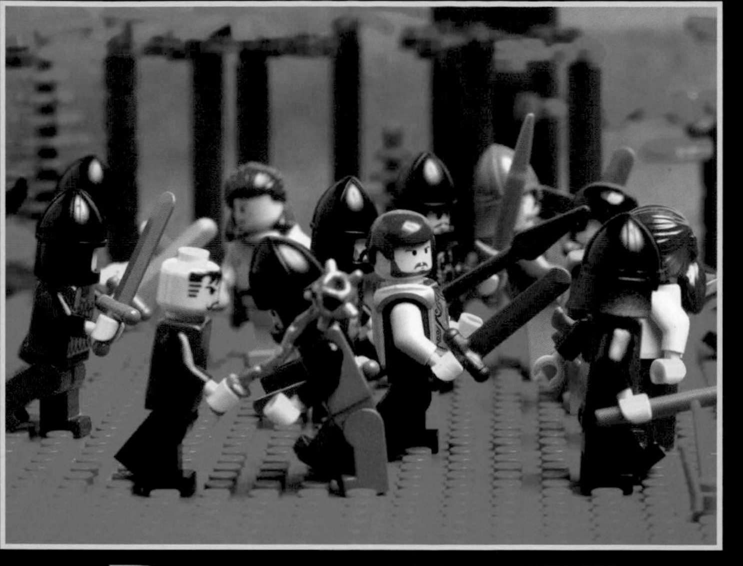

SERGEANT (cont.)
For brave Macbeth—well he deserves that name—
Disdaining Fortune, with his brandished steel,
Which smoked with bloody execution,
Like valour's minion carved out his passage
Till he faced the slave;
Which ne'er shook hands, nor bade farewell to him,
Till he unseamed him from the nave to th' chops,
And fixed his head upon our battlements.

SERGEANT
As whence the sun 'gins his reflection
Shipwrecking storms and direful thunders break,
So from that spring whence comfort seemed to come
Discomfort swells. Mark, King of Scotland, mark.
No sooner justice had, with valour armed,
Compelled these skipping kerns to trust their heels,
But the Norweyan lord, surveying vantage,
With furbished arms and new supplies of men
Began a fresh assault.
DUNCAN
Dismayed not this our captains, Macbeth and Banquo?

SERGEANT
Yes, as sparrows eagles, or the hare the lion.
If I say sooth, I must report they were
As cannons overcharged with double cracks,
So they doubly redoubled strokes upon the foe.
Except they meant to bathe in reeking wounds
Or memorise another Golgotha,
I cannot tell.

MALCOLM
The worthy Thane of Ross.
LENNOX
What a haste looks through his eyes!
So should he look that seems to speak things strange.

ROSS
God save the king!
DUNCAN
Whence cam'st thou, worthy thane?
ROSS
From Fife, great King,
Where the Norweyan banners flout the sky
And fan our people cold.
Norway himself, with terrible numbers,
Assisted by that most disloyal traitor,
The Thane of Cawdor, began a dismal conflict;
Till that Bellona's bridegroom, lapped in proof,
Confronted him with self-comparisons,
Point against point, rebellious arm 'gainst arm,
Curbing his lavish spirit; and to conclude,
The victory fell on us.

DUNCAN
Great happiness!
ROSS
That now
Sweno, the Norways' king, craves composition;
Nor would we deign him burial of his men
Till he disbursèd at Saint Colme's Inch
Ten thousand dollars to our general use.

DUNCAN
No more that Thane of Cawdor shall deceive
Our bosom interest. Go pronounce his present death,
And with his former title greet Macbeth.
ROSS
I'll see it done.

ACT I. Scene III (30–149).

ALL
The Weird Sisters, hand in hand,
Posters of the sea and land,
Thus do go about, about,
Thrice to thine, and thrice to mine,
And thrice again, to make up nine.
Peace! The charm's wound up.

BANQUO
How far is't called to Forres?—What are these,
So withered and so wild in their attire,
That look not like th'inhabitants o'th'earth
And yet are on't?—Live you? Or are you aught
That man may question? You seem to understand me
By each at once her choppy finger laying
Upon her skinny lips. You should be women,
And yet your beards forbid me to interpret
That you are so.
MACBETH
Speak, if you can. What are you?

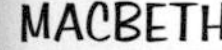

BANQUO
Good sir, why do you start and seem to fear
Things that do sound so fair?—I'th' name of truth,
Are ye fantastical or that indeed
Which outwardly ye show? My noble partner
You greet with present grace and great prediction
Of noble having and of royal hope,
That he seems rapt withal. To me you speak not.
If you can look into the seeds of time
And say which grain will grow and which will not,
Speak then to me, who neither beg nor fear
Your favours nor your hate.

FIRST WITCH
Lesser than Macbeth, and greater.

SECOND WITCH
Not so happy, yet much happier.

THIRD WITCH
Thou shalt get kings, though thou be none:
So all hail, Macbeth and Banquo!
FIRST WITCH
Banquo and Macbeth, all hail!

MACBETH
Stay, you imperfect speakers, tell me more!
By Sinel's death I know I am thane of Glamis,
But how of Cawdor? The Thane of Cawdor lives
A prosperous gentleman; and to be king
Stands not within the prospect of belief,
No more than to be Cawdor. Say from whence
You owe this strange intelligence, or why
Upon this blasted heath you stop our way
With such prophetic greeting? Speak, I charge you.

BANQUO
The earth hath bubbles, as the water has,
And these are of them. Whither are they vanished?
MACBETH
Into the air; and what seemed corporal melted,
As breath into the wind. Would they had stayed!
BANQUO
Were such things here as we do speak about?
Or have we eaten on the insane root
That takes the reason prisoner?

MACBETH
Your children shall be kings.
BANQUO
You shall be king.
MACBETH
And Thane of Cawdor too. Went it not so?
BANQUO
To th' selfsame tune and words—

BANQUO (cont.)
Who's here?
ROSS
The king hath happily received, Macbeth,
The news of thy success; and when he reads
Thy personal venture in the rebels' fight,
His wonders and his praises do contend
Which should be thine or his. Silenced with that,
In viewing o'er the rest o'th' selfsame day
He finds thee in the stout Norweyan ranks,
Nothing afeard of what thyself didst make,
Strange images of death. As thick as tale
Came post with post; and every one did bear
Thy praises in his kingdom's great defence,
And poured them down before him.
ANGUS
We are sent
To give thee from our royal master thanks,
Only to herald thee into his sight,
Not pay thee.

ROSS
And, for an earnest of a greater honour,
He bade me, from him, call thee Thane of Cawdor;
In which addition, hail, most worthy thane,
For it is thine.
BANQUO
What, can the devil speak true?

ANGUS
Who was the thane lives yet,
But under heavy judgment bears that life
Which he deserves to lose. Whether he was combined
With those of Norway, or did line the rebel
With hidden help and vantage, or that with both
He laboured in his country's wrack, I know not;
But treasons capital, confessed and proved,
Have overthrown him.

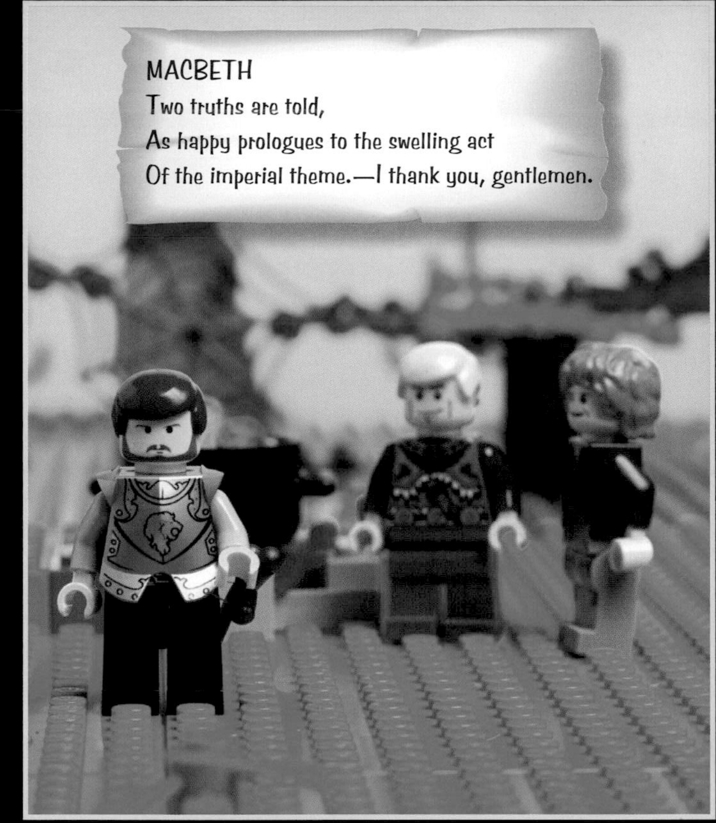

MACBETH (cont.)
This supernatural soliciting
Cannot be ill, cannot be good. If ill,
Why hath it given me earnest of success
Commencing in a truth? I am Thane of Cawdor.
If good, why do I yield to that suggestion
Whose horrid image doth unfix my hair
And make my seated heart knock at my ribs,
Against the use of nature? Present fears
Are less than horrible imaginings.
My thought, whose murder yet is but fantastical,
Shakes so my single state of man
That function is smothered in surmise,
And nothing is but what is not.

BANQUO
Look how our partner's rapt.

MACBETH
If chance will have me king, why, chance may crown me,
Without my stir.

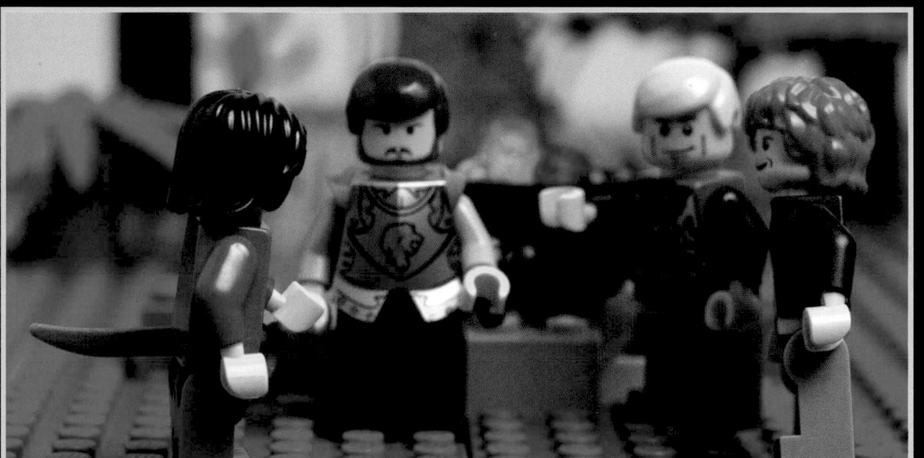
BANQUO
New honors come upon him,
Like our strange garments, cleave not to their mould
But with the aid of use.

MACBETH
Come what come may,
Time and the hour runs through the roughest day.

ACT I. Scene V (1–73).

Shortly after the witches foretell Macbeth and Banquo's royal prophecies, the pair meets up with King Duncan, who praises their loyalty and bravery. The traitorous Thane of Cawdor has been executed, and as promised by the witches, Macbeth will take his place. King Duncan jovially tells the men that his son, Malcolm, will be Prince of Cumberland, and therefore next in line to the throne. As King Duncan makes short-notice plans to visit Macbeth's castle at Inverness in celebration, Macbeth is struck by this new obstruction—Malcolm—in his seemingly straight line to the crown. In response to this unforeseen difficulty, Macbeth whispers to himself, "Stars, hide your fires;/Let not light see my black and deep desires./The eye wink at the hand; yet let that be/Which the eye fears, when it is done, to see" (I.iv.50–53). The first of many dark thoughts stir in Macbeth's head as he realizes that he must wear the mask of devotion to the King, tricking even himself, while secretly plotting to usurp the throne at any cost. With this dark seed sprouting, Macbeth goes ahead of the group to notify Lady Macbeth and his servants that King Duncan will be coming to his castle at Inverness shortly.

LADY MACBETH
"They met me in the day of success:
and I have learned by the perfect'st report
they have more in them than mortal knowledge. When I
burnt in desire to question them further, they made
themselves air, into which they vanished. Whiles I
stood rapt in the wonder of it came missives from the
King, who all-hailed me 'Thane of Cawdor,' by which
title, before, these Weird Sisters saluted me, and re-
ferred me to the coming on of time with 'Hail, king
that shalt be!' This have I thought good to deliver thee,
my dearest partner of greatness, that thou mightst not
lose the dues of rejoicing by being ignorant of
what greatness is promised thee. Lay it to thy heart, and
farewell."

LADY MACBETH (cont.)
Glamis thou art, and Cawdor; and shalt be
What thou art promised. Yet do I fear thy nature;
It is too full o'th' milk of human kindness
To catch the nearest way. Thou wouldst be great,
Art not without ambition, but without
The illness should attend it. What thou wouldst highly,
That wouldst thou holily; wouldst not play false,
And yet wouldst wrongly win. Thou'dst have, great Glamis,
That which cries "Thus thou must do," if thou have it;
And that which rather thou dost fear to do
Than wishest should be undone. Hie thee hither,
That I may pour my spirits in thine ear
And chastise with the valour of my tongue
All that impedes thee from the golden round
Which fate and metaphysical aid doth seem
To have thee crowned withal.

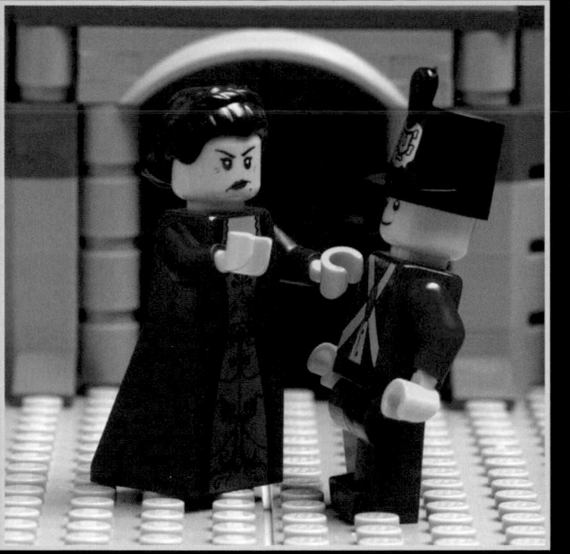

LADY MACBETH
Thou'rt mad to say it!
Is not thy master with him, who, were't so,
Would have informed for preparation?

MESSENGER
So please you, it is true. Our thane is coming.
One of my fellows had the speed of him,
Who, almost dead for breath, had scarcely more
Than would make up his message.
LADY MACBETH
Give him tending;
He brings great news.

LADY MACBETH (cont.)
The raven himself is hoarse
That croaks the fatal entrance of Duncan
Under my battlements. Come, you spirits
That tend on mortal thoughts, unsex me here
And fill me from the crown to the toe top-full
Of direst cruelty! Make thick my blood;
Stop up th'access and passage to remorse,
That no compunctious visitings of nature
Shake my fell purpose, nor keep peace between
The effect and it! Come to my woman's breasts
And take my milk for gall, you murd'ring ministers,
Wherever in your sightless substances
You wait on nature's mischief! Come, thick night,
And pall thee in the dunnest smoke of hell,
That my keen knife see not the wound it makes,
Nor heaven peep through the blanket of the dark
To cry "Hold, hold!"

LADY MACBETH
O, never
Shall sun that morrow see!
Your face, my thane, is as a book where men
May read strange matters. To beguile the time,
Look like the time; bear welcome in your eye,
Your hand, your tongue. Look like the innocent flower,
But be the serpent under't. He that's coming
Must be provided for; and you shall put
This night's great business into my dispatch;
Which shall to all our nights and days to come
Give solely sovereign sway and masterdom.

ACT I. Scene VII (1–83).

King Duncan and his entourage arrive at Macbeth's castle, and all are greeted by a saccharine Lady Macbeth. Duncan buoyantly praises Lady Macbeth for receiving them on such short notice, and Lady Macbeth responds in kind, despite the wheels of treachery that are already turning in her head. They all prepare for a celebration as the hosts of the party begin to plot the demise of the throne.

MACBETH

If it were done when 'tis done, then 'twere well
It were done quickly. If th'assassination
Could trammel up the consequence, and catch
With his surcease success—that but this blow
Might be the be-all and the end-all!—here,
But here, upon this bank and shoal of time,
We'd jump the life to come. But in these cases
We still have judgment here, that we but teach
Bloody instructions, which, being taught, return
To plague th'inventor. This evenhanded justice
Commends th'ingredients of our poisoned chalice
To our own lips. He's here in double trust:

MACBETH (cont.)

First, as I am his kinsman and his subject,
Strong both against the deed; then, as his host,
Who should against his murderer shut the door,
Not bear the knife myself. Besides, this Duncan
Hath borne his faculties so meek, hath been
So clear in his great office, that his virtues
Will plead like angels, trumpet-tongued, against
The deep damnation of his taking-off;
And Pity, like a naked newborn babe
Striding the blast, or heaven's cherubin, horsed
Upon the sightless couriers of the air,
Shall blow the horrid deed in every eye,
That tears shall drown the wind. I have no spur
To prick the sides of my intent, but only
Vaulting ambition, which o'erleaps itself
And falls on th'other.

MACBETH
We will proceed no further in this business.
He hath honoured me of late, and I have bought
Golden opinions from all sorts of people,
Which would be worn now in their newest gloss,
Not cast aside so soon.
LADY MACBETH
Was the hope drunk
Wherein you dressed yourself? Hath it slept since?
And wakes it now, to look so green and pale
At what it did so freely? From this time
Such I account thy love. Art thou afeard
To be the same in thine own act and valour
As thou art in desire? Wouldst thou have that
Which thou esteem'st the ornament of life,
And live a coward in thine own esteem,
Letting "I dare not" wait upon "I would,"
Like the poor cat i'th' adage?

MACBETH
Prithee, peace:
I dare do all that may become a man;
Who dares do more is none.
LADY MACBETH
What beast was't, then,
That made you break this enterprise to me?
When you durst do it, then you were a man;
And, to be more than what you were, you would
Be so much more the man. Nor time nor place
Did then adhere, and yet you would make both.
They have made themselves, and that their fitness now
Does unmake you. I have given suck, and know
How tender 'tis to love the babe that milks me;
I would, while it was smiling in my face,
Have plucked my nipple from his boneless gums
And dashed the brains out, had I so sworn as you
Have done to this.

LADY MACBETH
We fail?
But screw your courage to the sticking place
And we'll not fail. When Duncan is asleep—
Whereto the rather shall his day's hard journey
Soundly invite him—his two chamberlains
Will I with wine and wassail so convince
That memory, the warder of the brain,
Shall be a fume, and the receipt of reason
A limbeck only. When in swinish sleep
Their drenchèd natures lies as in a death,
What cannot you and I perform upon
Th'unguarded Duncan? What not put upon
His spongy officers, who shall bear the guilt
Of our great quell?

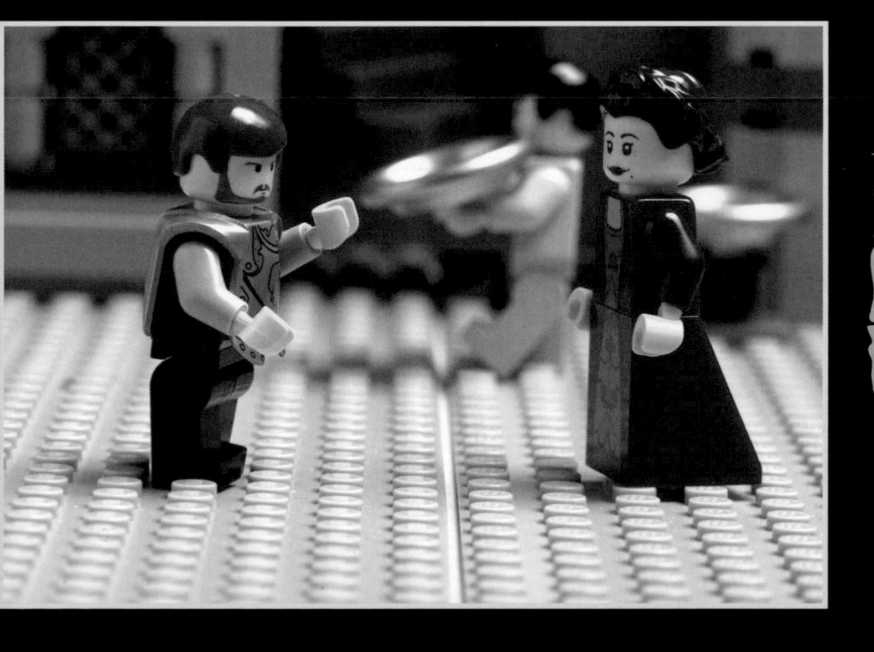

MACBETH
I am settled, and bend up
Each corporal agent to this terrible feat.
Away, and mock the time with fairest show.
False face must hide what the false heart doth know.

ACT II. Scene I (34–65).

Late that evening, Banquo and his son Fleance are walking the halls of Macbeth's castle and bump into the toiling Macbeth. Banquo describes how happy King Duncan was throughout the evening, having given out many gifts to Macbeth's household for their hospitality. Banquo gives Macbeth a large diamond, which is a gift from the King to Lady Macbeth for being such a welcoming hostess. Banquo then mentions a dream he had about the three witches' prophecies and tries to discuss it with Macbeth, who waves him off and tells him they can talk another time. Banquo and his son head to bed, and Macbeth continues to wander the corridors, still preoccupied with his plans for murder.

MACBETH (cont.)
I have thee not, and yet I see thee still.
Art thou not, fatal vision, sensible
To feeling as to sight? Or art thou but
A dagger of the mind, a false creation,
Proceeding from the heat-oppressèd brain?

MACBETH (cont.)
I see thee yet, in form as palpable
As this which now I draw.
Thou marshall'st me the way that I was going,
And such an instrument I was to use.
Mine eyes are made the fools o'th'other senses,
Or else worth all the rest. I see thee still,
And on thy blade and dudgeon gouts of blood,
Which was not so before. There's no such thing.
It is the bloody business which informs
Thus to mine eyes. Now o'er the one half world
Nature seems dead, and wicked dreams abuse
The curtained sleep.

MACBETH (cont.)
Witchcraft celebrates
Pale Hecate's offerings, and withered Murder,
Alarumed by his sentinel, the wolf,
Whose howl's his watch, thus with his stealthy pace,
With Tarquin's ravishing strides, towards his design
Moves like a ghost. Thou sure and firm-set earth,

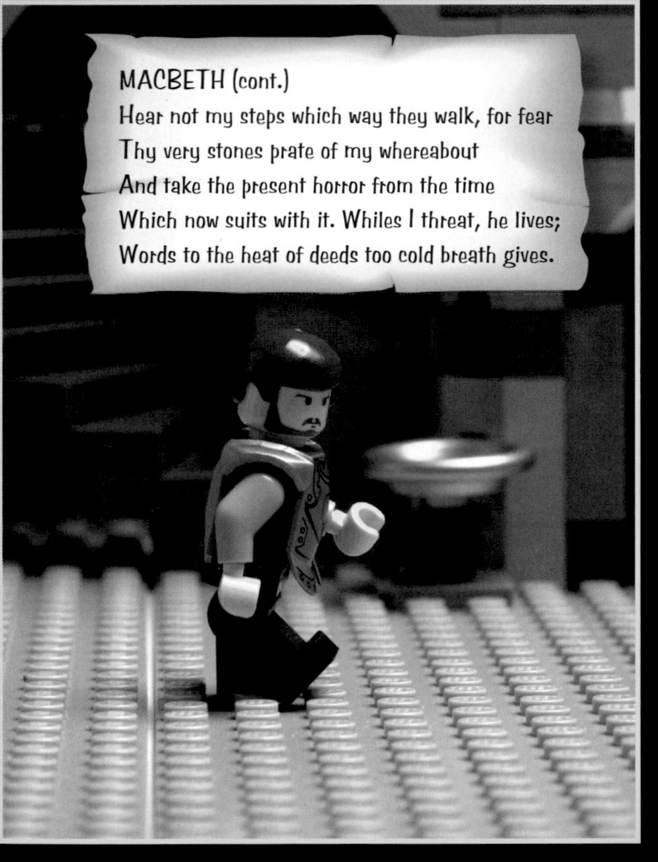
MACBETH (cont.)
Hear not my steps which way they walk, for fear
Thy very stones prate of my whereabout
And take the present horror from the time
Which now suits with it. Whiles I threat, he lives;
Words to the heat of deeds too cold breath gives.

MACBETH (cont.)
I go, and it is done. The bell invites me.
Hear it not, Duncan, for it is a knell
That summons thee to heaven or to hell.

M

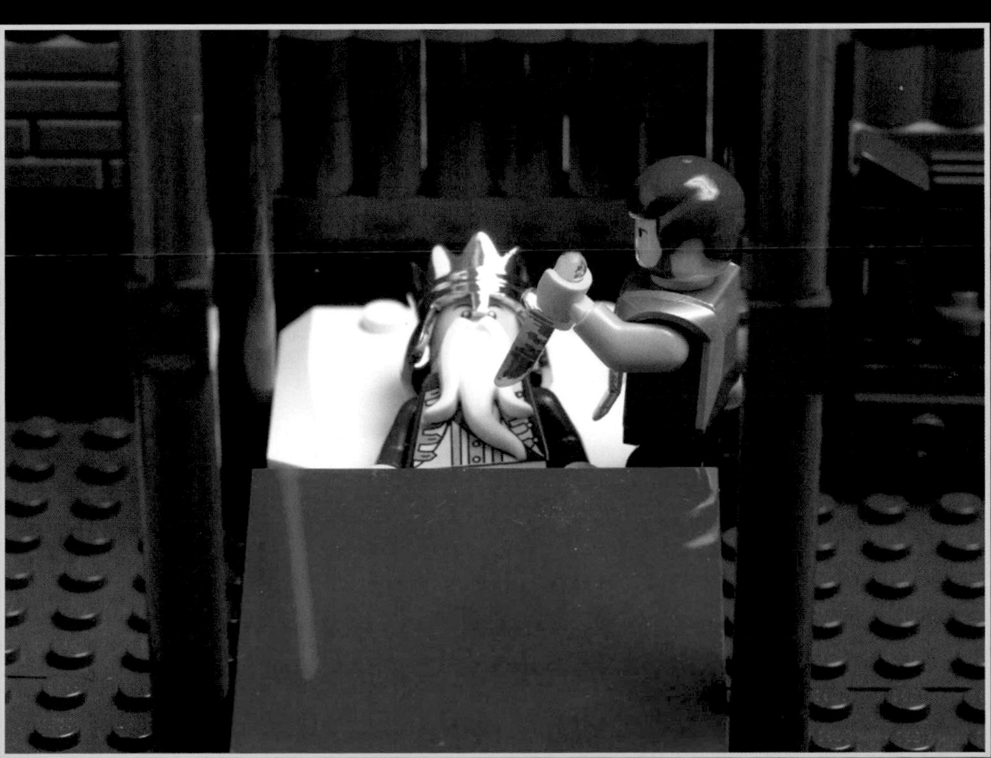

LADY MACBETH (cont.)
Hark! Peace!
It was the owl that shrieked, the fatal bellman,
Which gives the stern'st good-night. He is about it.
The doors are open; and the surfeited grooms
Do mock their charge with snores: I have drugged their possets,
That death and nature do contend about them,
Whether they live or die.

MACBETH
[Within] Who's there? What, ho!
LADY MACBETH
Alack, I am afraid they have awaked,
And 'tis not done. Th'attempt and not the deed
Confounds us. Hark! I laid their daggers ready;
He could not miss 'em. Had he not resembled
My father as he slept, I had done't.

LADY MACBETH
I heard the owl scream and the crickets cry.
Did not you speak?
MACBETH
When?
LADY MACBETH
Now.

MACBETH
As I descended?
LADY MACBETH
Ay.

MACBETH
Hark!
Who lies i'th' second chamber?
LADY MACBETH
Donalbain.

MACBETH
There's one did laugh in 's sleep, and one cried "Murder!"
That they did wake each other: I stood and heard them.
But they did say their prayers, and addressed them
Again to sleep.
LADY MACBETH
There are two lodged together.

MACBETH
One cried "God bless us!" and "Amen" the other,
As they had seen me with these hangman's hands.
List'ning their fear, I could not say "Amen,"
When they did say "God bless us!"

LADY MACBETH
Consider it not so deeply.
MACBETH
But wherefore could not I pronounce "Amen"?
I had most need of blessing, and "Amen"
Stuck in my throat.

MACBETH
Methought I heard a voice cry "Sleep no more!
Macbeth does murder sleep," the innocent sleep,
Sleep that knits up the raveled sleeve of care,
The death of each day's life, sore labour's bath,
Balm of hurt minds, great nature's second course,
Chief nourisher in life's feast—

LADY MACBETH
What do you mean?

MACBETH
Still it cried "Sleep no more!" to all the house;
"Glamis hath murdered sleep, and therefore Cawdor
Shall sleep no more; Macbeth shall sleep no more."

LADY MACBETH
Who was it that thus cried? Why, worthy thane,
You do unbend your noble strength, to think
So brainsickly of things. Go get some water
And wash this filthy witness from your hand.
Why did you bring these daggers from the place?
They must lie there. Go carry them and smear
The sleepy grooms with blood.

MACBETH
Whence is that knocking?
How is't with me, when every noise appalls me?
What hands are here? Ha! They pluck out mine eyes.
Will all great Neptune's ocean wash this blood
Clean from my hand? No, this my hand will rather
The multitudinous seas in incarnadine,
Making the green one red.

LADY MACBETH
My hands are of your colour; but I shame
To wear a heart so white.

LADY MACBETH (cont.)
I hear a knocking
At the south entry. Retire we to our chamber;
A little water clears us of this deed.
How easy is it, then! Your constancy
Hath left you unattended.

LADY MACBETH (cont.)
Hark! More knocking.
Get on your nightgown, lest occasion call us
And show us to be watchers. Be not lost
So poorly in your thoughts.

MACBETH
To know my deed, 'twere best not know myself.
Wake Duncan with thy knocking! I would thou couldst!

ACT II. Scene III (41–148).

It is the early morning and the knocking that startled Macbeth and Lady Macbeth amidst their violent crime continues. The castle's porter attends to the knocking, though not without a drunken monologue likening himself to the gatekeeper of Hell. His slurred speech is not so far from the truth, though no one knows what has occurred in the castle just yet. The porter lets in Macduff and Lennox, who are there to wake King Duncan for the day ahead. Macbeth joins the chatting group, feigning that he was awoken by the loud knocking, which will be his first of many lies about the coming discovery of King Duncan's death.

LENNOX
Good morrow, noble sir.
MACBETH
Good morrow, both.
MACDUFF
Is the King stirring, worthy thane?
MACBETH
Not yet.
MACDUFF
He did command me to call timely on him.
I have almost slipped the hour.

MACBETH
The labour we delight in physics pain.
This is the door.
MACDUFF
I'll make so bold to call,
For 'tis my limited service.

LENNOX
Goes the King hence today?
MACBETH
He does; he did appoint so.
LENNOX
The night has been unruly. Where we lay,
Our chimneys were blown down, and, as they say,
Lamentings heard i'th'air, strange screams of death,
And prophesying with accents terrible
Of dire combustion and confused events
New hatched to the woeful time. The obscure bird
Clamoured the livelong night. Some say the earth
Was feverous and did shake.
MACBETH
'Twas a rough night.
LENNOX
My young remembrance cannot parallel
A fellow to it.

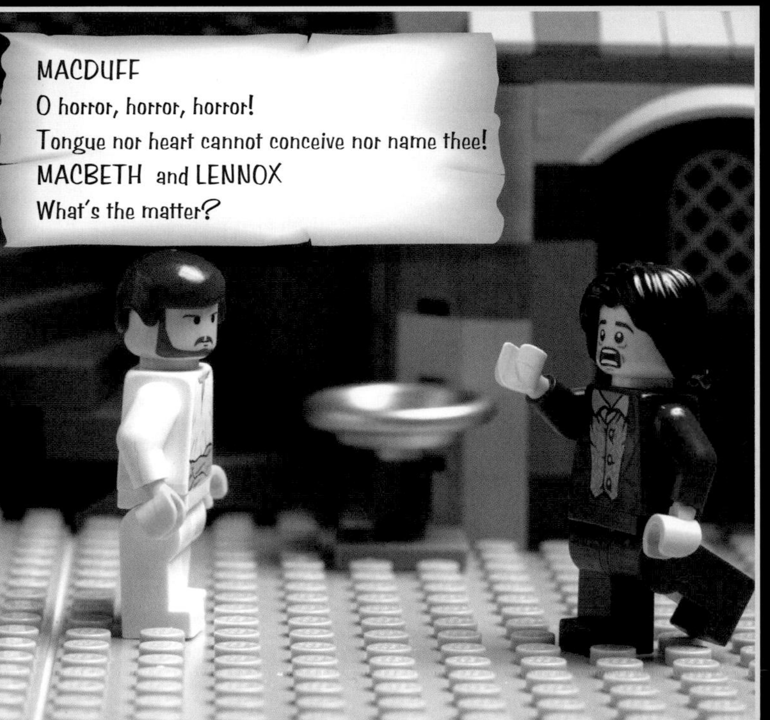

MACDUFF
Confusion now hath made his masterpiece!
Most sacrilegious murder hath broke ope
The Lord's anointed temple, and stole thence
The life o'th' building!

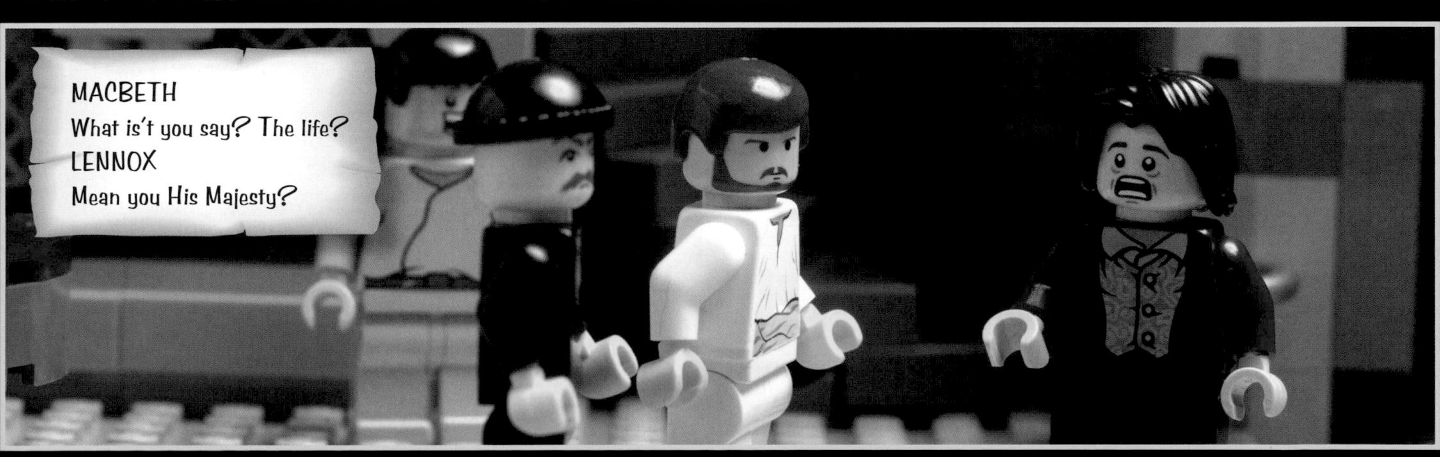

MACDUFF (cont.)
Awake, awake!
Ring the alarum bell. Murder and treason!
Banquo and Donalbain, Malcolm, awake!
Shake off this downy sleep, death's counterfeit,
And look on death itself! Up, up, and see
The great doom's image! Malcolm, Banquo,
As from your graves rise up and walk like sprites
To countenance this horror! Ring the bell.

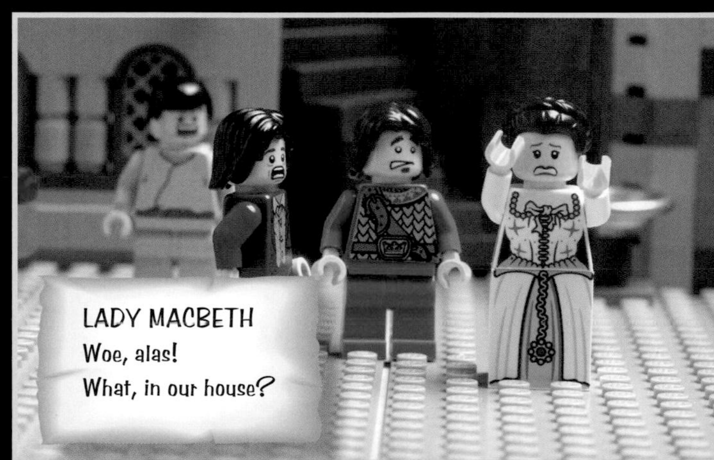

BANQUO
Too cruel anywhere.
Dear Duff, I prithee, contradict thyself
And say it is not so.

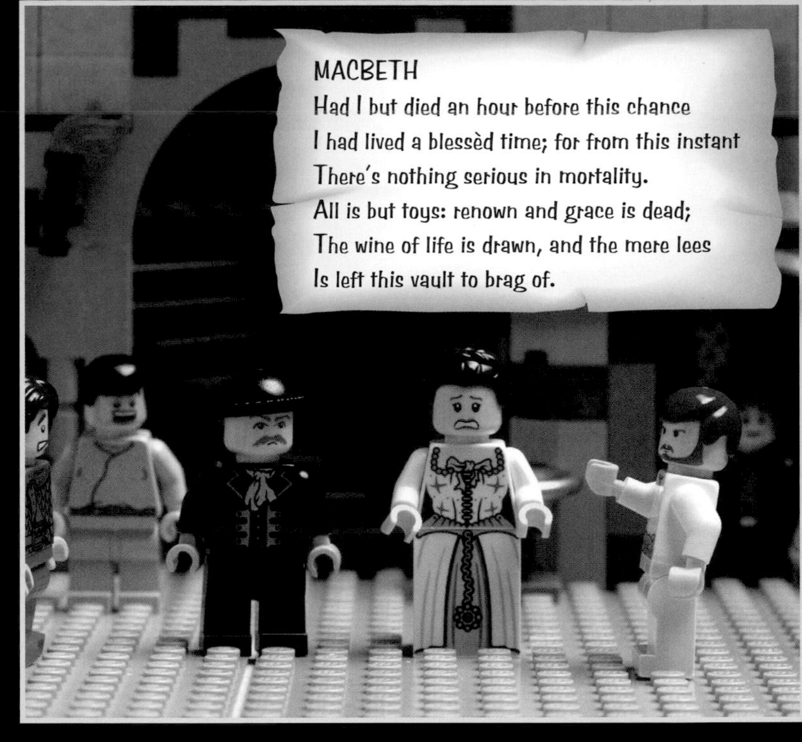
MACBETH
Had I but died an hour before this chance
I had lived a blessèd time; for from this instant
There's nothing serious in mortality.
All is but toys: renown and grace is dead;
The wine of life is drawn, and the mere lees
Is left this vault to brag of.

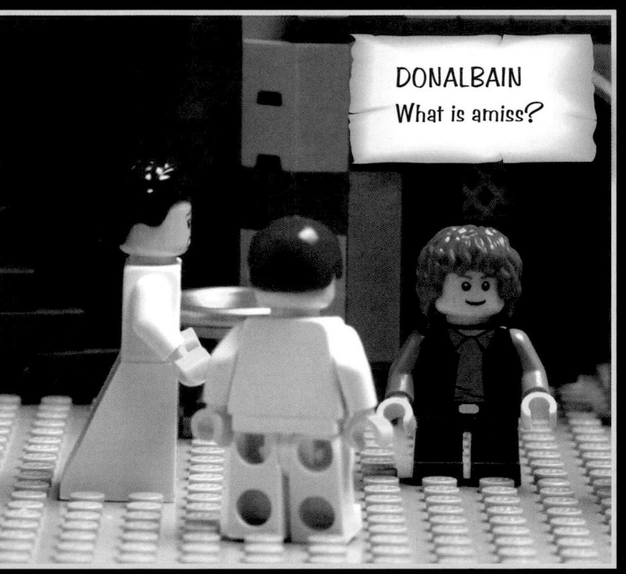
DONALBAIN
What is amiss?

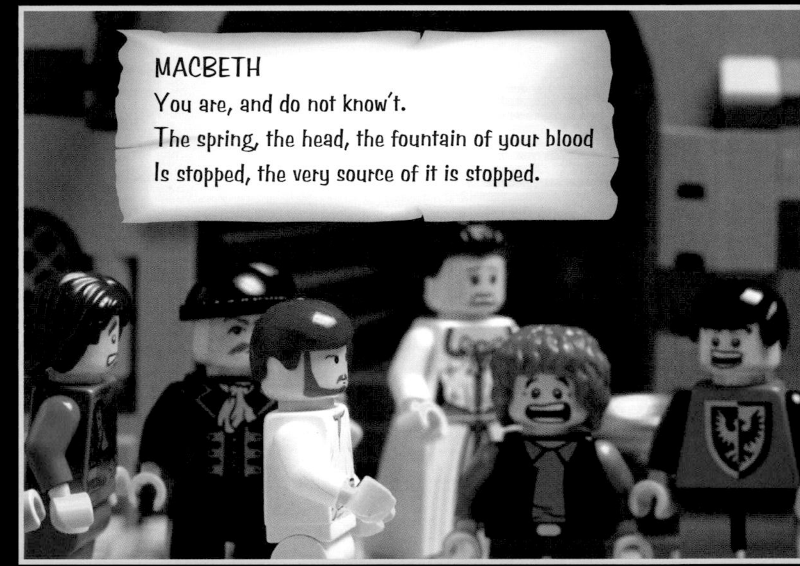
MACBETH
You are, and do not know't.
The spring, the head, the fountain of your blood
Is stopped, the very source of it is stopped.

MACDUFF
Your royal father's murdered.

MALCOLM
O, by whom?

LENNOX
Those of his chamber, as it seemed, had done't.
Their hands and faces were all badged with blood;
So were their daggers, which unwiped we found
Upon their pillows. They stared, and were distracted;
No man's life was to be trusted with them.

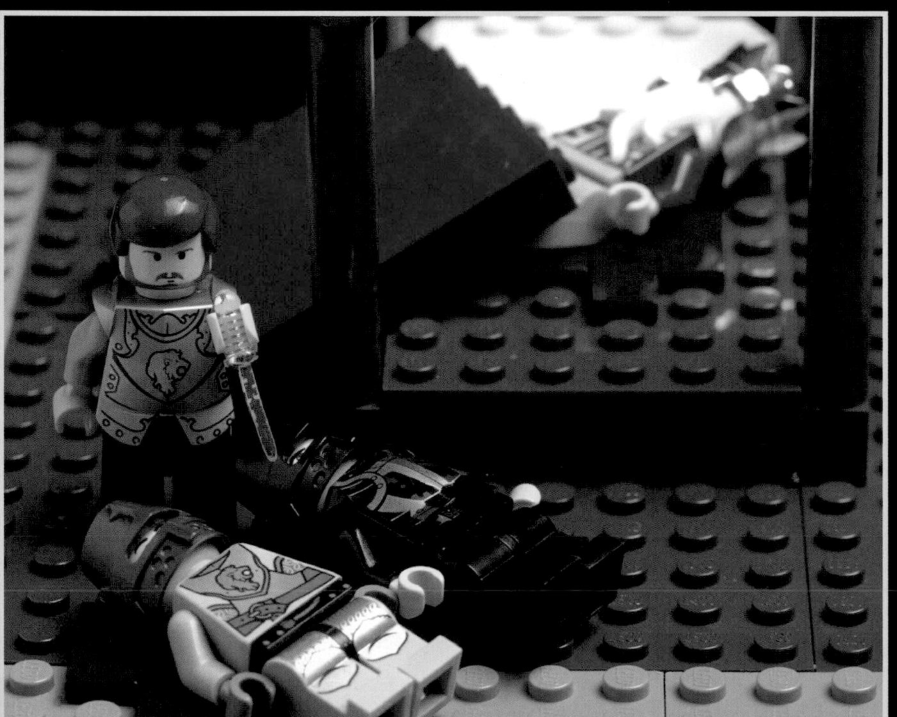

MACBETH (cont.)
Th'expedition my violent love
Outrun the pauser, reason. Here lay Duncan,
His silver skin laced with his golden blood,
And his gashed stabs looked like a breach in nature
For ruin's wasteful entrance; there, the murderers,
Steeped in the colours of their trade, their daggers
Unmannerly breeched with gore. Who could refrain
That had a heart to love, and in that heart
Courage to make 's love known?

BANQUO (cont.)
And when we have our naked frailties hid,
That suffer in exposure, let us meet
And question this most bloody piece of work
To know it further. Fears and scruples shake us.
In the great hand of God I stand, and thence
Against the undivulged pretence I fight
Of treasonous malice.
MACDUFF
And so do I.
ALL
So all.

MALCOLM
What will you do? Let's not consort with them.
To show an unfelt sorrow is an office
Which the false man does easy. I'll to England.

DONALBAIN
To Ireland, I; our separated fortune
Shall keep us both the safer. Where we are,
There's daggers in men's smiles; the nea'er in blood,
The nearer bloody.

MALCOLM
This murderous shaft that's shot
Hath not yet lighted, and our safest way
Is to avoid the aim. Therefore to horse,
And let us not be dainty of leave-taking,
But shift away. There's warrant in that theft
Which steals itself when there's no mercy left.

Act III. Scene I (1–143).

In the early wake of King Duncan's violent murder, an old man, Ross, and Macduff discuss the horror of the crime and what it means for Scotland. Macbeth has led them to believe that the guards in King Duncan's chamber were responsible for his death, and that he killed them in a seemingly loyal fit of rage for having supposedly murdered his beloved King. He has also planted the idea that King Duncan's sons, Malcolm and Donalbain, paid the two guards to kill their father, and that their subsequent flight is indicative of their guilt. In this discussion, it is revealed that Macbeth will go to Scone to be crowned as King, while the body of King Duncan will go to Colmekill to be buried in his family tomb. The witches' initial prophecy is now fulfilled.

BANQUO
Thou hast it now—King, Cawdor, Glamis, all
As the weird women promised, and I fear
Thou played'st most foully for't. Yet it was said
It should not stand in thy posterity,
But that myself should be the root and father
Of many kings. If there come truth from them—
As upon thee, Macbeth, their speeches shine—
Why, by the verities on thee made good,
May they not be my oracles as well
And set me up in hope? But hush, no more.

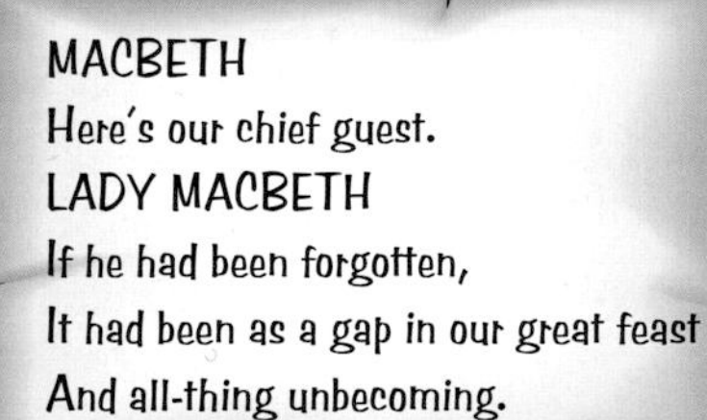

MACBETH
Tonight we hold a solemn supper, sir,
And I'll request your presence.
BANQUO
Let Your Highness
Command upon me, to the which my duties
Are with a most indissoluble tie
Forever knit.

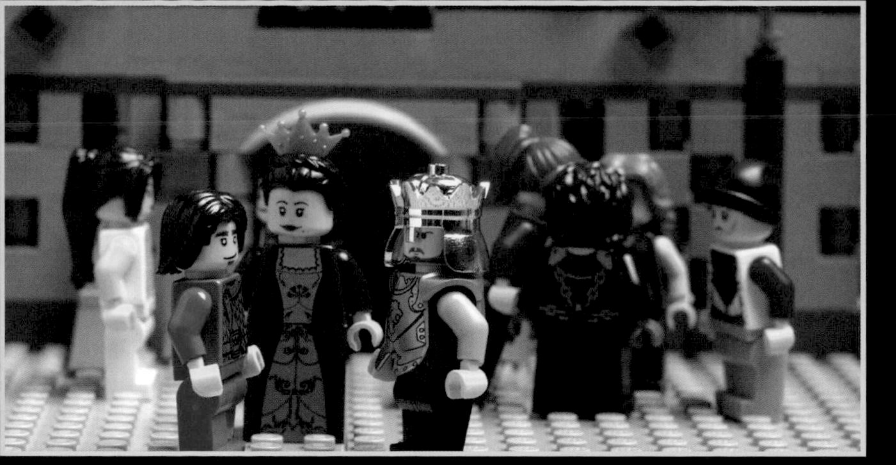
MACBETH
We should have else desired your good advice,
Which still hath been both grave and prosperous,
In this day's council; but we'll take tomorrow.
Is't far you ride?
BANQUO
As far, my lord, as will fill up the time
Twixt this and supper. Go not my horse the better,
I must become a borrower of the night
For a dark hour or twain.

MACBETH
Fail not our feast.
BANQUO
My lord, I will not.

MACBETH
We hear our bloody cousins are bestowed
In England and in Ireland, not confessing
Their cruel parricide, filling their hearers
With strange invention. But of that tomorrow,
When therewithal we shall have cause of state
Craving us jointly. Hie you to horse. Adieu,
Till you return at night. Goes Fleance with you?

BANQUO
Ay, my good lord: our time does call upon 's.

MACBETH
I wish your horses swift and sure of foot,
And so I do commend you to their backs.
Farewell.

MACBETH (cont.)
Let every man be master of his time
Till seven at night. To make society
The sweeter welcome, we will keep ourself
Till supper-time alone. While then, God be with you!

MACBETH (cont.)
Sirrah, a word with you. Attend those men
Our pleasure?
ATTENDANT
They are, my lord, without the palace gate.
MACBETH
Bring them before us.

MACBETH (cont.)
To be thus is nothing;
But to be safely thus.—Our fears in Banquo
Stick deep, and in his royalty of nature
Reigns that which would be feared. 'Tis much he dares;
And to that dauntless temper of his mind
He hath a wisdom that doth guide his valour
To act in safety. There is none but he
Whose being I do fear; and under him
My genius is rebuked, as it is said
Mark Antony's was by Caesar. He chid the sisters
When first they put the name of king upon me,
And bade them speak to him. Then, prophetlike,
They hailed him father to a line of kings.
Upon my head they placed a fruitless crown
And put a barren sceptre in my grip,
Thence to be wrenched with an unlineal hand,
No son of mine succeeding. If't be so,

MACBETH (cont.)
For Banquo's issue have I filed my mind;
For them the gracious Duncan have I murdered,
Put rancours in the vessel of my peace
Only for them, and mine eternal jewel
Given to the common enemy of man
To make them kings, the seeds of Banquo kings.
Rather than so, come fate into the list,
And champion me to th'utterance!—

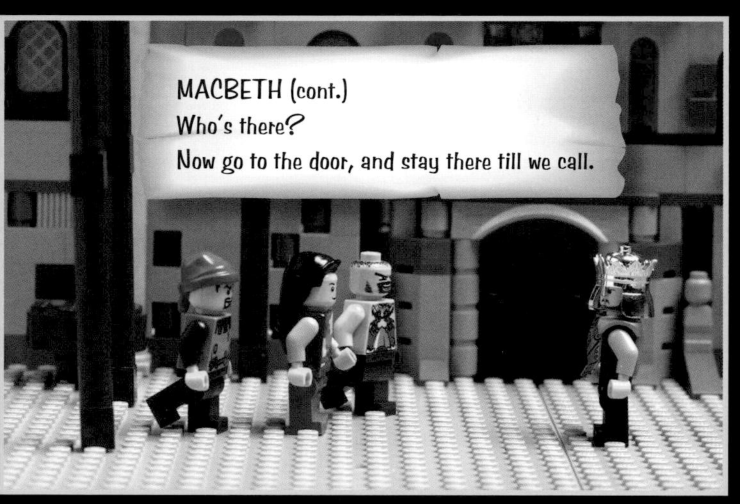

MACBETH
Well then, now
Have you considered of my speeches? Know
That it was he in the times past which held you
So under fortune, which you thought had been
Our innocent self. This I made good to you
In our last conference, passed in probation with you
How you were borne in hand, how crossed, the instruments,
Who wrought with them, and all things else that might
To half a soul and to a notion crazed
Say "Thus did Banquo."
FIRST MURDERER
You made it known to us.

MACBETH
I did so, and went further, which is now
Our point of second meeting. Do you find
Your patience so predominant in your nature
That you can let this go? Are you so gospeled
To pray for this good man and for his issue,
Whose heavy hand hath bowed you to the grave
And beggared yours forever?

MACBETH
Ay, in the catalogue ye go for men,
As hounds and greyhounds, mongrels, spaniels, curs,
Shoughs, water-rugs, and demi-wolves are clept
All by the name of dogs. The valued file
Distinguishes the swift, the slow, the subtle,
The housekeeper, the hunter, every one
According to the gift which bounteous nature
Hath in him closed, whereby he does receive
Particular addition from the bill
That writes them all alike; and so of men.
Now, if you have a station in the file,
Not i'th' worst rank of manhood, say't;
And I will put that business in your bosoms
Whose execution takes your enemy off,
Grapples you to the heart and love of us,
Who wear our health but sickly in his life,
Which in his death were perfect.

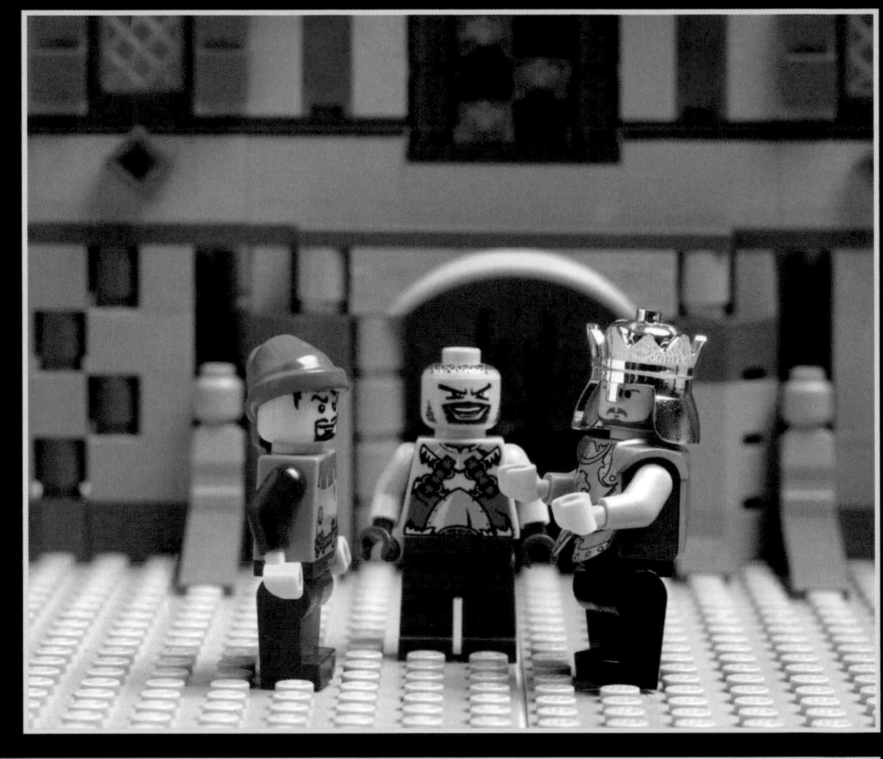

MACBETH
Both of you
Know Banquo was your enemy.
BOTH MURDERERS
True, my lord.
MACBETH
So is he mine, and in such bloody distance
That every minute of his being thrusts
Against my near'st of life. And though I could
With barefaced power sweep him from my sight
And bid my will avouch it, yet I must not,
For certain friends that are both his and mine,
Whose loves I may not drop, but wail his fall
Who I myself struck down. And thence it is
That I to your assistance do make love,
Masking the business from the common eye
For sundry weighty reasons.

MACBETH
Your spirits shine through you. Within this hour at most
I will advise you where to plant yourselves,
Acquaint you with the perfect spy o'th' time,
The moment on't, for't must be done tonight,
And something from the palace; always thought
That I require a clearness. And with him—
To leave no rubs nor botches in the work—
Fleance his son, that keeps him company,
Whose absence is no less material to me
Than is his father's, must embrace the fate
Of that dark hour. Resolve yourselves apart;
I'll come to you anon.
BOTH MURDERERS
We are resolved, my lord.

ACT III. Scene III (1–28).

After Macbeth plots to have Banquo killed, he and Lady Macbeth react quietly with one another to the results of their crime. Likening King Duncan's throne to a snake, Macbeth comments to his wife that they have "scorched the snake, not killed it./She'll close and be herself" (III.ii.15–16). In other words, though they have killed King Duncan, their plan was shortsighted and they are still vulnerable. Macbeth hints of his plans to kill Banquo but refuses to shed any more light on the plan, so that Lady Macbeth can applaud him when it is done.

FIRST MURDERER
But who did bid thee join with us?
THIRD MURDERER
Macbeth.
SECOND MURDERER
He needs not our mistrust, since he delivers
Our offices and what we have to do
To the direction just.

FIRST MURDERER
Then stand with us.
The west yet glimmers with some streaks of day:
Now spurs the lated traveler apace
To gain the timely inn, and near approaches
The subject of our watch.
THIRD MURDERER
Hark, I hear horses.
BANQUO
[Within] Give us a light there, ho!

FIRST MURDERER
Stand to't.

BANQUO
It will be rain tonight.

FIRST MURDERER
Let it come down!

BANQUO
O, treachery! Fly, good Fleance, fly, fly, fly!
Thou mayst revenge. O slave!

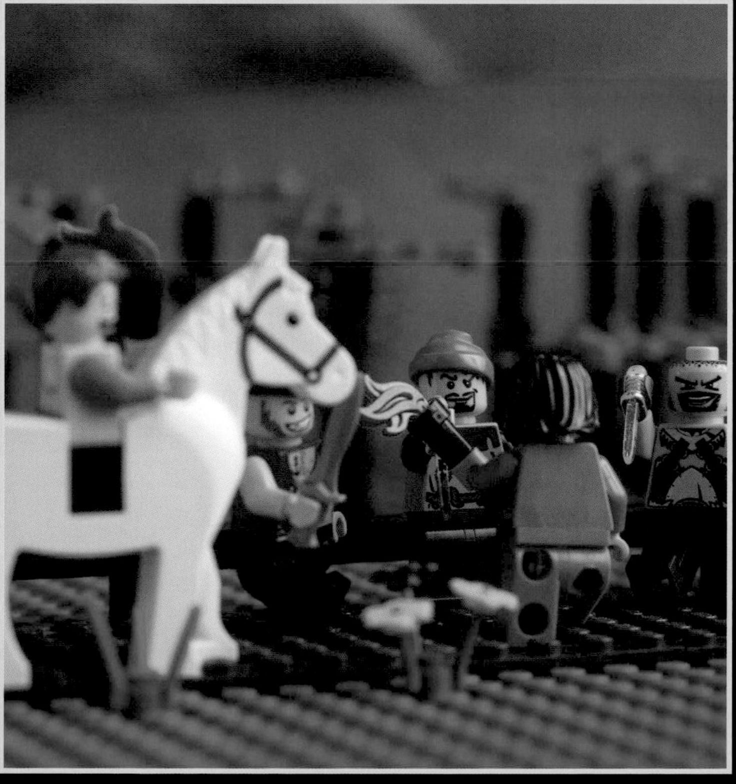

THIRD MURDERER
Who did strike out the light?
FIRST MURDERER
Was't not the way?

THIRD MURDERER
There's but one down; the son is fled.
SECOND MURDERER
We have lost best half of our affair.

FIRST MURDERER
Well, let's away and say how much is done.

ACT III. Scene IV (40–145).

The First Murderer shares the news with Macbeth that they have successfully killed Banquo, but that his son, Fleance, has fled. Macbeth thanks the murderer for killing Banquo but expresses concern that Fleance lives. While Fleance is young and harmless now, he is sure to grow up with vengeance for his father's death heavy on his mind. For the time being, Macbeth decides to put his anxieties aside and proceed to the party he is hosting.

MACBETH
Here had we now our country's honour roofed
Were the graced person of our Banquo present,
Who may I rather challenge for unkindness
Than pity for mischance.

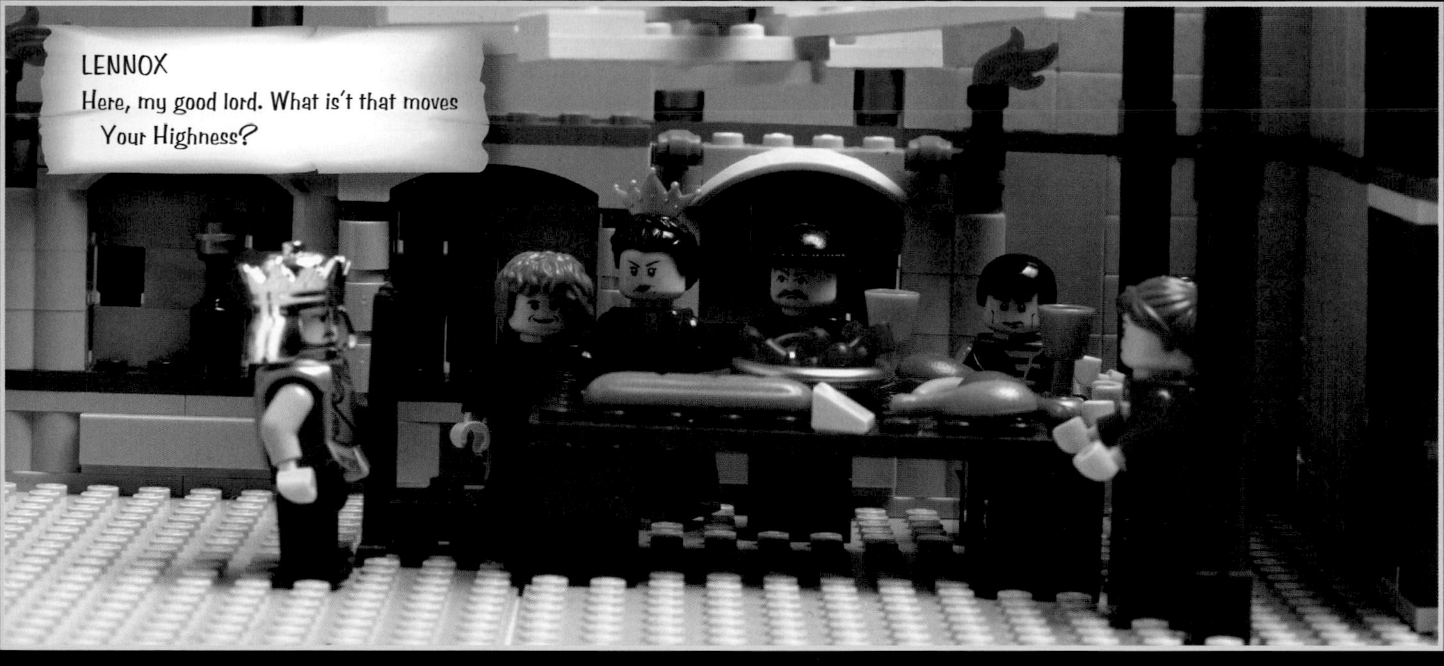

MACBETH
Thou canst not say I did it. Never shake
Thy gory locks at me.
ROSS
Gentlemen, rise. His Highness is not well.
LADY MACBETH
Sit, worthy friends. My lord is often thus,
And hath been from his youth. Pray you,
keep seat.
The fit is momentary; upon a thought
He will again be well. If much you note him
You shall offend him and extend his passion.
Feed, and regard him not.

LADY MACBETH (cont.)
Are you a man?
MACBETH
Ay, and a bold one, that dare look on that
Which might appall the devil.

LADY MACBETH
O, proper stuff.
This is the very painting of your fear:
This is the air-drawn dagger which, you said,
Led you to Duncan. O, these flaws and starts,
Impostors to true fear, would well become
A woman's story at a winter's fire,
Authorized by her grandam. Shame itself!
Why do you make such faces? When all's done,
You look but on a stool.

MACBETH
Prithee, see there!
Behold! look! Lo, how say you?—
Why, what care I? If thou canst nod, speak too.
If charnel houses and our graves must send
Those that we bury back, our monuments
Shall be the maws of kites.

LADY MACBETH
What, quite unmanned in folly?
MACBETH
If I stand here, I saw him.
LADY MACBETH
Fie, for shame!

MACBETH
Blood hath been shed ere now, i'th'olden time,
Ere humane statute purged the gentle weal;
Ay, and since too, murders have been performed
Too terrible for the ear. The time has been
That, when the brains were out, the man would die,
And there an end; but now they rise again
With twenty mortal murders on their crowns,
And push us from our stools. This is more strange
Than such a murder is.
LADY MACBETH
My worthy lord,
Your noble friends do lack you.

MACBETH
I do forget.
Do not muse at me, my most worthy friends;
I have a strange infirmity, which is nothing
To those that know me. Come, love and health to all!
Then I'll sit down. Give me some wine. Fill full.

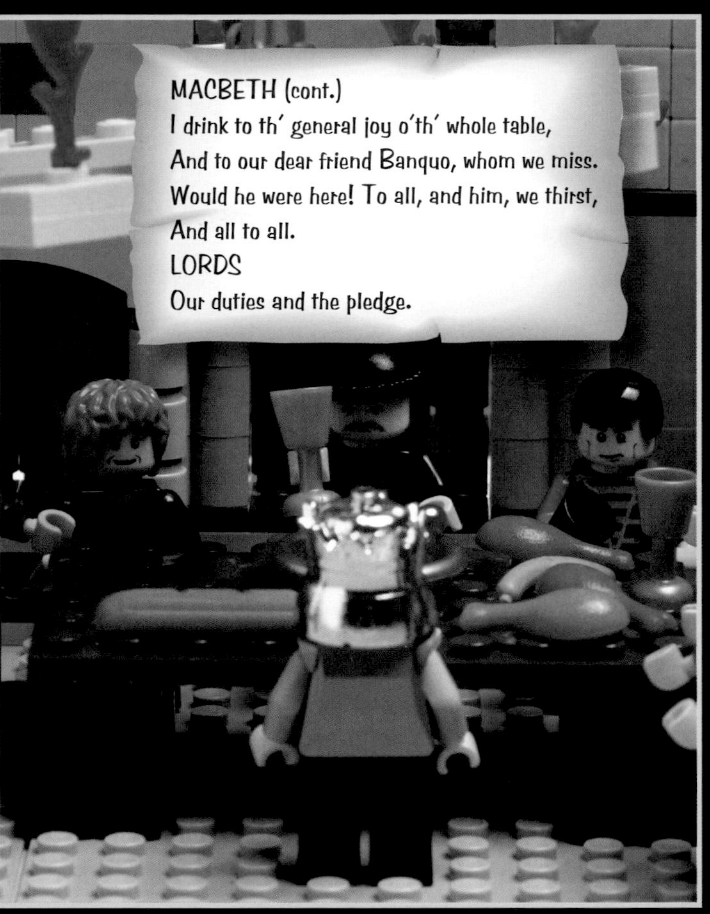

LADY MACBETH
Think of this, good peers,
But as a thing of custom. 'Tis no other;
Only it spoils the pleasure of the time.

MACBETH
What man dare, I dare.
Approach thou like the rugged Russian bear,
The armed rhinoceros, or th' Hyrcan tiger;
Take any shape but that, and my firm nerves
Shall never tremble. Or be alive again,
And dare me to the desert with thy sword.
If trembling I inhabit then, protest me
The baby of a girl. Hence, horrible shadow!
Unreal mockery, hence!

MACBETH
Can such things be,
And overcome us like a summer's cloud,
Without our special wonder? You make me strange
Even to the disposition that I owe,
When now I think you can behold such sights
And keep the natural ruby of your cheeks
When mine is blanched with fear.

MACBETH
It will have blood, they say; blood will have blood.
Stones have been known to move and trees to speak;
Augurs and understood relations have
By maggotpies and choughs and rooks brought forth
The secret'st man of blood. What is the night?
LADY MACBETH
Almost at odds with morning, which is which.

LADY MACBETH
Did you send to him, sir?
MACBETH
I hear it by the way; but I will send.
There's not a one of them but in his house
I keep a servant fee'd. I will tomorrow—
And betimes I will—to the Weird Sisters.
More shall they speak, for now I am bent to know
By the worst means the worst. For mine own good
All causes shall give way. I am in blood
Stepped in so far that, should I wade no more,
Returning were as tedious as go o'er.
Strange things I have in head, that will to hand,
Which must be acted ere they may be scanned.

LADY MACBETH
You lack the season of all natures, sleep.

MACBETH
Come, we'll to sleep. My strange and self-abuse
Is the initiate fear that wants hard use.
We are yet but young in deed.

ACT IV. Scene I (1–156).

The three witches assemble on a heath with Hecate, the Goddess of Witchcraft. Hecate scolds the Weird Sisters for having enlightened Macbeth to his prophecy, especially because his use of the knowledge has been destructive and self-serving. Hecate decides that they should appear to Macbeth in the coming day and provide him with an even greater spectacle of his fate, complete with a bubbling cauldron and magical illusions to further draw him in. Hecate hopes to elicit Macbeth's hubris, allowing the witches' prophecies to steer his dark sail to its own demise.

In the subsequent scene, Lennox and another Lord discuss the recent murders, and it becomes clear that they see through Macbeth's guise of benevolence and loyalty to the prior throne. They reveal that King Edward of England has allowed King Duncan's sons, Malcolm and Donalbain, to take refuge with him. Macduff has also gone to King Edward for assistance, but rather than refuge, he seeks to form an alliance and prepare a battle to free Scotland of Macbeth and his terrible reign.

FIRST WITCH
Thrice the brinded cat hath mewed.
SECOND WITCH
Thrice, and once the hedge-pig whined.
THIRD WITCH
Harpier cries, "'Tis time, 'tis time!"

FIRST WITCH
Round about the cauldron go;
In the poisoned entrails throw.
Toad, that under cold stone
Days and nights has thirty-one
Sweltered venom sleeping got,
Boil thou first i'th' charmed pot.

SECOND WITCH
Fillet of a fenny snake,
In the cauldron boil and bake;
Eye of newt and toe of frog,
Wool of bat and tongue of dog,
Adder's fork and blindworm's sting,
Lizard's leg and owlet's wing,
For a charm of powerful trouble,
Like a hell-broth boil and bubble.

THIRD WITCH
Scale of dragon, tooth of wolf,
Witches' mummy, maw and gulf
Of the ravined salt-sea shark,
Root of hemlock digged i'th' dark,
Liver of blaspheming Jew,
Gall of goat, and slips of yew
Silvered in the moon's eclipse,
Nose of Turk and Tartar's lips,
Finger of birth-strangled babe
Ditch-delivered by a drab,
Make the gruel thick and slab.
Add thereto a tiger's chaudron
For th'ingredience of our cauldron.

SECOND WITCH
Cool it with a baboon's blood,
Then the charm is firm and good.

HECATE
O, well done! I commend your pains,
And every one shall share i'th' gains.
And now about the cauldron sing
Live elves and fairies in a ring,
Enchanting all that you put in.
SECOND WITCH
By the pricking of my thumbs,
Something wicked this way comes.
Open, locks,
Whoever knocks!

MACBETH
How now, you secret, black, and midnight hags!
What is't you do?
ALL
A deed without a name.

MACBETH
I conjure you, by that which you profess,
Howe'er you come to know it, answer me.
Though you untie the winds and let them fight
Against the churches, though the yeasty waves
Confound and swallow navigation up,
Though bladed corn be lodged and trees blown down,
Though castles topple on their warders' heads,
Though palaces and pyramids do slope
Their heads to their foundations, though the treasure
Of nature's germens tumble all together
Even till destruction sicken, answer me
To what I ask you.

FIRST WITCH
Speak.
SECOND WITCH
Demand.
THIRD WITCH
We'll answer.
FIRST WITCH
Say, if thou'dst rather hear it from our mouths
Or from our masters?

FIRST WITCH
Pour in sow's blood, that hath eaten
Her nine farrow; grease that's sweaten
From the murderer's gibbet throw
Into the flame.

SECOND APPARITION
Macbeth! Macbeth! Macbeth!
MACBETH
Had I three ears, I'd hear thee.
SECOND APPARITION
Be bloody, bold, and resolute; laugh to scorn
The power of man, for none of woman born
Shall harm Macbeth.

MACBETH (cont.)
What is this
That rises like the issue of a king
And wears upon his baby brow the round
And top of sovereignty?
ALL
Listen, but speak not to't.
THIRD APPARITION
Be lion-mettled, proud; and take no care
Who chafes, who frets, or where conspirers are.
Macbeth shall never vanquished be until
Great Birnam Wood to high Dunsinane Hill
Shall come against him.

MACBETH
That will never be.
Who can impress the forest, bid the tree
Unfix his earthbound root? Sweet bodements, good!
Rebellious dead, rise never till the wood
Of Birnam rise, and our high-placed Macbeth
Shall live the lease of nature, pay his breath
To time and mortal custom. Yet my heart
Throbs to know one thing. Tell me, if your art
Can tell so much: shall Banquo's issue ever
Reign in this kingdom?
ALL
Seek to know no more.
MACBETH
I will be satisfied. Deny me this,
And an eternal curse fall on you! Let me know.
Why sinks that cauldron? And what noise is this?

ALL
Show his eyes, and grieve his heart;
Come like shadows, so depart!

MACBETH
Thou art too like the spirit of Banquo. Down!
Thy crown does sear mine eyeballs. And thy hair,
Thou other gold-bound brow, is like the first.
A third is like the former. Filthy hags,
Why do you show me this? A fourth? Start, eyes!
What, will the line stretch out to th' crack of doom?
Another yet? A seventh? I'll see no more.
And yet the eighth appears, who bears a glass
Which shows me many more; and some I see
That two-fold balls and treble sceptres carry.
Horrible sight! Now, I see, 'tis true,
For the blood-boltered Banquo smiles upon me
And points at them for his.

MACBETH (cont.)
What, is this so?
FIRST WITCH
Ay, sir, all this is so. But why
Stands Macbeth thus amazedly?
Come, sisters, cheer we up his sprites,
And show the best of our delights.
I'll charm the air to give a sound,
While you perform your antic round,
That this great king may kindly say,
Our duties did his welcome pay.

MACBETH
Where are they? Gone? Let this pernicious hour
Stand aye accursèd in the calendar!
Come in, without there!
LENNOX
What's Your Grace's will?

MACBETH
Saw you the Weird Sisters?
LENNOX
No, my lord.
MACBETH
Came they not by you?
LENNOX
No, indeed, my lord.
MACBETH
Infected be the air whereon they ride,
And damned all those that trust them! I did hear
The galloping of horse. Who was't came by?
LENNOX
'Tis two or three, my lord, that bring you word
Macduff is fled to England.

MACBETH
Fled to England!
LENNOX
Ay, my good lord.
MACBETH
Time, thou anticipat'st my dread exploits.
The flighty purpose never is o'ertook
Unless the deed go with it. From this moment
The very firstlings of my heart shall be
The firstlings of my hand. And even now,
To crown my thoughts with acts, be it thought and done:
The castle of Macduff I will surprise,
Seize upon Fife, give to th'edge o'th' sword
His wife, his babes, and all unfortunate souls
That trace him in his line. No boasting like a fool;
This deed I'll do before this purpose cool.
But no more sights!—Where are these gentlemen?
Come, bring me where they are.

ACT IV. Scene II (66–86).

Over at Macduff's castle, Ross and Lady Macduff lament the absence of Macduff, who has fled to England for assistance. His abrupt journey casts an air of suspicion over him, making him look traitorous to his family and his country. Ross implores Lady Macduff to see the good in the situation and leaves before he can become too emotional. Lady Macduff is left to field the many questions her young son has for her about his father's absence, what they will do without him, and what it means if he is in fact a traitor. They make jokes with one another to quell their growing anxiety, and it is at this point that they are interrupted by a messenger.

MESSENGER
Bless you, fair dame! I am not to you known,
Though in your state of honour I am perfect.
I doubt some danger does approach you nearly.
If you will take a homely man's advice,
Be not found here. Hence, with your little ones.
To fright you thus, methinks, I am too savage;
To do worse to you were fell cruelty,
Which is too nigh your person. Heaven preserve you!
I dare abide no longer.

LADY MACDUFF
Whither should I fly?
I have done no harm. But I remember now
I am in this earthly world, where to do harm
Is often laudable, to do good sometime
Accounted dangerous folly. Why then, alas,
Do I put up that womanly defence
To say I have done no harm?

LADY MACDUFF (cont.)
What are these faces?
FIRST MURDERER
Where is your husband?

LADY MACDUFF
I hope in no place so unsanctified
Where such as thou mayst find him.
FIRST MURDERER
He's a traitor.

SON
Thou liest, thou shag-haired villain!
FIRST MURDERER
What, you egg?

FIRST MURDERER (cont.)
Young fry of treachery!

SON
He has killed me, mother.
Run away, I pray you!

ACT V. Scene I (1–80).

Malcolm and Macduff are in distress over the state of Scotland and Macbeth's ever-worsening reign of slaughter. Macduff tries to encourage Malcolm to take his rightful seat on the throne, but as he does so, Malcolm tests Macduff's motives by divulging heinous vices that could be worsened by kingly power. Macduff recoils in horror, rebuking Malcolm and saying that he must have been mistaken for thinking he should be the one to overthrow Macbeth. Malcolm is relieved by this reaction and assures Macduff that he is in fact virtuous and has the best interest of Scotland and its people in mind.

Ross joins the conversation and the three despair over the terrible crimes being committed under Macbeth's rule. Alarmed, Macduff asks Ross if his family is okay, and Ross tries to appease him by saying that all are well in the Macduff castle. After some prodding, Ross reveals that Macduff's entire family and household have been viciously murdered by Macbeth's men. Overcome by the mayhem he has caused, the men resolve to bring the fight to Macbeth.

DOCTOR
I have two nights watched with you, but can perceive no truth in your report. When was it she last walked?
GENTLEWOMAN
Since his majesty went into the field, I have seen her rise from her bed, throw her nightgown upon her, unlock her closet, take forth paper, fold it, write upon't, read it, afterwards seal it, and again return to bed; yet all this while in a most fast sleep.
DOCTOR
A great perturbation in nature, to receive at once the benefit of sleep and do the effects of watching! In this slumbery agitation, besides her walking and other actual performances, what, at any time, have you heard her say?
GENTLEWOMAN
That, sir, which I will not report after her.
DOCTOR
You may to me, and 'tis most meet you should.
GENTLEWOMAN
Neither to you nor any one; having no witness to confirm my speech.

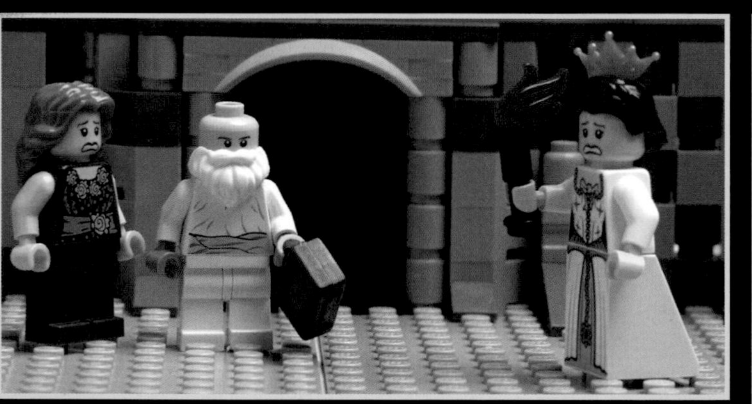

GENTLEWOMAN (cont.)
Lo you, here she comes! This is her very guise, and, upon my life, fast asleep. Observe her. Stand close.
DOCTOR
How came she by that light?
GENTLEWOMAN
Why, it stood by her. She has light by her continually. 'Tis her command.
DOCTOR
You see her eyes are open.
GENTLEWOMAN
Ay, but their sense are shut.

DOCTOR
What is it she does now? Look, how she rubs her hands.
GENTLEWOMAN
It is an accustomed action with her to seem thus washing her hands. I have known her continue in this a quarter of an hour.
LADY MACBETH
Yet here's a spot.

DOCTOR
Hark, she speaks: I will set down what comes from her, to satisfy my remembrance the more strongly.
LADY MACBETH
Out, damned spot! Out, I say! One—
Two—why then, 'tis time to do't. Hell is murky.—
Fie, my lord, fie, a soldier, and afeard? What need we fear who knows it, when none can call our power to account? Yet who would have thought the old man to have had so much blood in him?

DOCTOR
Do you mark that?
LADY MACBETH
The Thane of Fife had a wife. Where is she now?—What, will these hands ne'er be clean?—No more o'that, my lord, no more o'that; you mar all with this starting.
DOCTOR
Go to, go to. You have known what you should not.
GENTLEWOMAN
She has spoke what she should not, I am sure of that. Heaven knows what she has known!

LADY MACBETH
Here's the smell of the blood still. All the perfumes of Arabia will not sweeten this little hand.
Oh, oh, oh!
DOCTOR
What a sigh is there! The heart is sorely charged.
GENTLEWOMAN
I would not have such a heart in my bosom for the dignity of the whole body.
DOCTOR
Well, well, well.
GENTLEWOMAN
Pray God it be, sir.

DOCTOR
This disease is beyond my practice. Yet I have known those which have walked in their sleep who have died holily in their beds.
LADY MACBETH
Wash your hands, put on your night-gown; look not so pale! I tell you yet again, Banquo's buried. He cannot come out on 's grave.
DOCTOR
Even so?
LADY MACBETH
To bed, to bed! There's knocking at the Gate. Come, come, come, come, give me your hand. What's done cannot be undone. To bed, to bed, to bed!

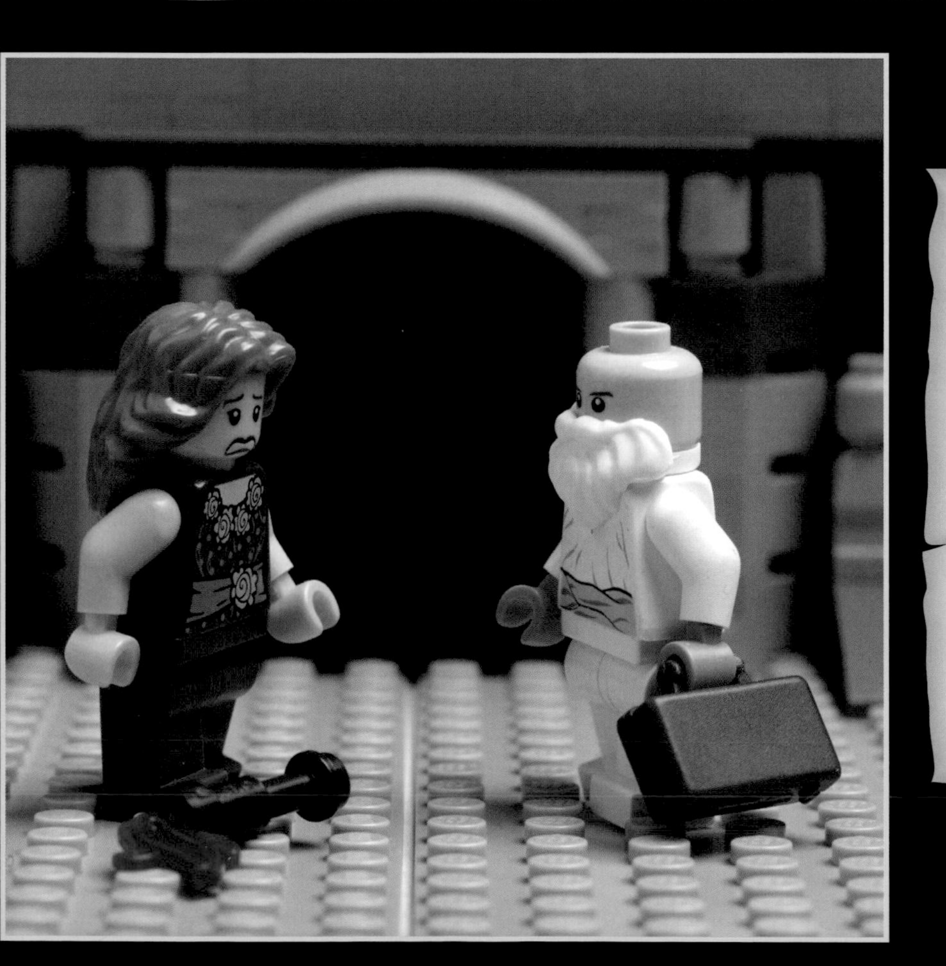

DOCTOR
Will she go now to bed?
GENTLEWOMAN
Directly.
DOCTOR
Foul whisperings are abroad: unnatural deeds
Do breed unnatural troubles. Infected minds
To their deaf pillows will discharge their secrets.
More needs she the divine than the physician.
God, God forgive us all! Look after her;
Remove from her the means of all annoyance,
And still keep eyes upon her. So, good night.
My mind she has mated, and amazed my sight.
I think, but dare not speak.
GENTLEWOMAN
Good night, good doctor.

ACT V. Scene VI (1–10).

With the coming help of the English, the leaders of the Scottish forces begin the march toward Dunsinane Hill to overthrow Macbeth. They profess their allegiance to the rightful heir to the throne, Malcolm, and wonder about Macbeth's violent psychosis. They lead the march to Birnam Wood.

Meanwhile, at Dunsinane, Macbeth is learning that Scottish thanes are abandoning him in loyalty to Malcolm. Despite this, Macbeth is confident that he will not be overthrown, because the witches' prophecy said that such could only happen if Birnam Wood were to move from its current location to the palace, which of course is impossible. More than ten thousand English soldiers assemble outside in preparation for a fight.

Out at Birnam Wood, Malcolm, Siward, and their men plot their approach to the castle. Malcolm decides to camouflage the soldiers by having them carry branches from the forest, which will confuse Macbeth and his men as to how many men they are up against.

Up at Dunsinane, Macbeth is given two reports of bad news. Lady Macbeth has died from her paranoid insanity, and the forest has seemingly moved to the foot of the palace. Macbeth waves off his wife's death and becomes horrorstruck and angry at the news that Birnam Wood has shifted locations. The ostensibly impossible prophecy that Macbeth should only worry if the forest moves has come true.

MALCOLM
Now near enough. Your leafy screens throw down,
And show like those you are. You, worthy uncle,
Shall with my cousin, your right noble son,
Lead our first battle. Worthy Macduff and we
Shall take upon 's what else remains to do,
According to our order.

MACDUFF
Make all our trumpets speak! Give them all breath,
Those clamorous harbingers of blood and death!

ACT V. Scene VII (1–30).

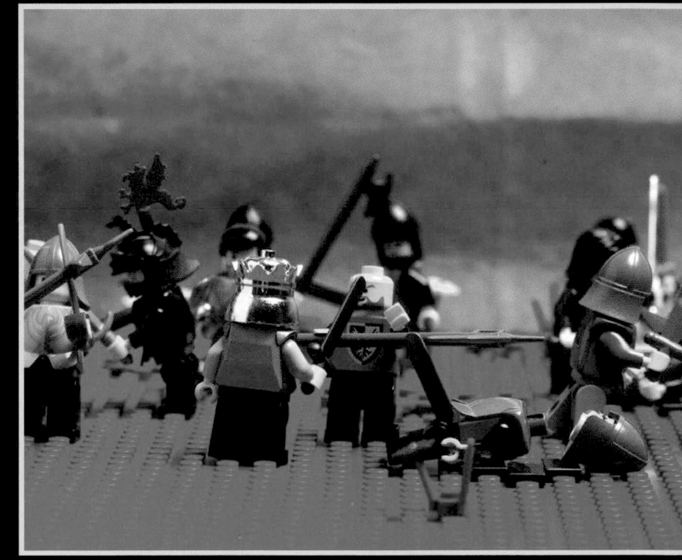

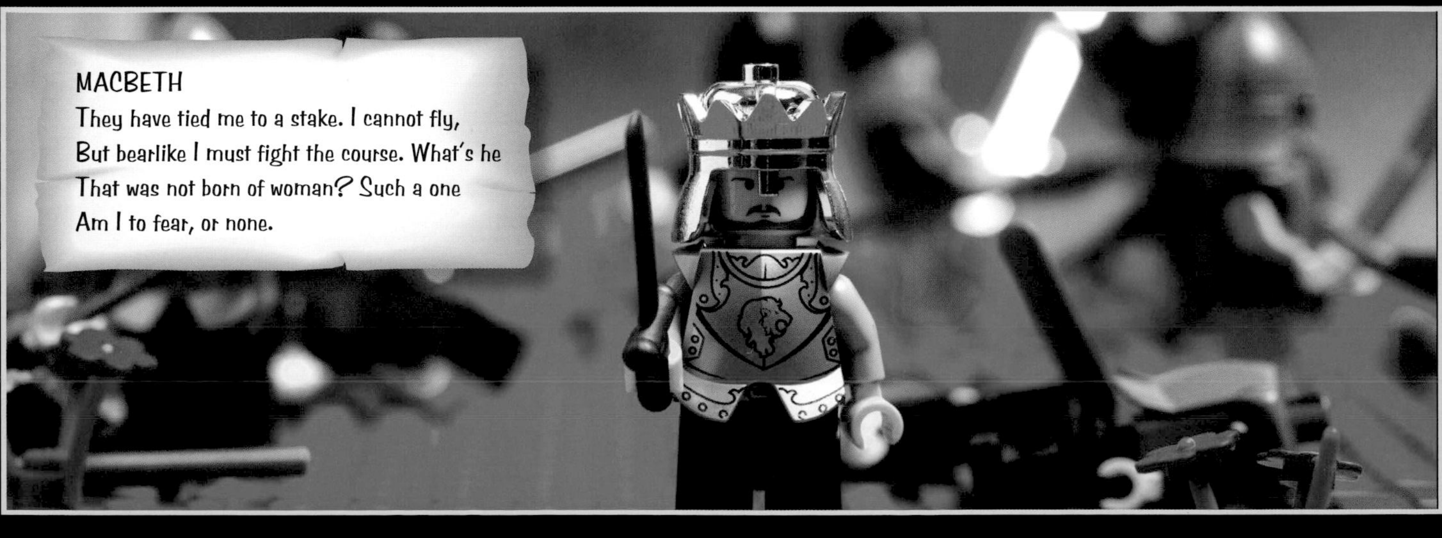
MACBETH
They have tied me to a stake. I cannot fly,
But bearlike I must fight the course. What's he
That was not born of woman? Such a one
Am I to fear, or none.

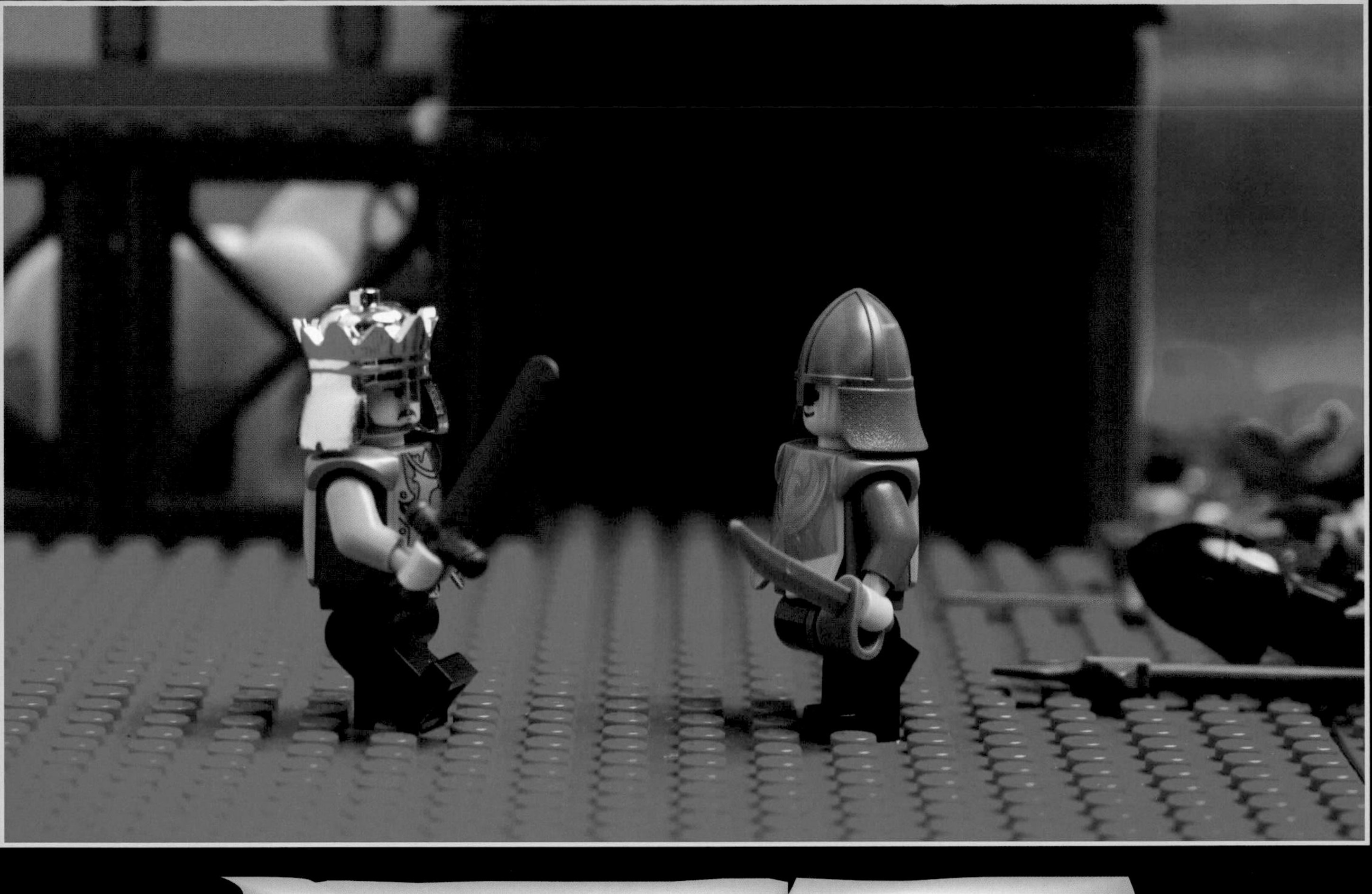

YOUNG SIWARD
What is thy name?
MACBETH
Thou'lt be afraid to hear it.
YOUNG SIWARD
No, though thou call'st thyself a hotter name
Than any is in hell.
MACBETH
My name's Macbeth.
YOUNG SIWARD
The devil himself could not pronounce a title
More hateful to mine ear.
MACBETH
No, nor more fearful.
YOUNG SIWARD
Thou liest, abhorrèd tyrant. With my sword
I'll prove the lie thou speak'st.

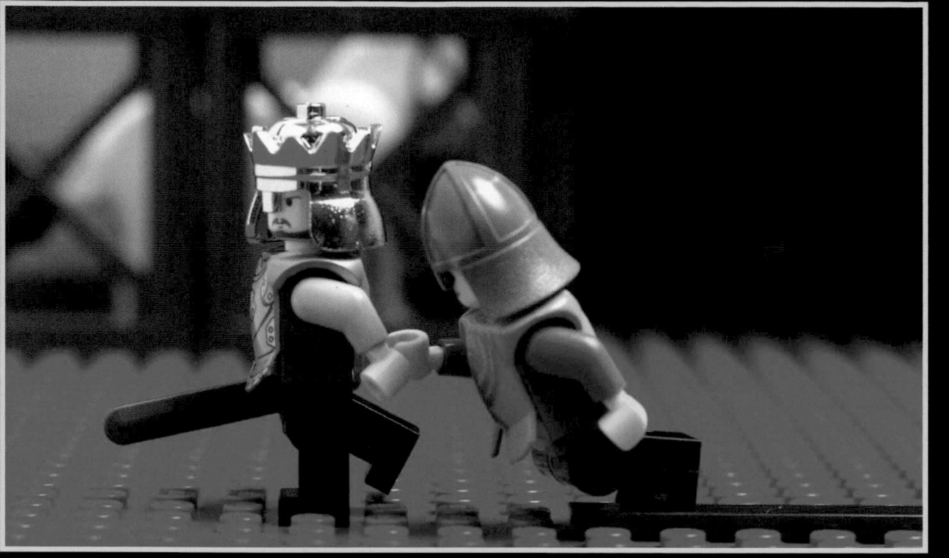

MACBETH
Thou wast born of woman
But swords I smile at, weapons laugh to scorn,
Brandished by man that's of a woman born.

MACDUFF
That way the noise is. Tyrant, show thy face!
If thou be'st slain, and with no stroke of mine,
My wife and children's ghosts will haunt me still.
I cannot strike at wretched kerns, whose arms
Are hired to bear their staves. Either thou, Macbeth,
Or else my sword with an unbattered edge
I sheathe again undeeded. There thou shouldst be;
By this great clatter one of greatest note
Seems bruited. Let me find him, Fortune!
And more I beg not.

SIWARD
This way, my lord. The castle's gently rendered:
The tyrant's people on both sides do fight,
The noble thanes do bravely in the war,
The day almost itself professes yours,
And little is to do.
MALCOLM
We have met with foes
That strike beside us.
SIWARD
Enter, sir, the castle.

ACT V. Scene VIII (1–76).

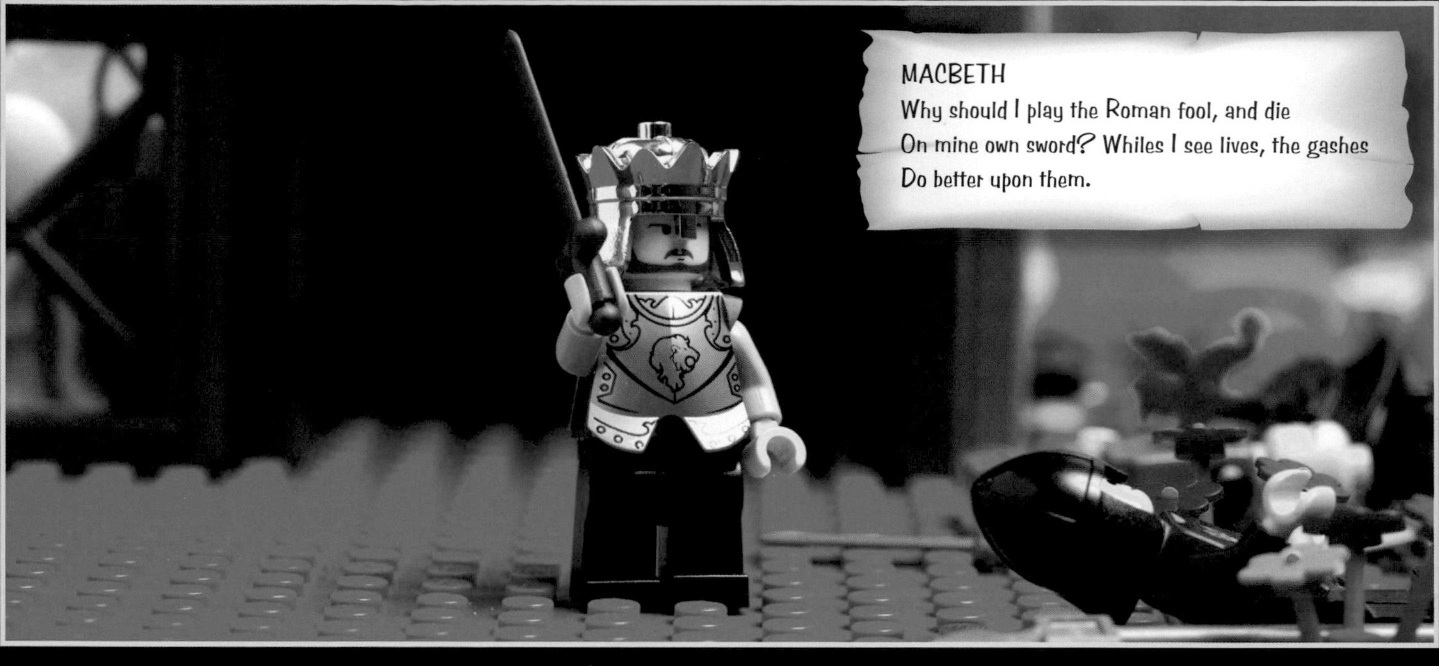
MACBETH
Why should I play the Roman fool, and die
On mine own sword? Whiles I see lives, the gashes
Do better upon them.

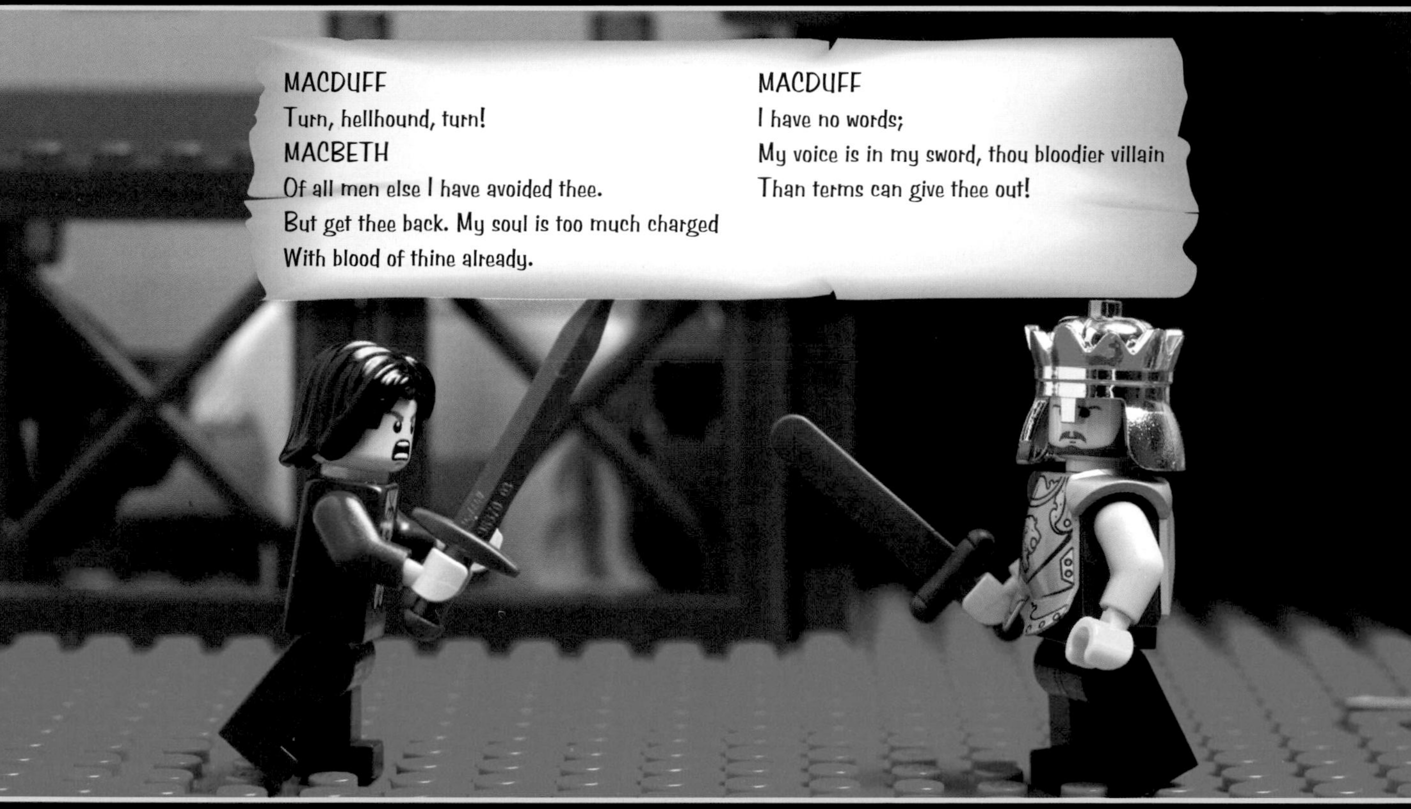
MACDUFF
Turn, hellhound, turn!
MACBETH
Of all men else I have avoided thee.
But get thee back. My soul is too much charged
With blood of thine already.
MACDUFF
I have no words;
My voice is in my sword, thou bloodier villain
Than terms can give thee out!

MACBETH
Thou losest labour.
As easy mayst thou the intrenchant air
With thy keen sword impress as make me bleed.
Let fall thy blade on vulnerable crests;
I bear a charmèd life, which must not yield,
To one of woman born.

MACDUFF
Despair thy charm,
And let the angel whom thou still hast served
Tell thee, Macduff was from his mother's womb
Untimely ripped.

MACBETH
Accursèd be that tongue that tells me so,
For it hath cowed my better part of man!
And be these juggling fiends no more believed
That palter with us in a double sense,
That keep the word of promise to our ear
And break it to our hope. I'll not fight with thee.

MACDUFF
Then yield thee, coward,
And live to be the show and gaze o'th' time!
We'll have thee, as our rarer monsters are,
Painted on a pole, and underwrit,
"Here may you see the tyrant."

MACBETH
I will not yield,
To kiss the ground before young Malcolm's feet
And to be baited with the rabble's curse.
Though Birnam Wood be come to Dunsinane,
And thou opposed, being of no woman born,
Yet I will try the last. Before my body
I throw my warlike shield. Lay on, Macduff,
And damned be him that first cries, "Hold, enough!"

ROSS
Your son, my lord, has paid a soldier's debt.
He only lived but till he was a man,
The which no sooner had his prowess confirmed
In the unshrinking station where he fought,
But like a man he died.
SIWARD
Then he is dead?
ROSS
Ay, and brought off the field. Your cause of sorrow
Must not be measured by his worth, for then
It hath no end.

SIWARD
Had he his hurts before?
ROSS
Ay, on the front.
SIWARD
Why then, God's soldier be he!
Had I as many sons as I have hairs,
I would not wish them to a fairer death.
And so, his knell is knolled.
MALCOLM
He's worth more sorrow,
And that I'll spend for him.
SIWARD
He's worth no more
They say he parted well and paid his score,
And so, God be with him! Here comes newer comfort.

MACDUFF
Hail, King! For so thou art. Behold where stands
The usurper's cursèd head. The time is free.
I see thee compassed with thy kingdom's pearl,
That speak my salutation in their minds,
Whose voices I desire aloud with mine:
Hail, King of Scotland!

MALCOLM
We shall not spend a large expense of time
Before we reckon with your several loves
And make us even with you. My thanes and kinsmen,
Henceforth be earls, the first that ever Scotland
In such an honour named. What's more to do
Which would be planted newly with the time,
As calling home our exiled friends abroad
That fled the snares of watchful tyranny,
Producing forth the cruel ministers
Of this dead butcher and his fiendlike queen—
Who, as 'tis thought, by self and violent hands
Took off her life—this, and what needful else
That calls upon us, by the grace of Grace
We will perform in measure, time, and place.
So, thanks to all at once and to each one,
Whom we invite to see us crowned at Scone.

Romeo and Juliet

Introduction to Romeo and Juliet

Romeo and Juliet, first published in 1597, is far and away one of William Shakespeare's most recognized plays. Depicting the tragic love story between the only children of two warring noble families in the city of Verona, the Montagues and the Capulets, this tale redefined the Elizabethan audience's perception of the archetypal tragic play.

Before its time, tragedies were based on powerful historical figures, rather than lovesick teenagers and the feuds of nobility. A play centered around sacrilegious suicide, and an English patronage that had made the historical shift away from Catholicism, the Elizabethan audience was even less likely to relate to the play and its protagonists. The powerful use of astrology throughout the play, announced as early as the prologue by referring to the pair as "star-crossed," and filtered into the characters' language throughout, reeled in the sympathies of the Elizabethan audience by giving the pair cosmic authority. If the path of these two lovers is defined by the stars, and is one that might even cause a social shift amongst their warring parents, then their love story carries more weight than average misfortune.

The shift of tragic style was important, but Shakespeare's language plays a key role in the characterization of the protagonists and the movement of the plot. While he uses blank verse written in iambic pentameter for much of the play, Shakespeare toys with the growlingly trite Petrarchan sonnet form while Romeo expresses his superficial love for Rosaline and moves to more contemporary sonnet form while exchanging sincere affections for his true love, Juliet. The Friar speaks in sermon, the newly wedded Juliet uses epithalamium form (a bridal poem), and Mercutio plays with rhapsody form (a portion of an epic poem). Each of these poetic styles draws particular emphasis to the lines they speak, giving heavier significance to the underlying themes and changes in plot.

Romeo and Juliet begins as a comedy and dramatically pivots into a tragedy. Woven with linguistic and astrological significance through Shakespeare's language, it comments on how senseless feuds can lead to horrific consequences when left unchecked.

Dramatis Personae

ESCALUS (PRINCE), prince of Verona

PARIS, a young noblemen and kinsman to the prince

MONTAGUE, head of Montague house

CAPULET, head of Capulet house

ROMEO, son to Montague

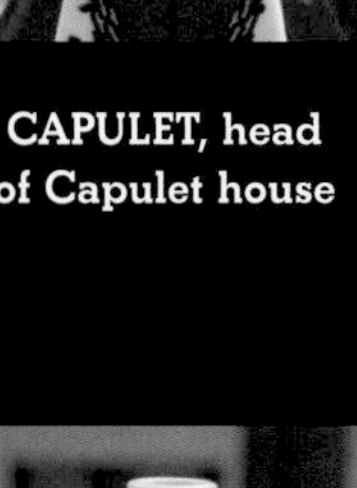

MERCUTIO, kinsman to the prince and friend to Romeo

BENVOLIO, nephew to Montague and friend to Romeo

TYBALT, nephew to Lady Capulet

FRIAR LAURENCE, Franciscan

FRIAR JOHN, Franciscan

BALTHASAR, servant to Romeo

SAMPSON, servant to Capulet

GREGORY, servant to Capulet

ABRAHAM, servant to Montague

APOTHECARY

LADY MONTAGUE, wife to Montague

LADY CAPULET, wife to Capulet

JULIET, daughter to Capulet

NURSE to Juliet

CHORUS

Not Pictured

PETER, servant to Juliet's Nurse
FIRST MUSICIAN
SECOND MUSICIAN
THIRD MUSICIAN
PAGE to Paris
Another PAGE
An OFFICER

Citizens of Verona, several Men and Women with relations to both houses, Maskers,

ACT I.

Prologue.

R & J

CHORUS
Two households, both alike in dignity,
In fair Verona, where we lay our scene,
From ancient grudge break to new mutiny,
Where civil blood makes civil hands unclean.
From forth the fatal loins of these two foes
A pair of star-cross'd lovers take their life;
Whose misadventured piteous overthrows
Do with their death bury their parents' strife.
The fearful passage of their death-mark'd love,
And the continuance of their parents' rage,
Which, but their children's end, naught could remove,
Is now the two hours' traffic of our stage.
The which if you with patient ears attend,
What here shall miss, our toil shall strive to mend.

ACT I. Scene I (18–96).
Verona. A public place.

GREGORY
The quarrel is between our masters and us their men.
SAMPSON
'Tis all one, I will show myself a tyrant: when I have fought with the men, I will be cruel with the maids, and cut off their heads.
GREGORY
The heads of the maids?
SAMPSON
Ay, the heads of the maids, or their maidenheads; take it in what sense thou wilt.
GREGORY
They must take it in sense that feel it.
SAMPSON
Me they shall feel while I am able to stand: and 'tis known I am a pretty piece of flesh.

GREGORY
'Tis well thou art not fish; if thou hadst, thou hadst been poor John. Draw thy tool! here comes two of the house of the Montagues.
SAMPSON
My naked weapon is out: quarrel, I will back thee.
GREGORY
How! turn thy back and run?
SAMPSON
Fear me not.
GREGORY
No, marry; I fear thee!
SAMPSON
Let us take the law of our sides; let them begin.
GREGORY
I will frown as I pass by, and let them take it as they list.
SAMPSON
Nay, as they dare. I will bite my thumb at them; which is a disgrace to them, if they bear it.

ABRAHAM
Do you bite your thumb at us, sir?
SAMPSON
I do bite my thumb, sir.
ABRAHAM
Do you bite your thumb at us, sir?
SAMPSON
Is the law of our side, if I say ay?
GREGORY
No.
SAMPSON
No, sir, I do not bite my thumb at you, sir, but I
bite my thumb, sir.
GREGORY
Do you quarrel, sir?
ABRAHAM
Quarrel sir! no, sir.
SAMPSON
If you do, sir, I am for you: I serve as good a man as you.
ABRAHAM
No better.
SAMPSON
Well, sir.

GREGORY
Say "better:" here comes one of my master's kinsmen.
SAMPSON
Yes, better, sir.
ABRAHAM
You lie.
SAMPSON
Draw, if you be men. Gregory, remember thy swashing blow.

BENVOLIO
Part, fools!
Put up your swords; you know not what you do.

TYBALT
What, art thou drawn among these heartless hinds?
Turn thee, Benvolio, look upon thy death.
BENVOLIO
I do but keep the peace: put up thy sword,
Or manage it to part these men with me.
TYBALT
What, drawn, and talk of peace! I hate the word,
As I hate hell, all Montagues, and thee:
Have at thee, coward!

CAPULET
What noise is this? Give me my long sword, ho!
LADY CAPULET
A crutch, a crutch! why call you for a sword?
CAPULET
My sword, I say! Old Montague is come,
And flourishes his blade in spite of me.

MONTAGUE
Thou villain Capulet,—Hold me not, let me go.
LADY MONTAGUE
Thou shalt not stir a foot to seek a foe.

PRINCE
Rebellious subjects, enemies to peace,
Profaners of this neighbour-stained steel,—
Will they not hear? What, ho! you men, you beasts,
That quench the fire of your pernicious rage
With purple fountains issuing from your veins,
On pain of torture, from those bloody hands
Throw your mistemper'd weapons to the ground,
And hear the sentence of your moved prince.
Three civil brawls, bred of an airy word,
By thee, old Capulet, and Montague,
Have thrice disturb'd the quiet of our streets,
And made Verona's ancient citizens
Cast by their grave beseeming ornaments,
To wield old partisans, in hands as old,
Canker'd with peace, to part your canker'd hate:
If ever you disturb our streets again,
Your lives shall pay the forfeit of the peace.
For this time, all the rest depart away:
You Capulet; shall go along with me:
And, Montague, come you this afternoon,
To know our further pleasure in this case,
To old Free-town, our common judgment-place.
Once more, on pain of death, all men depart.

The first scene of the play sets the tone for the Capulet and Montague feud. These two families, who have undoubtedly been feuding for so long that they can no longer grasp its root, are so steeped in hatred that even the smallest provocation can end in turmoil and death. Prior to the coming action, Paris, a kinsman to the Prince, asks Capulet for Juliet's hand in marriage. Capulet favors the idea but, with his daughter being just fourteen, encourages Paris to woo her and patiently wait for her to be of a more suitable marrying age. Capulet prepares a costume party at the family home, to which all noble families in Verona (except the Montagues), are invited. Capulet thinks this sets the stage for Paris's courtship with his daughter, but in actuality, it will be the meeting of Romeo and Juliet and, in some ways, the beginning of the end.

Romeo and his friends decide to crash the Capulet party. They arrive in costume just minutes after the partygoers have finished dinner and in time for dancing. Romeo has just been burned by the object of his affections, Rosaline, and all of his friends see the party as an opportunity for him to meet another girl. While he talks of his heartbreak over Rosaline and disinterest in all other women, he touches on the "consequence yet hanging in the stars" that will lead to "some vile forfeit of untimely death" if he goes to the party (I.iv.105, 109). While these foreboding lines seem to come from nowhere, they are an example of a running habit of both Romeo and Juliet to foreshadow their own tragic ends. Romeo's good friends Benvolio and Mercutio wave off his fears, and they enter the Capulet party in better spirits.

ACT I. Scene V (47–155).

A hall in Capulet's house.

ROMEO
O, she doth teach the torches to burn bright!
It seems she hangs upon the cheek of night
Like a rich jewel in an Ethiope's ear;
Beauty too rich for use, for earth too dear!
So shows a snowy dove trooping with crows,
As yonder lady o'er her fellows shows.
The measure done, I'll watch her place of stand,
And, touching hers, make blessed my rude hand.
Did my heart love till now? forswear it, sight!
For I ne'er saw true beauty till this night.

CAPULET
Young Romeo is it?
TYBALT
'Tis he, that villain Romeo.
CAPULET
Content thee, gentle coz, let him alone;
He bears him like a portly gentleman;
And, to say truth, Verona brags of him
To be a virtuous and well-govern'd youth:
I would not for the wealth of all the town
Here in my house do him disparagement:
Therefore be patient, take no note of him:
It is my will, the which if thou respect,
Show a fair presence and put off these frowns,
And ill-beseeming semblance for a feast.

CAPULET
He shall be endured:
What, goodman boy! I say, he shall: go to;
Am I the master here, or you? go to.
You'll not endure him! God shall mend my soul!
You'll make a mutiny among my guests!
You will set cock-a-hoop! you'll be the man!
TYBALT
Why, uncle, 'tis a shame.

CAPULET
Go to, go to;
You are a saucy boy: is't so, indeed?
This trick may chance to scathe you, I know what:
You must contrary me! marry, 'tis time.
Well said, my hearts! You are a princox; go:
Be quiet, or—More light, more light! For shame!
I'll make you quiet. What, cheerly, my hearts!

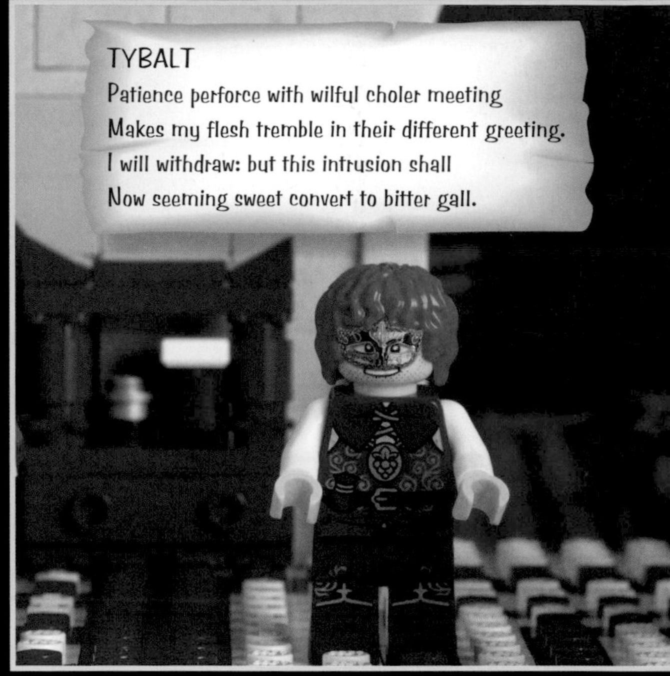
TYBALT
Patience perforce with wilful choler meeting
Makes my flesh tremble in their different greeting.
I will withdraw: but this intrusion shall
Now seeming sweet convert to bitter gall.

ROMEO
If I profane with my unworthiest hand
This holy shrine, the gentle fine is this:
My lips, two blushing pilgrims, ready stand
To smooth that rough touch with a tender kiss.
JULIET
Good pilgrim, you do wrong your hand too much,
Which mannerly devotion shows in this;
For saints have hands that pilgrims' hands do touch,
And palm to palm is holy palmers' kiss.

ROMEO
Have not saints lips, and holy palmers too?
JULIET
Ay, pilgrim, lips that they must use in prayer.

ROMEO
O, then, dear saint, let lips do what hands do;
They pray, grant thou, lest faith turn to despair.
JULIET
Saints do not move, though grant for prayers' sake.

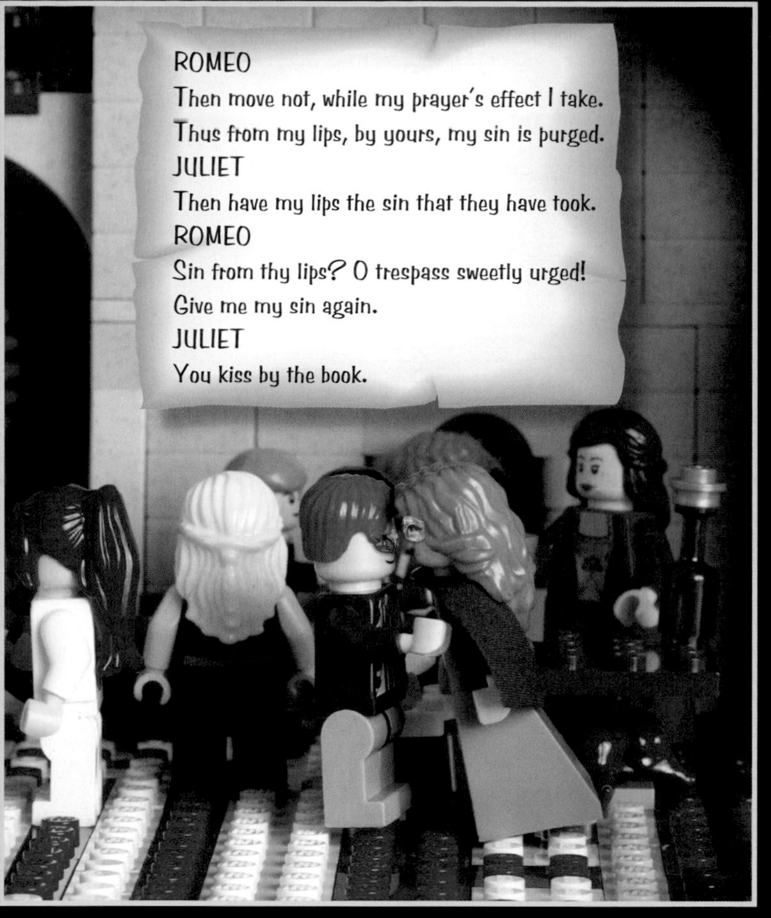
ROMEO
Then move not, while my prayer's effect I take.
Thus from my lips, by yours, my sin is purged.
JULIET
Then have my lips the sin that they have took.
ROMEO
Sin from thy lips? O trespass sweetly urged!
Give me my sin again.
JULIET
You kiss by the book.

NURSE
Madam, your mother craves a word with you.

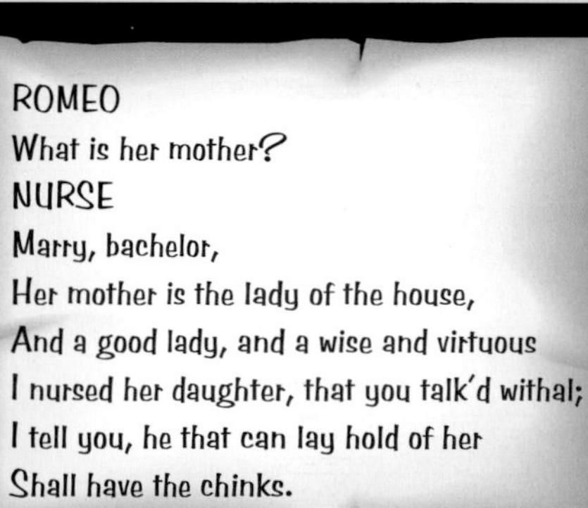
ROMEO
What is her mother?
NURSE
Marry, bachelor,
Her mother is the lady of the house,
And a good lady, and a wise and virtuous
I nursed her daughter, that you talk'd withal;
I tell you, he that can lay hold of her
Shall have the chinks.

ROMEO
Is she a Capulet?
O dear account! my life is my foe's debt.

CAPULET
Nay, gentlemen, prepare not to be gone;
We have a trifling foolish banquet towards.
Is it e'en so? why, then, I thank you all
I thank you, honest gentlemen; good night.
More torches here! Come on then, let's to bed.
Ah, sirrah, by my fay, it waxes late:
I'll to my rest.

JULIET
Come hither, nurse. What is yond gentleman?
NURSE
The son and heir of old Tiberio.
JULIET
What's he that now is going out of door?
NURSE
Marry, that, I think, be young Petrucio.
JULIET
What's he that follows there, that would not dance?
NURSE
I know not.

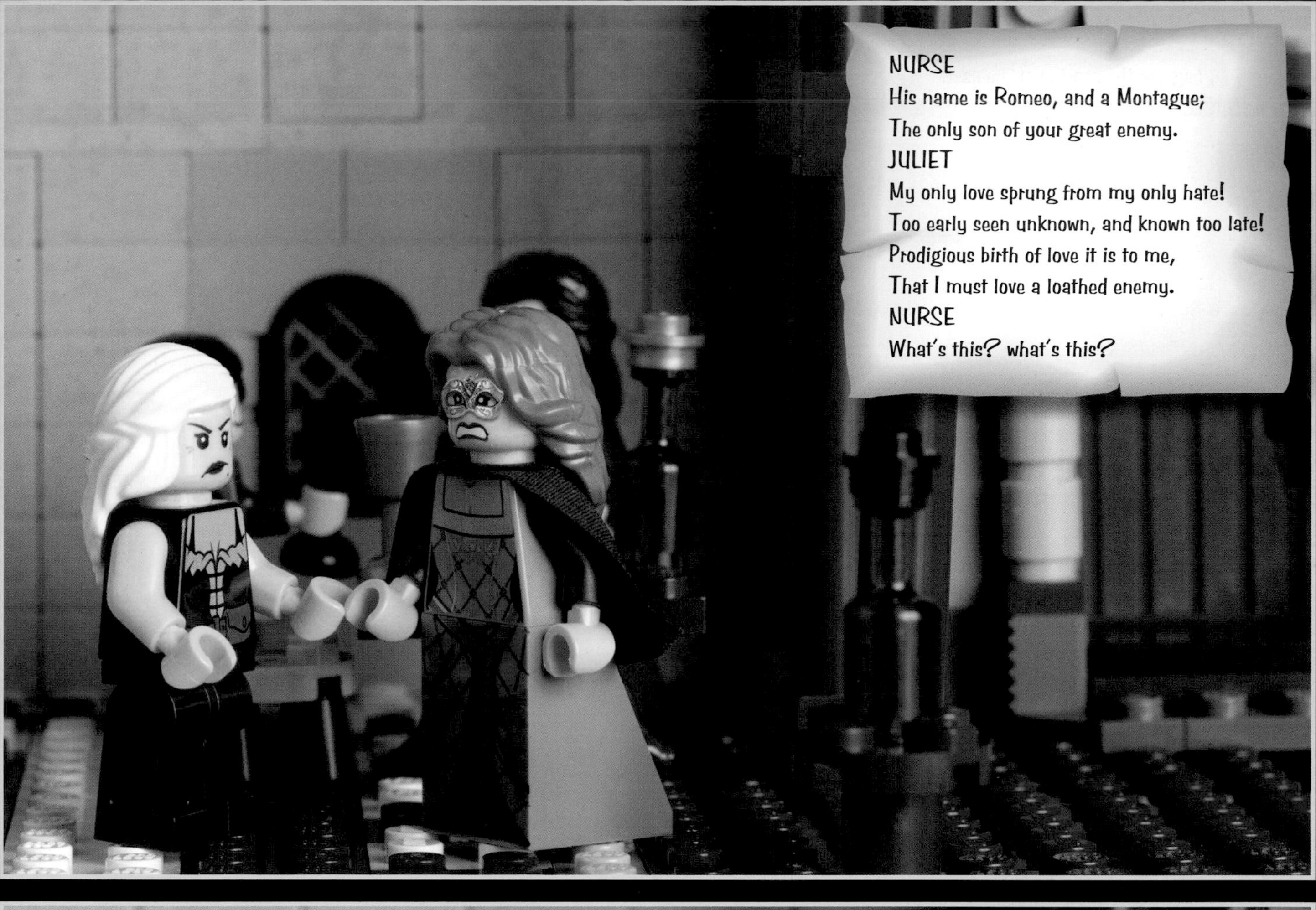
NURSE
His name is Romeo, and a Montague;
The only son of your great enemy.
JULIET
My only love sprung from my only hate!
Too early seen unknown, and known too late!
Prodigious birth of love it is to me,
That I must love a loathed enemy.
NURSE
What's this? what's this?

JULIET
A rhyme I learn'd even now
Of one I danced withal.
NURSE
Anon, anon!
Come, let's away; the strangers all are gone.

ACT II. Scene II (1–204).
Capulet's orchard.

Romeo and Juliet have just met, fallen for one another, and discovered their misfortune of family ties. Romeo has moved from being the hopeless cast-off of Rosaline to love's torchbearer for Juliet. As he leaves the Capulets' party, Romeo remains stunned that he has found the love his life, and that this love is also completely off limits to him. His friends think he is still glum about Rosaline and try to cheer him up. Distracted and confused, Romeo runs off, leaping the Capulets' orchard walls in search for Juliet. In the coming portrayal, Romeo finds her alone, simultaneously gushing over him and toiling over their forbidden love.

ROMEO
He jests at scars that never felt a wound.

But, soft! what light through yonder window breaks?
It is the east, and Juliet is the sun.
Arise, fair sun, and kill the envious moon,
Who is already sick and pale with grief,
That thou her maid art far more fair than she:
Be not her maid, since she is envious;
Her vestal livery is but sick and green
And none but fools do wear it; cast it off.
It is my lady, O, it is my love!
O, that she knew she were!
She speaks yet she says nothing: what of that?
Her eye discourses; I will answer it.
I am too bold, 'tis not to me she speaks:
Two of the fairest stars in all the heaven,
Having some business, do entreat her eyes
To twinkle in their spheres till they return.
What if her eyes were there, they in her head?
The brightness of her cheek would shame those stars,
As daylight doth a lamp; her eyes in heaven
Would through the airy region stream so bright
That birds would sing and think it were not night.
See, how she leans her cheek upon her hand!
O, that I were a glove upon that hand,
That I might touch that cheek!

JULIET
Ay me!

ROMEO
She speaks:
O, speak again, bright angel! for thou art
As glorious to this night, being o'er my head
As is a winged messenger of heaven
Unto the white-upturned wondering eyes
Of mortals that fall back to gaze on him
When he bestrides the lazy-pacing clouds
And sails upon the bosom of the air.

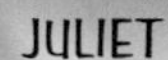

JULIET
O Romeo, Romeo! wherefore art thou Romeo?
Deny thy father and refuse thy name;
Or, if thou wilt not, be but sworn my love,
And I'll no longer be a Capulet.
ROMEO
Shall I hear more, or shall I speak at this?
JULIET
'Tis but thy name that is my enemy;
Thou art thyself, though not a Montague.
What's Montague? it is nor hand, nor foot,
Nor arm, nor face, nor any other part
Belonging to a man. O, be some other name!
What's in a name? that which we call a rose
By any other name would smell as sweet;
So Romeo would, were he not Romeo call'd,
Retain that dear perfection which he owes
Without that title. Romeo, doff thy name,
And for that name which is no part of thee
Take all myself.

ROMEO
I take thee at thy word:
Call me but love, and I'll be new baptized;
Henceforth I never will be Romeo.
JULIET
What man art thou that thus bescreen'd in night
So stumblest on my counsel?
ROMEO
By a name
I know not how to tell thee who I am:
My name, dear saint, is hateful to myself,
Because it is an enemy to thee;
Had I it written, I would tear the word.
JULIET
My ears have not yet drunk a hundred words
Of that tongue's utterance, yet I know the sound:
Art thou not Romeo and a Montague?

ROMEO
Neither, fair saint, if either thee dislike.
JULIET
How camest thou hither, tell me, and wherefore?
The orchard walls are high and hard to climb,
And the place death, considering who thou art,
If any of my kinsmen find thee here.
ROMEO
With love's light wings did I o'er-perch these walls;
For stony limits cannot hold love out,
And what love can do that dares love attempt;
Therefore thy kinsmen are no let to me.

ROMEO
Alack, there lies more peril in thine eye
Than twenty of their swords: look thou but sweet,
And I am proof against their enmity.
JULIET
I would not for the world they saw thee here.
ROMEO
I have night's cloak to hide me from their sight;
And but thou love me, let them find me here:
My life were better ended by their hate,
Than death prorogued, wanting of thy love.
JULIET
By whose direction found'st thou out this place?
ROMEO
By love, who first did prompt me to inquire;
He lent me counsel and I lent him eyes.
I am no pilot; yet, wert thou as far
As that vast shore wash'd with the farthest sea,
I would adventure for such merchandise.
JULIET
Thou know'st the mask of night is on my face,
Else would a maiden blush bepaint my cheek
For that which thou hast heard me speak to-night
Fain would I dwell on form, fain, fain deny
What I have spoke: but farewell compliment!
Dost thou love me? I know thou wilt say "Ay,"
And I will take thy word: yet if thou swear'st,
Thou mayst prove false; at lovers' perjuries
Then say, Jove laughs. O gentle Romeo,
If thou dost love, pronounce it faithfully:
Or if thou think'st I am too quickly won,
I'll frown and be perverse an say thee nay,
So thou wilt woo; but else, not for the world.
In truth, fair Montague, I am too fond,
And therefore thou mayst think my 'havior light:
But trust me, gentleman, I'll prove more true
Than those that have more cunning to be strange.
I should have been more strange, I must confess,
But that thou overheard'st, ere I was ware,
My true love's passion: therefore pardon me,
And not impute this yielding to light love,
Which the dark night hath so discovered.

ROMEO
Lady, by yonder blessed moon I swear
That tips with silver all these fruit-tree tops—
JULIET
O, swear not by the moon, the inconstant moon,
That monthly changes in her circled orb,
Lest that thy love prove likewise variable.
ROMEO
What shall I swear by?
JULIET
Do not swear at all;
Or, if thou wilt, swear by thy gracious self,
Which is the god of my idolatry,
And I'll believe thee.

JULIET
Well, do not swear: although I joy in thee,
I have no joy of this contract to-night:
It is too rash, too unadvised, too sudden;
Too like the lightning, which doth cease to be
Ere one can say "It lightens." Sweet, good night!
This bud of love, by summer's ripening breath,
May prove a beauteous flower when next we meet.
Good night, good night! as sweet repose and rest
Come to thy heart as that within my breast!
ROMEO
O, wilt thou leave me so unsatisfied?
JULIET
What satisfaction canst thou have to-night?
ROMEO
The exchange of thy love's faithful vow for mine.

JULIET
I gave thee mine before thou didst request it:
And yet I would it were to give again.
ROMEO
Wouldst thou withdraw it? for what purpose, love?
JULIET
But to be frank, and give it thee again.
And yet I wish but for the thing I have:
My bounty is as boundless as the sea,
My love as deep; the more I give to thee,
The more I have, for both are infinite.

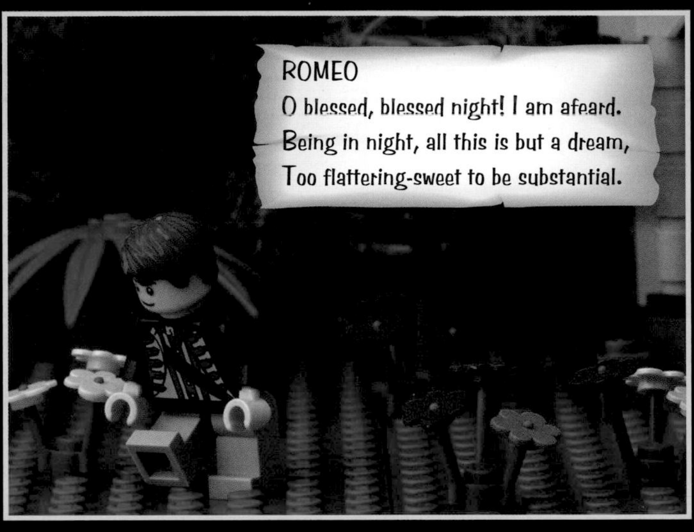

JULIET
Three words, dear Romeo, and good night indeed.
If that thy bent of love be honourable,
Thy purpose marriage, send me word to-morrow,
By one that I'll procure to come to thee,
Where and what time thou wilt perform the rite;
And all my fortunes at thy foot I'll lay
And follow thee my lord throughout the world.
NURSE
Madam!
JULIET
I come, anon.—But if thou mean'st not well,
I do beseech thee—
NURSE
Madam!
JULIET
By and by, I come:—
To cease thy suit, and leave me to my grief:
To-morrow will I send.
ROMEO
So thrive my soul—
JULIET
A thousand times good night!

JULIET
Hist! Romeo, hist! O, for a falconer's voice,
To lure this tassel-gentle back again!
Bondage is hoarse, and may not speak aloud;
Else would I tear the cave where Echo lies,
And make her airy tongue more hoarse than mine,
With repetition of my Romeo's name.
ROMEO
It is my soul that calls upon my name:
How silver-sweet sound lovers' tongues by night,
Like softest music to attending ears!

JULIET
Romeo!
ROMEO
My dear?
JULIET
At what o'clock to-morrow
Shall I send to thee?
ROMEO
At the hour of nine.
JULIET
I will not fail: 'tis twenty years till then.
I have forgot why I did call thee back.
ROMEO
Let me stand here till thou remember it.
JULIET
I shall forget, to have thee still stand there,
Remembering how I love thy company.
ROMEO
And I'll still stay, to have thee still forget,
Forgetting any other home but this.

JULIET
'Tis almost morning; I would have thee gone:
And yet no further than a wanton's bird;
Who lets it hop a little from her hand,
Like a poor prisoner in his twisted gyves,
And with a silk thread plucks it back again,
So loving-jealous of his liberty.
ROMEO
I would I were thy bird.
JULIET
Sweet, so would I:
Yet I should kill thee with much cherishing.
Good night, good night! parting is such sweet sorrow,
That I shall say good night till it be morrow.
ROMEO
Sleep dwell upon thine eyes, peace in thy breast!
Would I were sleep and peace, so sweet to rest!
Hence will I to my ghostly father's cell,
His help to crave, and my dear hap to tell.

ACT II. Scene III (1–97).
Friar Laurence's cell.

FRIAR LAURENCE
The grey-eyed morn smiles on the frowning night,
Chequering the eastern clouds with streaks of light,
And flecked darkness like a drunkard reels
From forth day's path and Titan's fiery wheels:
Now, ere the sun advance his burning eye,
The day to cheer and night's dank dew to dry,
I must up-fill this osier cage of ours
With baleful weeds and precious-juiced flowers.
The earth that's nature's mother is her tomb;
What is her burying grave that is her womb,
And from her womb children of divers kind
We sucking on her natural bosom find,
Many for many virtues excellent,
None but for some and yet all different.
O, mickle is the powerful grace that lies
In herbs, plants, stones, and their true qualities:
For nought so vile that on the earth doth live
But to the earth some special good doth give,
Nor aught so good but strain'd from that fair use
Revolts from true birth, stumbling on abuse:
Virtue itself turns vice, being misapplied;
And vice sometimes by action dignified.
Within the infant rind of this small flower
Poison hath residence and medicine power:
For this, being smelt, with that part cheers each part;
Being tasted, slays all senses with the heart.
Two such opposed kings encamp them still
In man as well as herbs, grace and rude will;
And where the worser is predominant,
Full soon the canker death eats up that plant.

ROMEO
Good morrow, father.
FRIAR LAURENCE
Benedicite!
What early tongue so sweet saluteth me?
Young son, it argues a distemper'd head
So soon to bid good morrow to thy bed:
Care keeps his watch in every old man's eye,
And where care lodges, sleep will never lie;
But where unbruised youth with unstuff'd brain
Doth couch his limbs, there golden sleep doth reign:
Therefore thy earliness doth me assure
Thou art up-roused by some distemperature;
Or if not so, then here I hit it right,
Our Romeo hath not been in bed to-night.

ROMEO
That last is true; the sweeter rest was mine.
FRIAR LAURENCE
God pardon sin! wast thou with Rosaline?
ROMEO
With Rosaline, my ghostly father? no;
I have forgot that name, and that name's woe.
FRIAR LAURENCE
That's my good son: but where hast thou been, then?

ROMEO
I'll tell thee, ere thou ask it me again.
I have been feasting with mine enemy,
Where on a sudden one hath wounded me,
That's by me wounded: both our remedies
Within thy help and holy physic lies:
I bear no hatred, blessed man, for, lo,
My intercession likewise steads my foe.
FRIAR LAURENCE
Be plain, good son, and homely in thy drift;
Riddling confession finds but riddling shrift.
ROMEO
Then plainly know my heart's dear love is set
On the fair daughter of rich Capulet:
As mine on hers, so hers is set on mine;
And all combined, save what thou must combine
By holy marriage: when and where and how
We met, we woo'd and made exchange of vow,
I'll tell thee as we pass; but this I pray,
That thou consent to marry us to-day.

FRIAR LAURENCE
Holy Saint Francis, what a change is here!
Is Rosaline, whom thou didst love so dear,
So soon forsaken? young men's love then lies
Not truly in their hearts, but in their eyes.
Jesu Maria, what a deal of brine
Hath wash'd thy sallow cheeks for Rosaline!
How much salt water thrown away in waste,
To season love, that of it doth not taste!
The sun not yet thy sighs from heaven clears,
Thy old groans ring yet in my ancient ears;
Lo, here upon thy cheek the stain doth sit
Of an old tear that is not wash'd off yet:
If e'er thou wast thyself and these woes thine,
Thou and these woes were all for Rosaline:
And art thou changed? pronounce this sentence then,
Women may fall, when there's no strength in men.
ROMEO
Thou chid'st me oft for loving Rosaline.
FRIAR LAURENCE
For doting, not for loving, pupil mine.

ROMEO
And bad'st me bury love.
FRIAR LAURENCE
Not in a grave,
To lay one in, another out to have.
ROMEO
I pray thee, chide not; she whom I love now
Doth grace for grace and love for love allow;
The other did not so.

FRIAR LAURENCE
O, she knew well
Thy love did read by rote and could not spell.
But come, young waverer, come, go with me,
In one respect I'll thy assistant be;
For this alliance may so happy prove,
To turn your households' rancour to pure love.
ROMEO
O, let us hence; I stand on sudden haste.
FRIAR LAURENCE
Wisely and slow; they stumble that run fast.

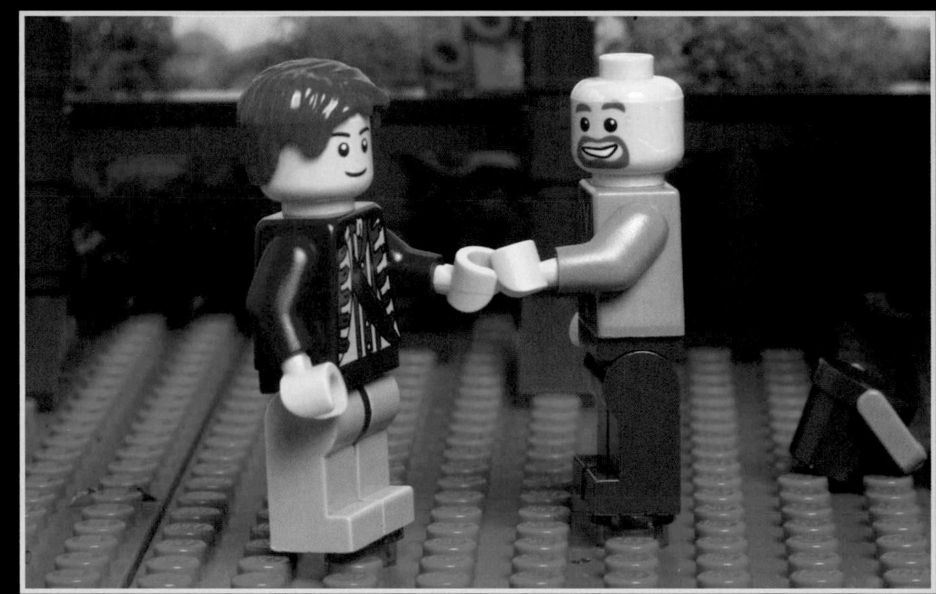

R

&

J

The Nurse has helped pass the message to Juliet that Friar Laurence and Romeo have set out a plan for the couple to marry. In private, the two wed, but the secrecy and family tension prevent them from enjoying their marital bliss for very long. Secret marriage aside, the kindling love between Romeo and Juliet has caused severe unrest amongst the warring Montagues and Capulets. Tybalt Capulet, cousin of Juliet, is the unwavering defender of their hatred of the Montagues. In the very first scene of the play, while discussing the potential peace between the families, he says, "I hate the word, as I hate hell, all Montagues, and thee" (I.i.64–65). Romeo and Juliet's "star-crossed" (I.Prologue.6) relationship—or one that is doomed by fate—is the catalyst to the coming duel as Tybalt sets out to break the couple apart. Romeo assembles his kinsman, Benvolio, and dear friend Mercutio to help defend him but is too hazy with his love for Juliet to understand the brevity of the situation.

Romeo, rather idly, tries to convince Tybalt that they should be friends rather than enemies. His explanation to Tybalt is vague at best, but the audience understands that he now sees Tybalt as his kinsman rather than his foe. Witty Mercutio verbally spars back and forth with Tybalt, making fun of his pretentious fashions and formal dueling style. Filtering his language with subtle insults about Tybalt's likeness to cats (the name "Tybalt" is taken from a play whose character is the "Prince of Cats") and homoerotic double-entendres, he slowly and steadily infuriates an already fuming Tybalt. In return, Tybalt serves Mercutio with belittling jabs of his role as "consort" to Romeo, which implies both a menial social standing and a sexual relationship. In spite of Romeo and Benvolio's pacifistic attempts to diffuse the situation, the group begins to fight.

TYBALT
Well, peace be with you, sir: here comes my man.
MERCUTIO
But I'll be hanged, sir, if he wear your livery:
Marry, go before to field, he'll be your follower;
Your worship in that sense may call him 'man.'

TYBALT
Romeo, the hate I bear thee can afford
No better term than this,—thou art a villain.
ROMEO
Tybalt, the reason that I have to love thee
Doth much excuse the appertaining rage
To such a greeting: villain am I none;
Therefore farewell; I see thou know'st me not.
TYBALT
Boy, this shall not excuse the injuries
That thou hast done me; therefore turn and draw.

MERCUTIO
O calm, dishonourable, vile submission!
Alla stoccata carries it away.
Tybalt, you rat-catcher, will you walk?
TYBALT
What wouldst thou have with me?

MERCUTIO
Good king of cats, nothing but one of your nine lives; that I mean to make bold withal, and as you shall use me hereafter, drybeat the rest of the eight. Will you pluck your sword out of his pitcher by the ears? make haste, lest mine be about your ears ere it be out.

TYBALT
I am for you.

ROMEO (cont.)
Gentlemen, for shame, forbear this outrage!
Tybalt, Mercutio, the prince expressly hath
Forbidden bandying in Verona streets:
Hold, Tybalt! good Mercutio!
MERCUTIO
I am hurt.
A plague o' both your houses! I am sped.
Is he gone, and hath nothing?

ROMEO
Courage, man; the hurt cannot be much.
MERCUTIO
No, 'tis not so deep as a well, nor so wide as a church-door; but 'tis enough, 'twill serve: ask for me to-morrow, and you shall find me a grave man. I am peppered, I warrant, for this world. A plague o' both your houses! 'Zounds, a dog, a rat, a mouse, a cat, to scratch a man to death! a braggart, a rogue, a villain, that fights by the book of arithmetic! Why the devil came you between us? I was hurt under your arm.
ROMEO
I thought all for the best.

ROMEO
This gentleman, the prince's near ally,
My very friend, hath got his mortal hurt
In my behalf; my reputation stain'd
With Tybalt's slander,—Tybalt, that an hour
Hath been my kinsman! O sweet Juliet,
Thy beauty hath made me effeminate
And in my temper soften'd valour's steel!

BENVOLIO
O Romeo, Romeo, brave Mercutio's dead!
That gallant spirit hath aspired the clouds,
Which too untimely here did scorn the earth.
ROMEO
This day's black fate on more days doth depend;
This but begins the woe, others must end.

BENVOLIO
Here comes the furious Tybalt back again.
ROMEO
Alive, in triumph! and Mercutio slain!
Away to heaven, respective lenity,
And fire-eyed fury be my conduct now!
Now, Tybalt, take the villain back again,
That late thou gavest me; for Mercutio's soul
Is but a little way above our heads,
Staying for thine to keep him company:
Either thou, or I, or both, must go with him.

BENVOLIO
Romeo, away, be gone!
The citizens are up, and Tybalt slain.
Stand not amazed: the prince will doom thee death,
If thou art taken: hence, be gone, away!

ROMEO
O, I am fortune's fool!

BENVOLIO
Why dost thou stay?

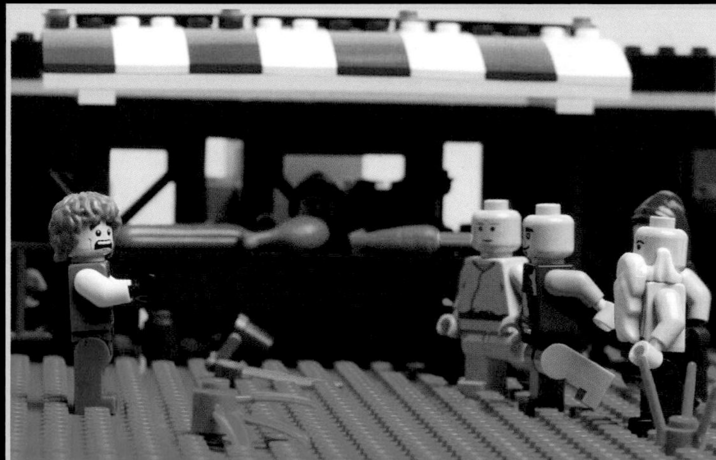

PRINCE
Where are the vile beginners of this fray?

BENVOLIO
O noble prince, I can discover all
The unlucky manage of this fatal brawl:
There lies the man, slain by young Romeo,
That slew thy kinsman, brave Mercutio.

LADY CAPULET
Tybalt, my cousin! O my brother's child!
O prince! O cousin! husband! O, the blood is spilt
O my dear kinsman! Prince, as thou art true,
For blood of ours, shed blood of Montague.
O cousin, cousin!

PRINCE
Benvolio, who began this bloody fray?

BENVOLIO
Tybalt, here slain, whom Romeo's hand did slay;
Romeo that spoke him fair, bade him bethink
How nice the quarrel was, and urged withal
Your high displeasure: all this uttered
With gentle breath, calm look, knees humbly bow'd,
Could not take truce with the unruly spleen
Of Tybalt deaf to peace, but that he tilts
With piercing steel at bold Mercutio's breast,
Who all as hot, turns deadly point to point,
And, with a martial scorn, with one hand beats
Cold death aside, and with the other sends
It back to Tybalt, whose dexterity,
Retorts it: Romeo he cries aloud,
"Hold, friends! friends, part!" and, swifter than his tongue,
His agile arm beats down their fatal points,
And 'twixt them rushes; underneath whose arm
An envious thrust from Tybalt hit the life
Of stout Mercutio, and then Tybalt fled;
But by and by comes back to Romeo,
Who had but newly entertain'd revenge,
And to 't they go like lightning, for, ere I
Could draw to part them, was stout Tybalt slain.
And, as he fell, did Romeo turn and fly.
This is the truth, or let Benvolio die.

LADY CAPULET
He is a kinsman to the Montague;
Affection makes him false; he speaks not true:
Some twenty of them fought in this black strife,
And all those twenty could but kill one life.
I beg for justice, which thou, prince, must give;
Romeo slew Tybalt, Romeo must not live.
PRINCE
Romeo slew him, he slew Mercutio;
Who now the price of his dear blood doth owe?

MONTAGUE
Not Romeo, prince, he was Mercutio's friend;
His fault concludes but what the law should end,
The life of Tybalt.
PRINCE
And for that offence
Immediately we do exile him hence:
I have an interest in your hate's proceeding,
My blood for your rude brawls doth lie a-bleeding;
But I'll amerce you with so strong a fine
That you shall all repent the loss of mine:
I will be deaf to pleading and excuses;
Nor tears nor prayers shall purchase out abuses:
Therefore use none: let Romeo hence in haste,
Else, when he's found, that hour is his last.
Bear hence this body and attend our will:
Mercy but murders, pardoning those that kill.

Still aglow from her wedding day, Juliet's Nurse brings her the news of the death of someone she loves. Misunderstanding the Nurse to mean Romeo, Juliet is inconsolable. The Nurse explains that her beloved cousin, Tybalt, was in fact slain at the hands of her new husband and that Romeo has been banished. Juliet is seriously troubled, saying "And death, not Romeo, take my maidenhead," meaning that Death has taken her innocence on her wedding night, rather than her husband (III.ii.138). She asks the Nurse to take her ring and give it to Romeo in solidarity.

Friar Laurence tells Romeo that he has been banished, and Romeo sees this as a fate worse than death because he will be unable to be with Juliet. The Nurse comes by to give Romeo Juliet's ring. Seeing that Romeo and Juliet are both equally inconsolable and heartbroken, they decide that Romeo will visit with Juliet through the night and then, in the morning, shall go to Mantua until the Prince can be convinced to pardon him. Romeo spends a blissful night with Juliet, and the two try to settle one another's fears for the future. In the meantime, Capulet has put a rush on Paris' request to marry Juliet, thinking that this will put her in better spirits after the death of Tybalt.

JULIET
Now, by Saint Peter's Church and Peter too,
He shall not make me there a joyful bride.
I wonder at this haste; that I must wed
Ere he, that should be husband, comes to woo.
I pray you, tell my lord and father, madam,
I will not marry yet; and, when I do, I swear,
It shall be Romeo, whom you know I hate,
Rather than Paris. These are news indeed!

CAPULET
When the sun sets, the air doth drizzle dew;
But for the sunset of my brother's son
It rains downright.
How now! a conduit, girl? what, still in tears?
Evermore showering? In one little body
Thou counterfeit'st a bark, a sea, a wind;
For still thy eyes, which I may call the sea,
Do ebb and flow with tears; the bark thy body is,
Sailing in this salt flood; the winds, thy sighs;
Who, raging with thy tears, and they with them,
Without a sudden calm, will overset
Thy tempest-tossed body. How now, wife!
Have you deliver'd to her our decree?

LADY CAPULET
Ay, sir; but she will none, she gives you thanks.
I would the fool were married to her grave!

CAPULET
How now, how now, chop-logic! What is this?
"Proud," and "I thank you," and 'I thank you not;"
And yet "not proud," mistress minion, you,
Thank me no thankings, nor, proud me no prouds,
But fettle your fine joints 'gainst Thursday next,
To go with Paris to Saint Peter's Church,
Or I will drag thee on a hurdle thither.
Out, you green-sickness carrion! out, you baggage!
You tallow-face!

CAPULET
Hang thee, young baggage! disobedient wretch!
I tell thee what: get thee to church o' Thursday,
Or never after look me in the face:
Speak not, reply not, do not answer me;
My fingers itch. Wife, we scarce thought us blest
That God had lent us but this only child;
But now I see this one is one too much,
And that we have a curse in having her:
Out on her, hilding!

ACT IV. Scene I (51–127).
Friar Laurence's cell.

Juliet's parents have informed her of her coming marriage to Paris. Grief-stricken and unable to tell them that she is in fact already married to Romeo, she makes another plan to commit suicide. The Nurse tells her she should concede to marry Tybalt, and pretending to take her advice, Juliet goes off to see Friar Laurence to discuss her fate. Arriving at the church, Paris is already there making wedding plans with the Friar, who is maintaining the guise that Romeo and Juliet are not married. Coming upon them, Juliet ushers Paris out of the church by telling him she needs to make her confession, per Catholic doctrine, in private. Paris's attempts to charm her are in vain, and Juliet sets forth to confess her intentions to Friar Laurence.

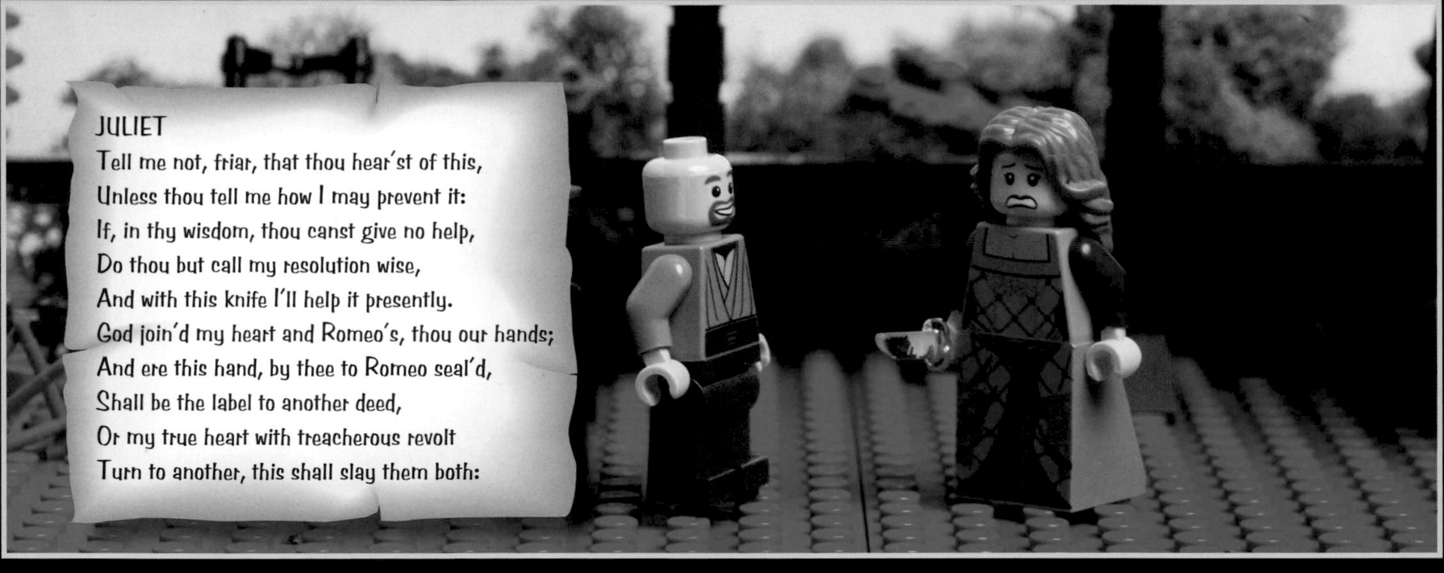

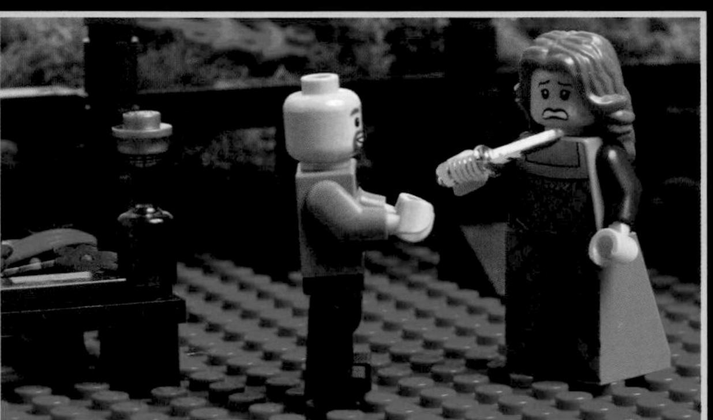

JULIET (cont.)
Therefore, out of thy long-experienced time,
Give me some present counsel, or, behold,
'Twixt my extremes and me this bloody knife
Shall play the umpire, arbitrating that
Which the commission of thy years and art
Could to no issue of true honour bring.
Be not so long to speak; I long to die,
If what thou speak'st speak not of remedy.

FRIAR LAURENCE
Hold, daughter: I do spy a kind of hope,
Which craves as desperate an execution.
As that is desperate which we would prevent.
If, rather than to marry County Paris,
Thou hast the strength of will to slay thyself,
Then is it likely thou wilt undertake
A thing like death to chide away this shame,
That copest with death himself to scape from it:
And, if thou darest, I'll give thee remedy.

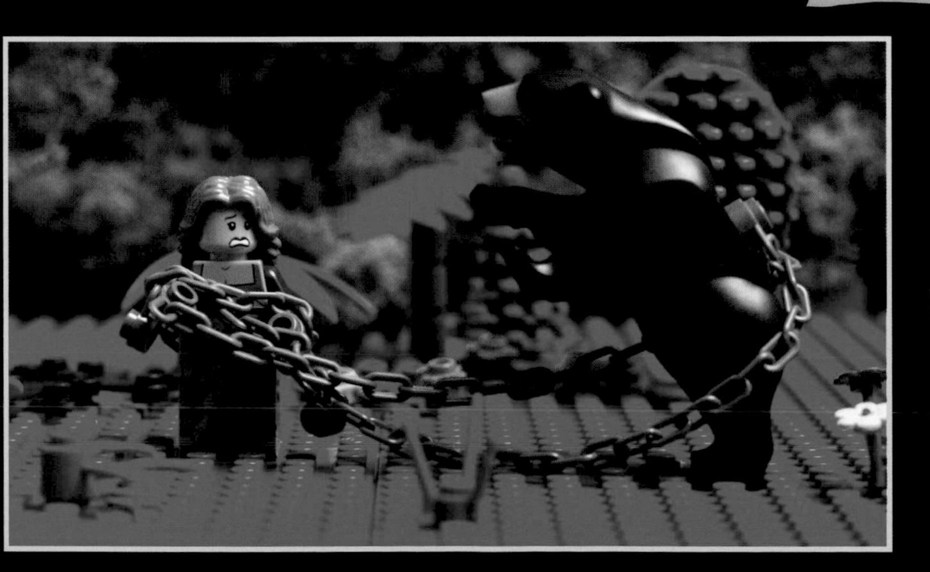

JULIET
O, bid me leap, rather than marry Paris,
From off the battlements of yonder tower;
Or walk in thievish ways; or bid me lurk
Where serpents are; chain me with roaring bears;

JULIET (cont.)
Or bid me go into a new-made grave
And hide me with a dead man in his shroud;
Things that, to hear them told, have made me tremble;
And I will do it without fear or doubt,
To live an unstain'd wife to my sweet love.

FRIAR LAURENCE
Hold, then; go home, be merry, give consent
To marry Paris: Wednesday is to-morrow:
To-morrow night look that thou lie alone;
Let not thy nurse lie with thee in thy chamber:
Take thou this vial, being then in bed,
And this distilled liquor drink thou off;

FRIAR LAURENCE (cont.)
When presently through all thy veins shall run
A cold and drowsy humour, for no pulse
Shall keep his native progress, but surcease:
No warmth, no breath, shall testify thou livest;
The roses in thy lips and cheeks shall fade
To paly ashes, thy eyes' windows fall,
Like death, when he shuts up the day of life;
Each part, deprived of supple government,
Shall, stiff and stark and cold, appear like death:
And in this borrow'd likeness of shrunk death
Thou shalt continue two and forty hours,
And then awake as from a pleasant sleep.
Now, when the bridegroom in the morning comes
To rouse thee from thy bed, there art thou dead:
Then, as the manner of our country is,
In thy best robes uncover'd on the bier
Thou shalt be borne to that same ancient vault
Where all the kindred of the Capulets lie.
In the mean time, against thou shalt awake,
Shall Romeo by my letters know our drift,
And hither shall he come: and he and I
Will watch thy waking, and that very night
Shall Romeo bear thee hence to Mantua.
And this shall free thee from this present shame;
If no inconstant toy, nor womanish fear,
Abate thy valour in the acting it.

JULIET
Give me, give me! O, tell not me of fear!

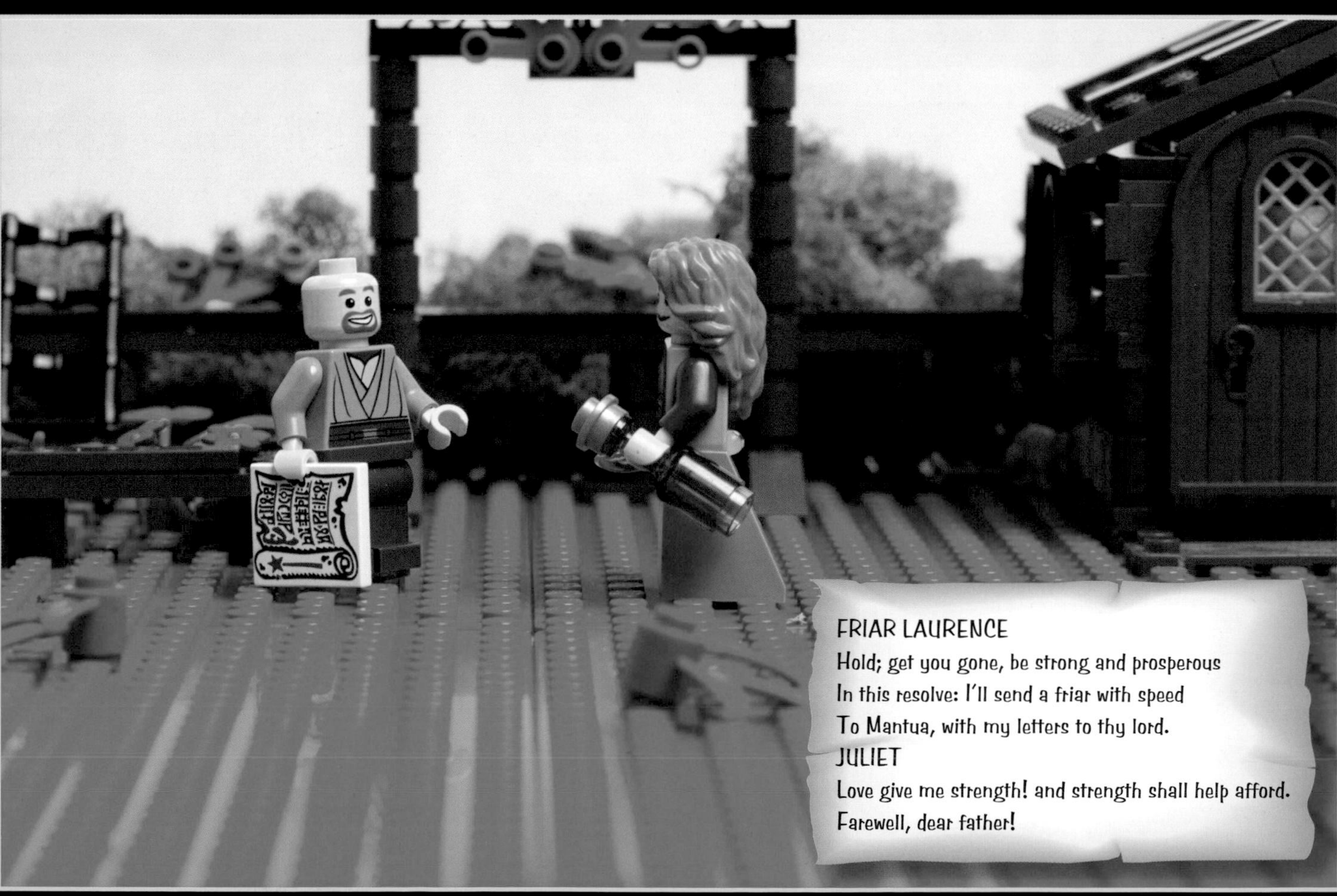
FRIAR LAURENCE
Hold; get you gone, be strong and prosperous
In this resolve: I'll send a friar with speed
To Mantua, with my letters to thy lord.
JULIET
Love give me strength! and strength shall help afford.
Farewell, dear father!

Having settled on a plan with Friar Laurence, Juliet returns home with her pseudo-poison in hand. She profusely apologizes to her parents for her prior behavior and tells them that she will happily marry Paris. Juliet's father is so pleased by the news that he decides to move the wedding up to Wednesday, the very next day. Juliet thanks her parents for keeping her best interests in mind and asks her Nurse to sleep in another room so that she can prepare for her nuptials. In truth, she is about the take the potion that mimics death.

JULIET (cont.)
Come, vial.
What if this mixture do not work at all?
Shall I be married then to-morrow morning?
No, no: this shall forbid it: lie thou there.

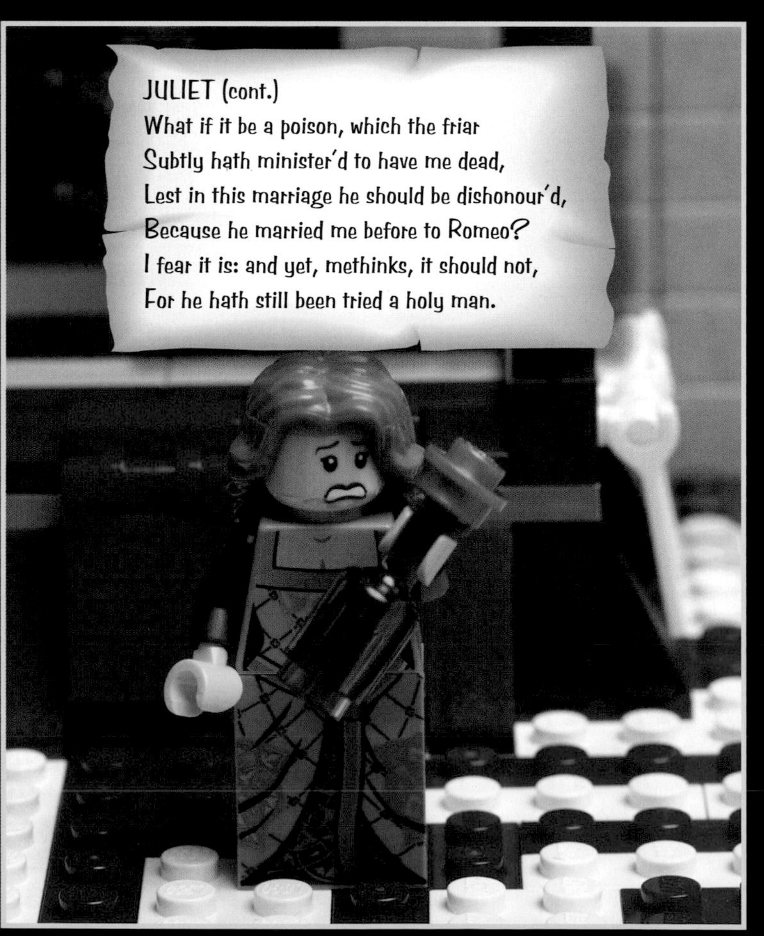

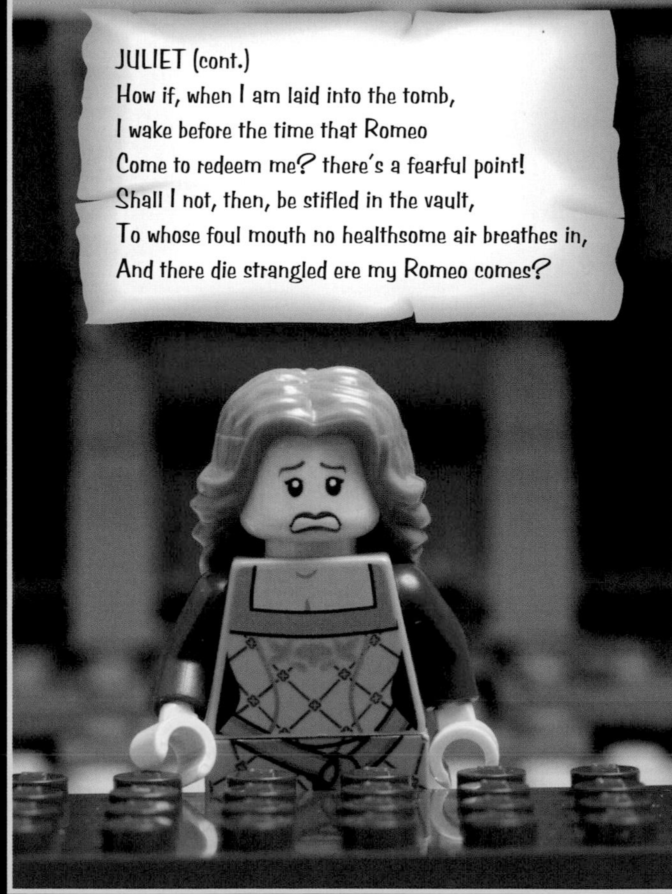

JULIET (cont.)
Or, if I live, is it not very like,
The horrible conceit of death and night,
Together with the terror of the place,—
As in a vault, an ancient receptacle,
Where, for these many hundred years, the bones
Of all my buried ancestors are packed:

JULIET (cont.)
Alack, alack, is it not like that I,
So early waking, what with loathsome smells,
And shrieks like mandrakes' torn out of the earth,
That living mortals, hearing them, run mad:—
O, if I wake, shall I not be distraught,
Environed with all these hideous fears?
And madly play with my forefather's joints?
And pluck the mangled Tybalt from his shroud?

JULIET (cont.)
And, in this rage, with some great kinsman's bone,
As with a club, dash out my desperate brains?
O, look! methinks I see my cousin's ghost
Seeking out Romeo, that did spit his body
Upon a rapier's point: stay, Tybalt, stay!

JULIET (cont.)
Romeo, I come! this do I drink to thee.

The next day, the day of Juliet's wedding with Paris, Capulet orders Nurse to wake Juliet and make her ready. Nurse is little prepared for what she discovers.

NURSE
Mistress! what, mistress! Juliet! fast, I warrant her, she:
Why, lamb! why, lady! fie, you slug-a-bed!
Why, love, I say! madam! sweet-heart! why, bride!
What, not a word? you take your pennyworths now;
Sleep for a week; for the next night, I warrant,
The County Paris hath set up his rest,
That you shall rest but little. God forgive me,
Marry, and amen, how sound is she asleep!
I must needs wake her. Madam, madam, madam!
Ay, let the county take you in your bed;
He'll fright you up, i' faith. Will it not be?

NURSE (cont.)
What, dress'd! and in your clothes! and down again!
I must needs wake you; Lady! lady! lady!
Alas, alas! Help, help! my lady's dead!
O, well-a-day, that ever I was born!
Some aqua vitae, ho! My lord! my lady!

LADY CAPULET
What noise is here?

NURSE
O lamentable day!
LADY CAPULET
What is the matter?
NURSE
Look, look! O heavy day!
LADY CAPULET
O me, O me! My child, my only life,
Revive, look up, or I will die with thee!
Help, help! Call help.

CAPULET
For shame, bring Juliet forth; her lord is come.

NURSE
She's dead, deceased, she's dead; alack the day!
LADY CAPULET
Alack the day, she's dead, she's dead, she's dead!

CAPULET
Ha! let me see her: out, alas! she's cold:
Her blood is settled, and her joints are stiff;
Life and these lips have long been separated:
Death lies on her like an untimely frost
Upon the sweetest flower of all the field.
NURSE
O lamentable day!
LADY CAPULET
O woful time!
CAPULET
Death, that hath ta'en her hence to make me wail,
Ties up my tongue, and will not let me speak.

FRIAR LAURENCE
Come, is the bride ready to go to church?

CAPULET
Ready to go, but never to return.
O son! the night before thy wedding-day
Hath Death lain with thy wife. There she lies,
Flower as she was, deflowered by him.
Death is my son-in-law, Death is my heir;
My daughter he hath wedded: I will die,
And leave him all; life, living, all is Death's.

LADY CAPULET
Accursed, unhappy, wretched, hateful day!
Most miserable hour that e'er time saw
In lasting labour of his pilgrimage!
But one, poor one, one poor and loving child,
But one thing to rejoice and solace in,
And cruel death hath catch'd it from my sight!

NURSE
O woe! O woful, woful, woful day!
Most lamentable day, most woful day,
That ever, ever, I did yet behold!
O day! O day! O day! O hateful day!
Never was seen so black a day as this:
O woful day, O woful day!
PARIS
Beguiled, divorced, wronged, spited, slain!
Most detestable death, by thee beguil'd,
By cruel cruel thee quite overthrown!
O love! O life! not life, but love in death!

CAPULET
Despised, distressed, hated, martyr'd, kill'd!
Uncomfortable time, why camest thou now
To murder, murder our solemnity?
O child! O child! my soul, and not my child!
Dead art thou! Alack! my child is dead;
And with my child my joys are buried.

FRIAR LAURENCE
Peace, ho, for shame! confusion's cure lives not
In these confusions. Heaven and yourself
Had part in this fair maid; now heaven hath all,
And all the better is it for the maid:
Your part in her you could not keep from death,
But heaven keeps his part in eternal life.
The most you sought was her promotion;
For 'twas your heaven she should be advanced:
And weep ye now, seeing she is advanced
Above the clouds, as high as heaven itself?

FRIAR LAURENCE (cont.)
O, in this love, you love your child so ill,
That you run mad, seeing that she is well:
She's not well married that lives married long;
But she's best married that dies married young.
Dry up your tears, and stick your rosemary
On this fair corse; and, as the custom is,
In all her best array bear her to church:
For though fond nature bids us an lament,
Yet nature's tears are reason's merriment.

CAPULET
All things that we ordained festival,
Turn from their office to black funeral;
Our instruments to melancholy bells,
Our wedding cheer to a sad burial feast,
Our solemn hymns to sullen dirges change,
Our bridal flowers serve for a buried corse,
And all things change them to the contrary.

ACT V. Scene I (1–90).
Mantua. A street.

ROMEO
If I may trust the flattering truth of sleep,
My dreams presage some joyful news at hand:
My bosom's lord sits lightly in his throne;
And all this day an unaccustom'd spirit
Lifts me above the ground with cheerful thoughts.
I dreamt my lady came and found me dead—
Strange dream, that gives a dead man leave
to think!—

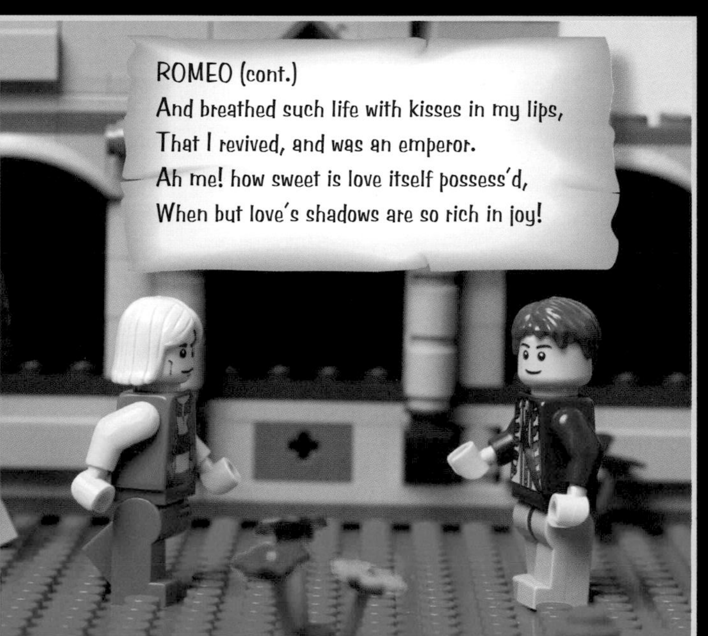

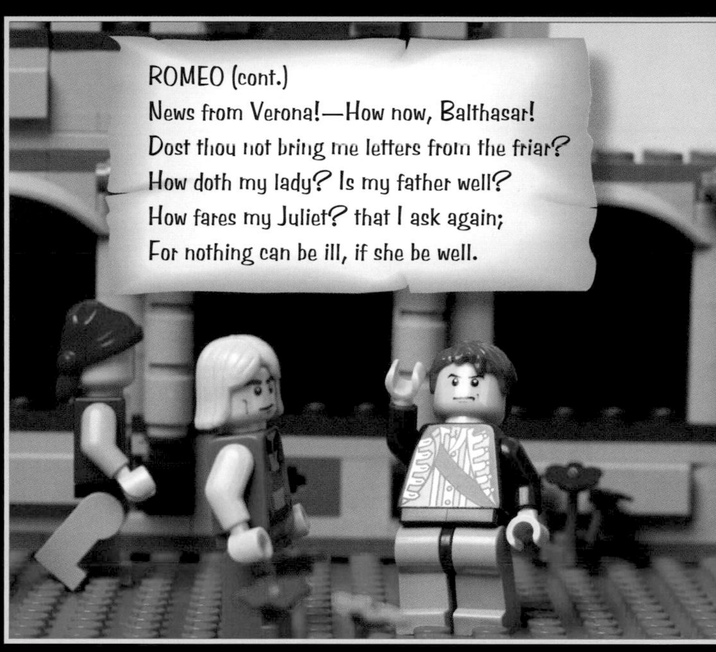

BALTHASAR
Then she is well, and nothing can be ill:
Her body sleeps in Capel's monument,
And her immortal part with angels lives.
I saw her laid low in her kindred's vault,
And presently took post to tell it you:
O, pardon me for bringing these ill news,
Since you did leave it for my office, sir.

ROMEO
Is it even so? then I defy you, stars!
Thou know'st my lodging: get me ink and paper,
And hire post-horses; I will hence to-night.
BALTHASAR
I do beseech you, sir, have patience:
Your looks are pale and wild, and do import
Some misadventure.

ROMEO (cont.)
Well, Juliet, I will lie with thee to-night.
Let's see for means: O mischief, thou art swift
To enter in the thoughts of desperate men!
I do remember an apothecary,—
And hereabouts he dwells,—which late I noted
In tatter'd weeds, with overwhelming brows,
Culling of simples; meagre were his looks,
Sharp misery had worn him to the bones:
And in his needy shop a tortoise hung,
An alligator stuff'd, and other skins
Of ill-shaped fishes; and about his shelves
A beggarly account of empty boxes,
Green earthen pots, bladders and musty seeds,
Remnants of packthread and old cakes of roses,
Were thinly scatter'd, to make up a show.
Noting this penury, to myself I said
"An if a man did need a poison now,
Whose sale is present death in Mantua,
Here lives a caitiff wretch would sell it him."
O, this same thought did but forerun my need;
And this same needy man must sell it me.

ROMEO
Come hither, man. I see that thou art poor:
Hold, there is forty ducats: let me have
A dram of poison, such soon-speeding gear
As will disperse itself through all the veins
That the life-weary taker may fall dead
And that the trunk may be discharged of breath
As violently as hasty powder fired
Doth hurry from the fatal cannon's womb.

APOTHECARY
Such mortal drugs I have; but Mantua's law
Is death to any he that utters them.
ROMEO
Art thou so bare and full of wretchedness,
And fear'st to die? famine is in thy cheeks,
Need and oppression starveth in thine eyes,
Contempt and beggary hangs upon thy back;
The world is not thy friend nor the world's law;
The world affords no law to make thee rich;
Then be not poor, but break it, and take this.

APOTHECARY
My poverty, but not my will, consents.
ROMEO
I pay thy poverty, and not thy will.

APOTHECARY
Put this in any liquid thing you will,
And drink it off; and, if you had the strength
Of twenty men, it would dispatch you straight.

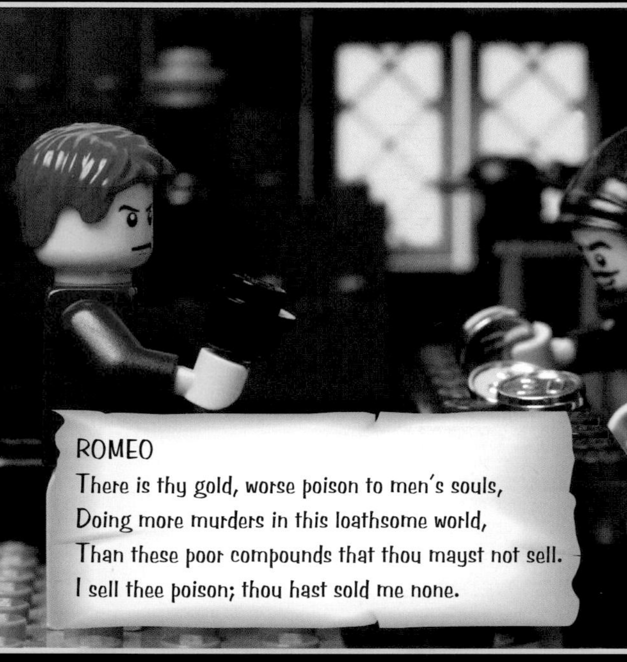
ROMEO
There is thy gold, worse poison to men's souls,
Doing more murders in this loathsome world,
Than these poor compounds that thou mayst not sell.
I sell thee poison; thou hast sold me none.

ROMEO (cont.)
Farewell: buy food, and get thyself in flesh.
Come, cordial and not poison, go with me
To Juliet's grave; for there must I use thee.

ACT V. Scene II (1–30).

Friar Laurence's cell.

FRIAR JOHN
Holy Franciscan friar! brother, ho!

FRIAR LAURENCE
This same should be the voice of Friar John.
Welcome from Mantua: what says Romeo?
Or, if his mind be writ, give me his letter.

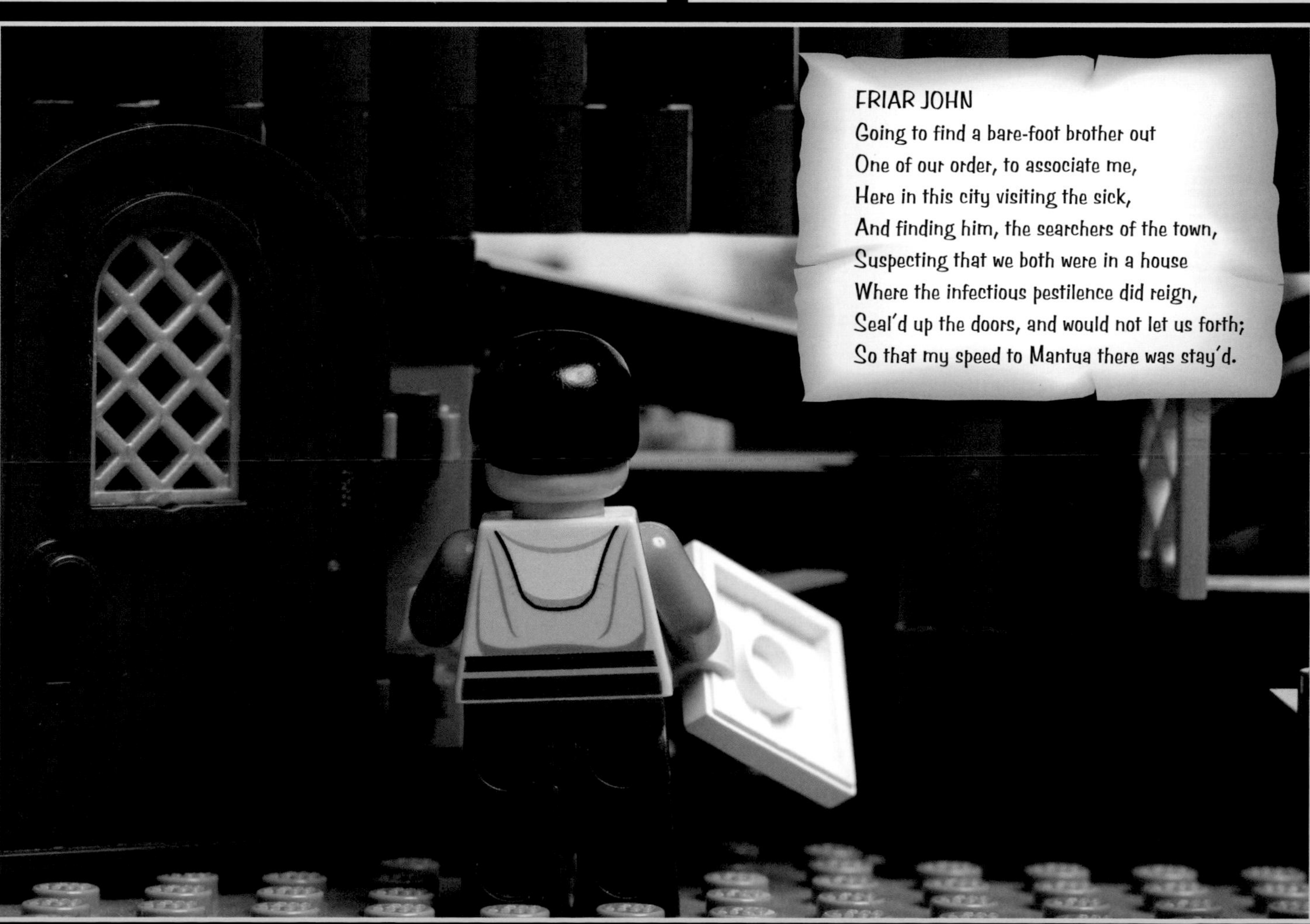
FRIAR JOHN
Going to find a bare-foot brother out
One of our order, to associate me,
Here in this city visiting the sick,
And finding him, the searchers of the town,
Suspecting that we both were in a house
Where the infectious pestilence did reign,
Seal'd up the doors, and would not let us forth;
So that my speed to Mantua there was stay'd.

FRIAR LAURENCE
Unhappy fortune! by my brotherhood,
The letter was not nice but full of charge
Of dear import, and the neglecting it
May do much danger. Friar John, go hence;
Get me an iron crow, and bring it straight
Unto my cell.
FRIAR JOHN
Brother, I'll go and bring it thee.

FRIAR LAURENCE
Now must I to the monument alone;
Within three hours will fair Juliet wake:
She will beshrew me much that Romeo
Hath had no notice of these accidents;
But I will write again to Mantua,
And keep her at my cell till Romeo come;
Poor living corse, closed in a dead man's tomb!

ACT V. Scene III (12–189).
A churchyard; in it a tomb belonging to the Capulets.

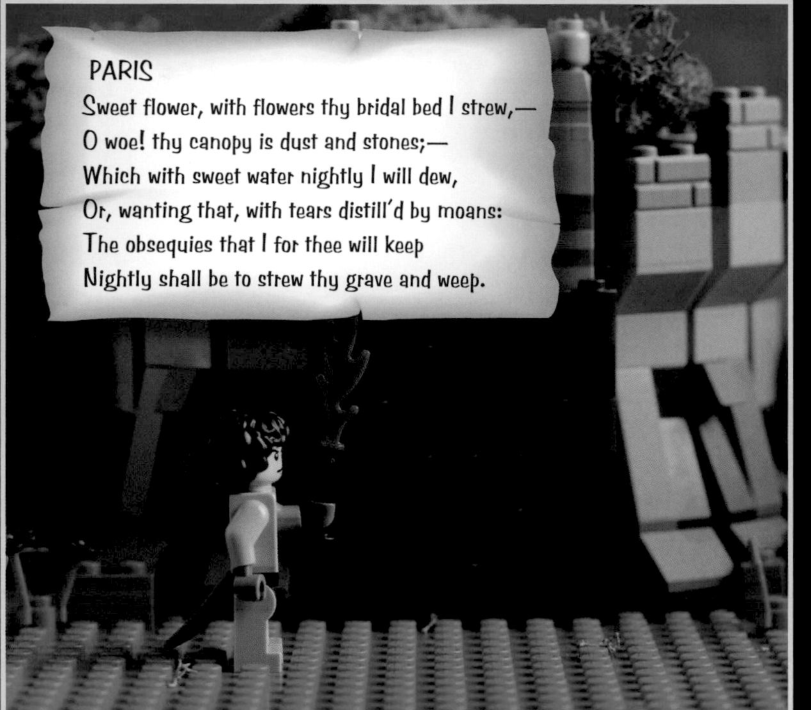
PARIS
Sweet flower, with flowers thy bridal bed I strew,—
O woe! thy canopy is dust and stones;—
Which with sweet water nightly I will dew,
Or, wanting that, with tears distill'd by moans:
The obsequies that I for thee will keep
Nightly shall be to strew thy grave and weep.

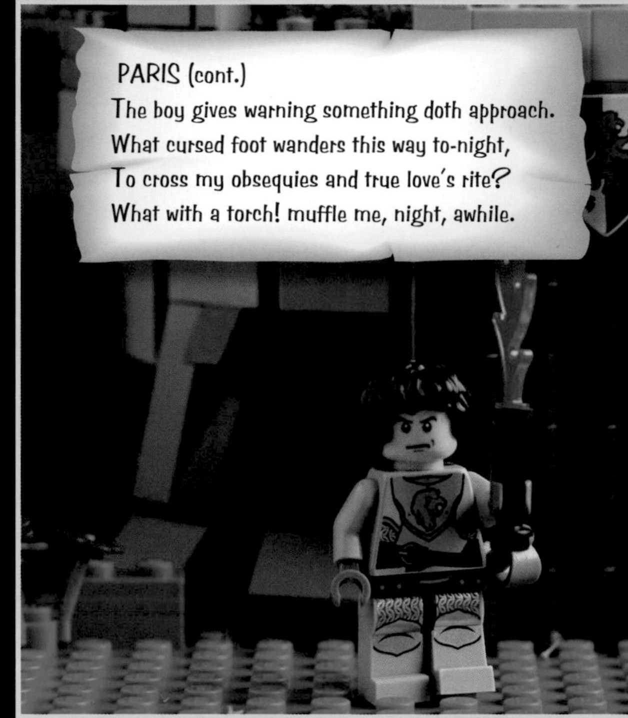
PARIS (cont.)
The boy gives warning something doth approach.
What cursed foot wanders this way to-night,
To cross my obsequies and true love's rite?
What with a torch! muffle me, night, awhile.

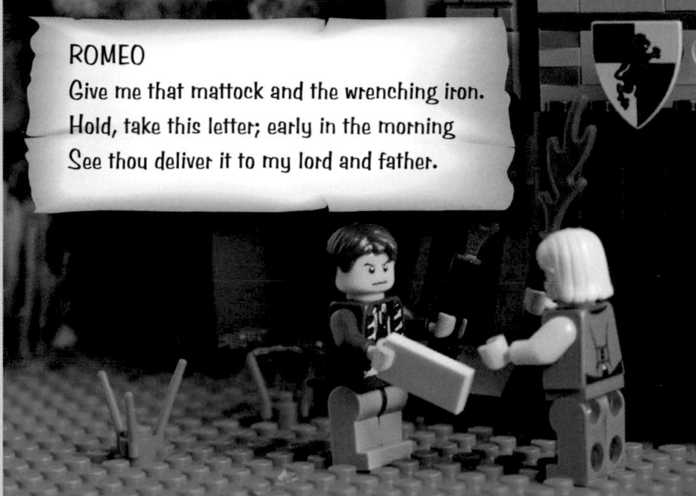
ROMEO
Give me that mattock and the wrenching iron.
Hold, take this letter; early in the morning
See thou deliver it to my lord and father.

ROMEO (cont.)
Give me the light: upon thy life, I charge thee,
Whate'er thou hear'st or seest, stand all aloof,
And do not interrupt me in my course.
Why I descend into this bed of death,
Is partly to behold my lady's face;
But chiefly to take thence from her dead finger
A precious ring, a ring that I must use
In dear employment: therefore hence, be gone:
But if thou, jealous, dost return to pry
In what I further shall intend to do,
By heaven, I will tear thee joint by joint
And strew this hungry churchyard with thy limbs:
The time and my intents are savage-wild,
More fierce and more inexorable far
Than empty tigers or the roaring sea.

BALTHASAR
I will be gone, sir, and not trouble you.
ROMEO
So shalt thou show me friendship. Take thou that:
Live, and be prosperous: and farewell, good fellow.

BALTHASAR
For all this same, I'll hide me hereabout:
His looks I fear, and his intents I doubt.

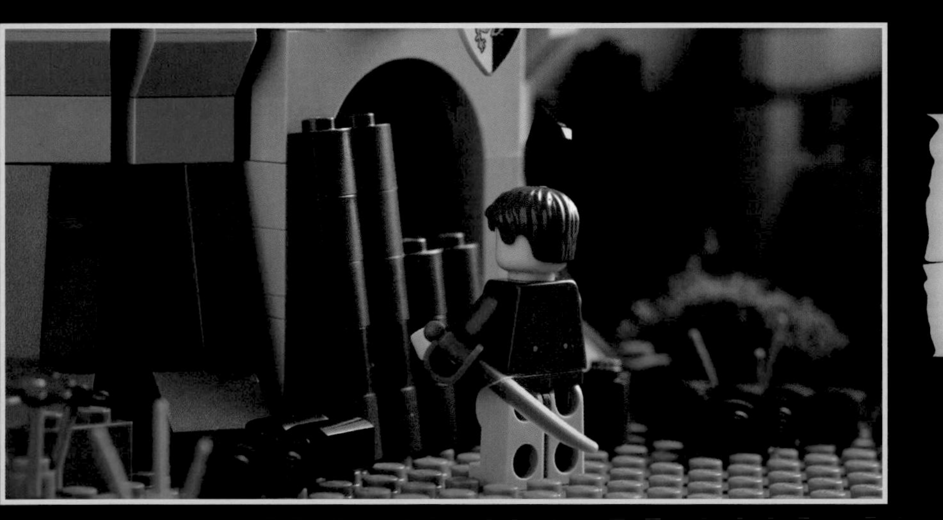

ROMEO
Thou detestable maw, thou womb of death,
Gorged with the dearest morsel of the earth,
Thus I enforce thy rotten jaws to open,
And, in despite, I'll cram thee with more food!

PARIS
This is that banish'd haughty Montague,
That murder'd my love's cousin, with which grief,
It is supposed, the fair creature died;
And here is come to do some villanous shame
To the dead bodies: I will apprehend him.

PARIS (cont.)
Stop thy unhallow'd toil, vile Montague!
Can vengeance be pursued further than death?
Condemned villain, I do apprehend thee:
Obey, and go with me; for thou must die.

ROMEO
I must indeed; and therefore came I hither.
Good gentle youth, tempt not a desperate man;
Fly hence, and leave me: think upon these gone;
Let them affright thee. I beseech thee, youth,
Put not another sin upon my head,
By urging me to fury: O, be gone!
By heaven, I love thee better than myself;
For I come hither arm'd against myself:
Stay not, be gone; live, and hereafter say,
A madman's mercy bade thee run away.

PARIS
I do defy thy conjurations,
And apprehend thee for a felon here.

ROMEO
Wilt thou provoke me? then have at thee, boy!

PAGE
O Lord, they fight! I will go call the watch.

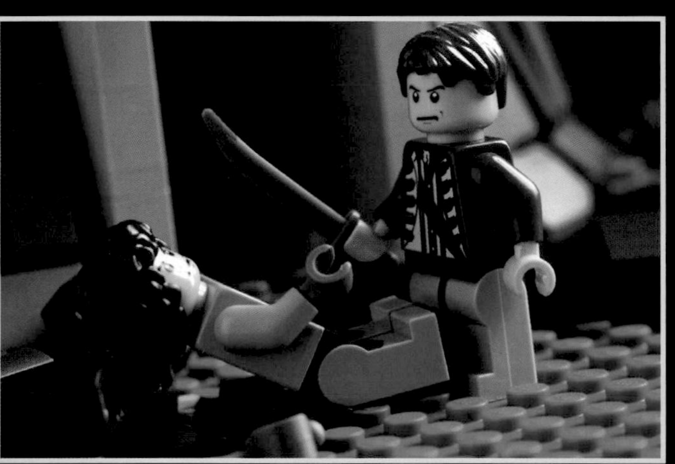

ROMEO
In faith, I will. Let me peruse this face.
Mercutio's kinsman, noble County Paris!
What said my man, when my betossed soul
Did not attend him as we rode? I think
He told me Paris should have married Juliet:
Said he not so? or did I dream it so?

ROMEO (cont.)
Or am I mad, hearing him talk of Juliet,
To think it was so? O, give me thy hand,
One writ with me in sour misfortune's book!
I'll bury thee in a triumphant grave;

ROMEO (cont.)
A grave? O no! a lantern, slaughter'd youth,
For here lies Juliet, and her beauty makes
This vault a feasting presence full of light.
Death, lie thou there, by a dead man interr'd.

ROMEO (cont.)
How oft when men are at the point of death
Have they been merry! which their keepers call
A lightning before death: O, how may I
Call this a lightning? O my love! my wife!
Death, that hath suck'd the honey of thy breath,
Hath had no power yet upon thy beauty:
Thou art not conquer'd; beauty's ensign yet
Is crimson in thy lips and in thy cheeks,
And death's pale flag is not advanced there.
Tybalt, liest thou there in thy bloody sheet?
O, what more favour can I do to thee,
Than with that hand that cut thy youth in twain
To sunder his that was thine enemy?

ROMEO (cont.)
Forgive me, cousin! Ah, dear Juliet,
Why art thou yet so fair? shall I believe
That unsubstantial death is amorous,
And that the lean abhorred monster keeps
Thee here in dark to be his paramour?
For fear of that, I still will stay with thee;
And never from this palace of dim night
Depart again: here, here will I remain
With worms that are thy chamber-maids; O, here
Will I set up my everlasting rest,
And shake the yoke of inauspicious stars
From this world-wearied flesh. Eyes, look your last!

ROMEO (cont.)
Arms, take your last embrace! and, lips, O you
The doors of breath, seal with a righteous kiss
A dateless bargain to engrossing death!
Come, bitter conduct, come, unsavoury guide!
Thou desperate pilot, now at once run on
The dashing rocks thy sea-sick weary bark!

ROMEO (cont.)
Here's to my love!

ROMEO (cont.)
O true apothecary!
Thy drugs are quick. Thus with a kiss I die.

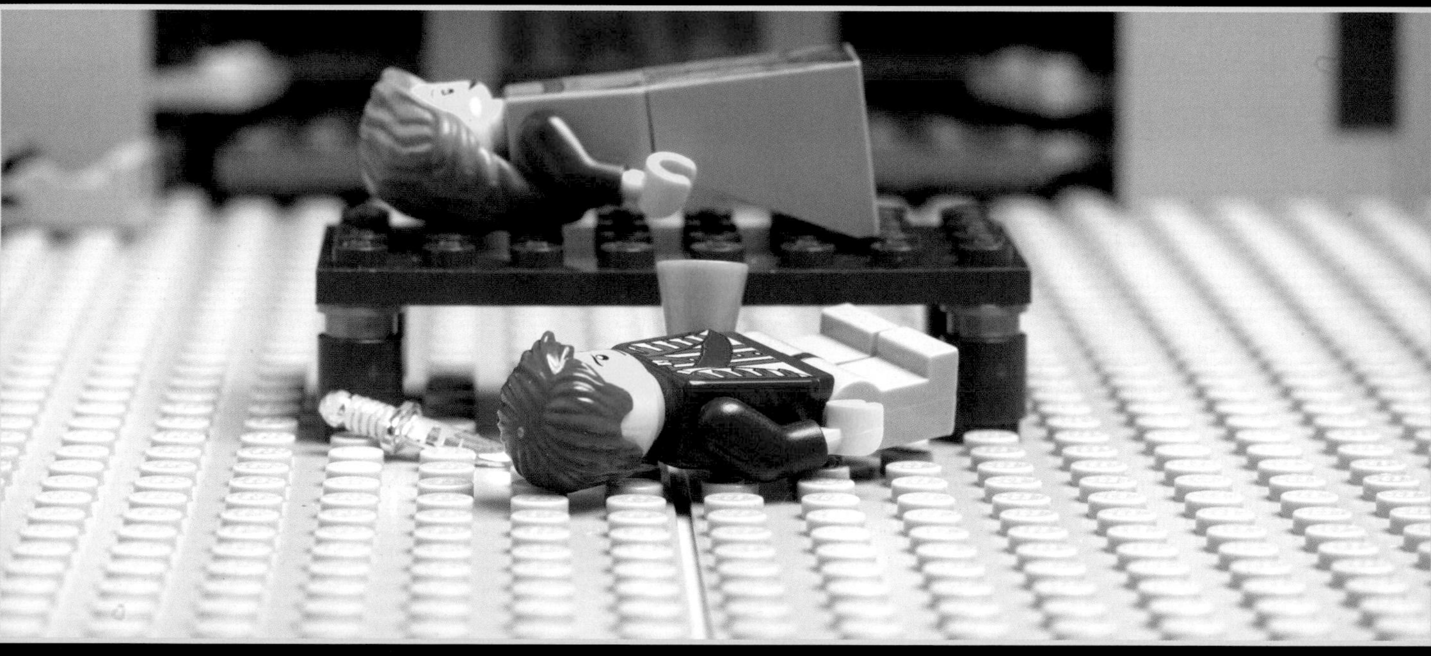

FRIAR LAURENCE
Saint Francis be my speed! how oft to-night
Have my old feet stumbled at graves! Who's there?

BALTHASAR
Here's one, a friend, and one that knows you well.

FRIAR LAURENCE
Bliss be upon you! Tell me, good my friend,
What torch is yond, that vainly lends his light
To grubs and eyeless skulls? as I discern,
It burneth in the Capel's monument.

BALTHASAR
It doth so, holy sir; and there's my master,
One that you love.

FRIAR LAURENCE
Who is it?

BALTHASAR
Romeo.

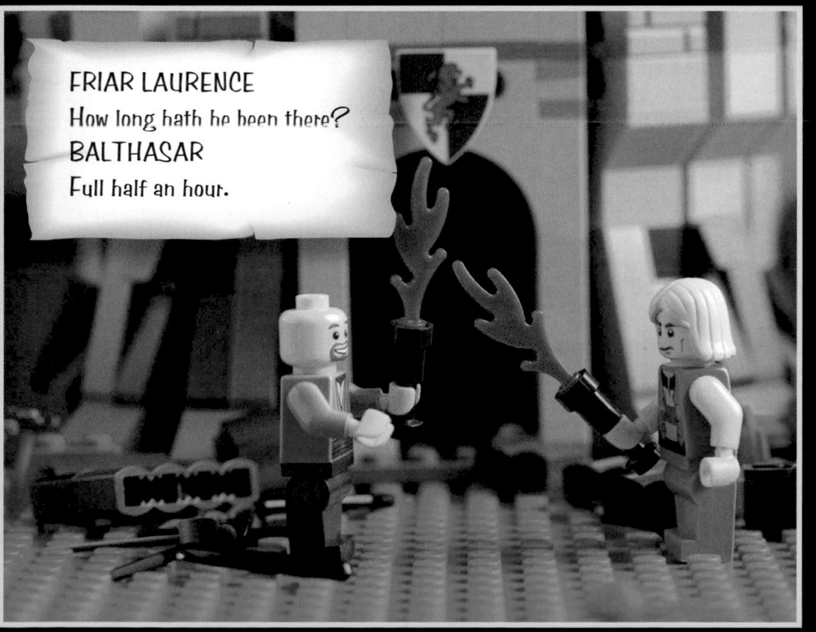
FRIAR LAURENCE
How long hath he been there?
BALTHASAR
Full half an hour.

FRIAR LAURENCE
Go with me to the vault.

FRIAR LAURENCE (cont.)
Alack, alack, what blood is this, which stains
The stony entrance of this sepulchre?
What mean these masterless and gory swords
To lie discolour'd by this place of peace?
Romeo! O, pale! Who else? what, Paris too?
And steep'd in blood? Ah, what an unkind hour
Is guilty of this lamentable chance!

FRIAR LAURENCE
I hear some noise. Lady, come from that nest
Of death, contagion, and unnatural sleep:
A greater power than we can contradict
Hath thwarted our intents. Come, come away.
Thy husband in thy bosom there lies dead;
And Paris too. Come, I'll dispose of thee
Among a sisterhood of holy nuns:

JULIET (cont.)
What's here? a cup, closed in my true love's hand?

JULIET (cont.)
Poison, I see, hath been his timeless end:
O churl! drunk all, and left no friendly drop
To help me after? I will kiss thy lips;

JULIET (cont.)
Haply some poison yet doth hang on them,
To make die with a restorative.

JULIET (cont.)
Thy lips are warm.

FIRST WATCHMAN
Lead, boy: which way?
JULIET
Yea, noise? then I'll be brief.

FIRST WATCHMAN
The ground is bloody; search about the churchyard:
Go, some of you, whoe'er you find attach.
Pitiful sight! here lies the county slain,
And Juliet bleeding, warm, and newly dead,
Who here hath lain these two days buried.
Go, tell the prince: run to the Capulets:
Raise up the Montagues: some others search:
We see the ground whereon these woes do lie;
But the true ground of all these piteous woes
We cannot without circumstance descry.

ACT V. Scene III (290–315).
A churchyard; in it a tomb belonging to the Capulets.

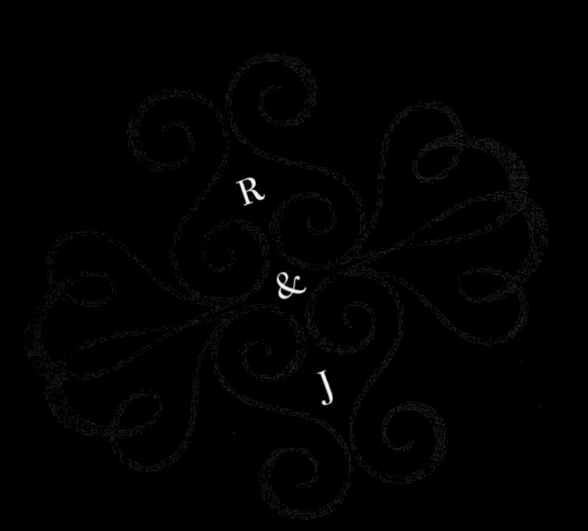

With all of the players at the scene of the couple's tragedy, fingers point to Friar Laurence. The watchmen saw that the Friar had come and gone to the Capulet tomb, bearing a "mattock," or a pickaxe, and the Prince and the two noble families of Verona try to decipher what this means (V.iii.190). Good Friar Laurence speaks at length about the events leading up to Romeo and Juliet's deaths, saying, "And here I stand, both to impeach and purge,/Myself condemned and myself excused" (V.iii.235–236). While he is innocent of committing any mortal sins, he still feels responsible for having unintentionally ushered Romeo and Juliet through their troubles and to untimely ends. Citing the letters that the Friar sent to Romeo in Mantua, Romeo's friend Balthasar helps exonerate Friar Laurence. With the air cleared, the Prince calls for the Montagues and the Capulets to take in the tragic scene that lies before them and look inward to see the heavy role their feud played

PRINCE

This letter doth make good the friar's words,
Their course of love, the tidings of her death:
And here he writes that he did buy a poison
Of a poor 'pothecary, and therewithal
Came to this vault to die, and lie with Juliet.
Where be these enemies? Capulet! Montague!
See, what a scourge is laid upon your hate,
That heaven finds means to kill your joys with love.
And I for winking at your discords too
Have lost a brace of kinsmen: all are punish'd.

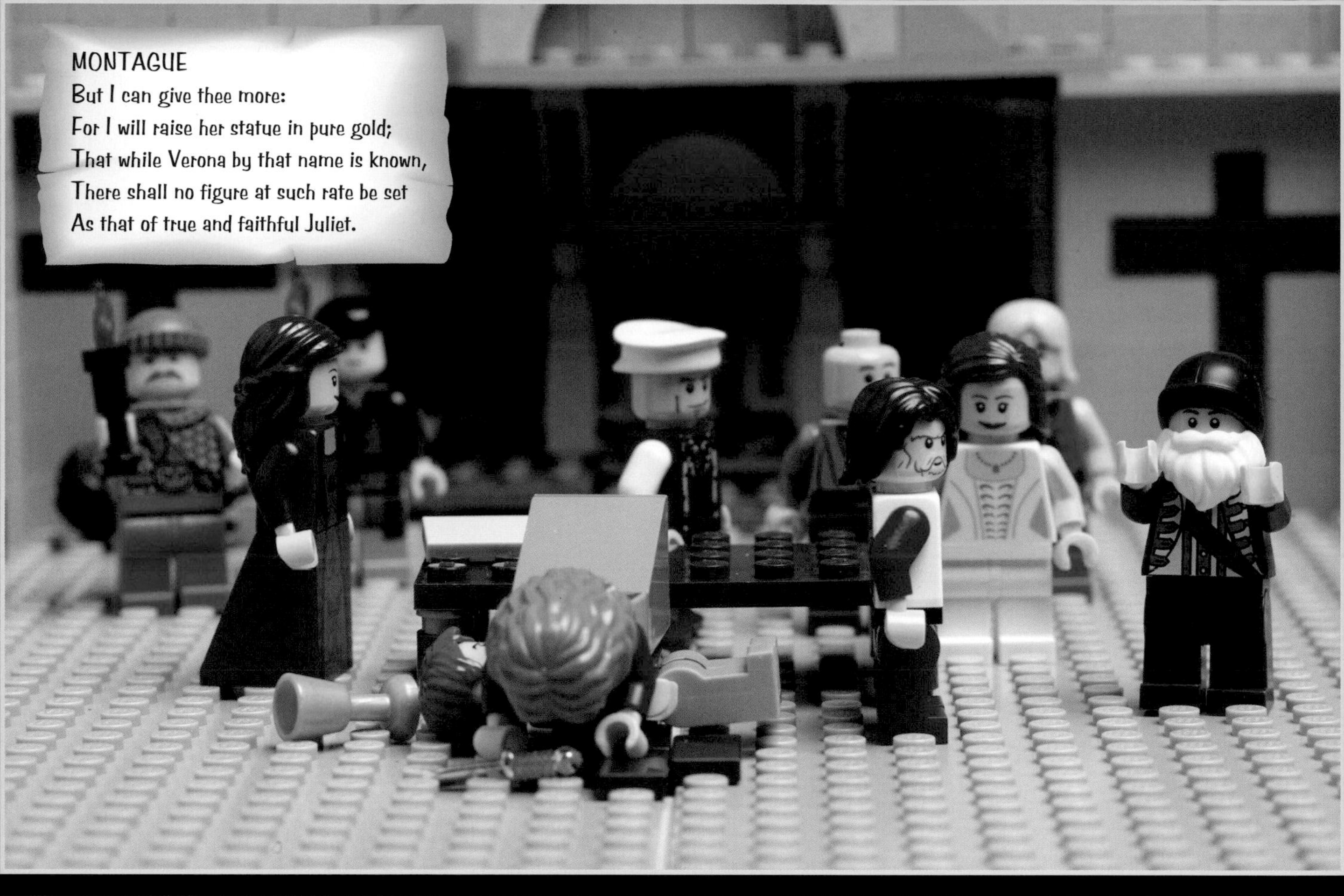
MONTAGUE
But I can give thee more:
For I will raise her statue in pure gold;
That while Verona by that name is known,
There shall no figure at such rate be set
As that of true and faithful Juliet.

CAPULET
As rich shall Romeo's by his lady's lie;
Poor sacrifices of our enmity!

PRINCE
A glooming peace this morning with it brings;
The sun, for sorrow, will not show his head:
Go hence, to have more talk of these sad things;
Some shall be pardon'd, and some punished:
For never was a story of more woe
Than this of Juliet and her Romeo.

Julius Caesar

Introduction to Julius Caesar

Julius Caesar is one of Shakespeare's most quoted plays: even those unfamiliar with the story know lines like "Cowards die many times before their deaths/The valiant never taste of death but once" (II.ii.32–33), or "Friends, Romans, countrymen, lend me your ears" (III.ii.73–74), or at the very least, Caesar's famous last words, "Et tu, Brutè" (III.i.77)?

Julius Caesar is a tragedy set at a key moment in history: Caesar's death also marks the death of the Roman republic and the birth of the Roman Empire. Up to this point, elected representatives and other politicians had governed Rome. As the empire expanded, however, the military gained more political sway, and generals and other military leaders began fighting amongst themselves for control. Eventually this erupted into civil war, from which Caesar eventually emerged as the unchallenged ruler of Rome.

As the play opens, Caesar has just returned from his recent victory against Pompey the Great, who had previously controlled Rome. Upon his homecoming the common people welcome him loudly, but many of the politicians and other powerful figures are wary of Caesar and fear his ambition. It is from these tensions that the play's main events unfold.

Shakespeare's audiences would have been familiar with the historical tale of Caesar's assassination, and would have known what to expect. Shakespeare highlights this dramatic irony, where the audience can see the tragedy unfolding well before the characters do, by playing with themes of superstition and destiny, as most famously illustrated by the character of the Soothsayer, the old fortune-teller who warns Caesar of his impending doom in the very first act of the play. To the same end, Shakespeare presents neither side of the conflict as the "villain" of the tale, but prefers to show how good men can become victims of their own pride and poor decisions.

Dramatis Personae

JULIUS CAESAR

CALPURNIA, Caesar's wife

MARK ANTONY, triumvir after Caesar's death

OCTAVIUS CAESAR, triumvir after Caesar's death

MARCUS BRUTUS

CAIUS CASSIUS

CASCA, conspirator

DECIUS BRUTUS, conspirator

CINNA, conspirator

METELLUS CIMBER, conspirator

TREBONIUS, conspirator

CICERO, senator

PUBLIUS, senator

POPILIUS LENA, senator

SOOTHSAYER

ARTEMIDORUS, a teacher of rhetoric

CINNA, a poet

LUCILIUS, soldier in Brutus's and Cassius's army

TITINIUS, soldier in Brutus's and Cassius's army

MESSALA, soldier in Brutus's and Cassius's army

YOUNG CATO, soldier in Brutus's and Cassius's army

VARRO, soldier in Brutus's and Cassius's army

VOLUMNIUS, soldier in Brutus's and Cassius's army

CLAUDIUS, soldier in Brutus's and Cassius's army

CLITUS, soldier in Brutus's and Cassius's army

DARDANIUS, soldier in Brutus's and Cassius's army

PINDARUS, Cassius's servant

LUCIUS, Brutus's servant

STRATO, Brutus's servant

Caesar's SERVANT

Not Pictured

LEPIDUS
CAIUS LIGARIUS, conspirator
PORTIA, Brutus's wife
FLAVIUS, tribune of the people
MARULLUS, tribune of the people
Another POET
LABEO, soldier in Brutus's and Cassius's army
FLAVIUS, soldier in Brutus's and Cassius's army
Antony's SERVANT
Octavius's SERVANT
CARPENTER
COBBLER
Five PLEBEIANS
Three SOLDIERS in Brutus's army
Two SOLDERS in Antony's army
MESSENGER

Senators, Plebeians, Officers, Soldiers, and Attendants

ACT I. Scene II (12–25).

Rome is bustling with activity as the people fill the streets to celebrate the Festival of Lupercal. Caesar and his train wait to watch young Mark Antony run the course: Caesar has just finished giving Antony some last-minute advice before sending him on his way.

CAESAR
Set on, and leave no ceremony out.

SOOTHSAYER
Caesar!

CAESAR
Ha! Who calls?

CASCA
Bid every noise be still. Peace yet again!

CAESAR
Who is it in the press that calls on me?
I hear a tongue shriller than all the music
Cry "Caesar!" Speak. Caesar is turned to hear.

SOOTHSAYER
Beware the ides of March.

CAESAR
What man is that?

BRUTUS
A soothsayer bids you beware the ides of March.
CAESAR
Set him before me. Let me see his face.

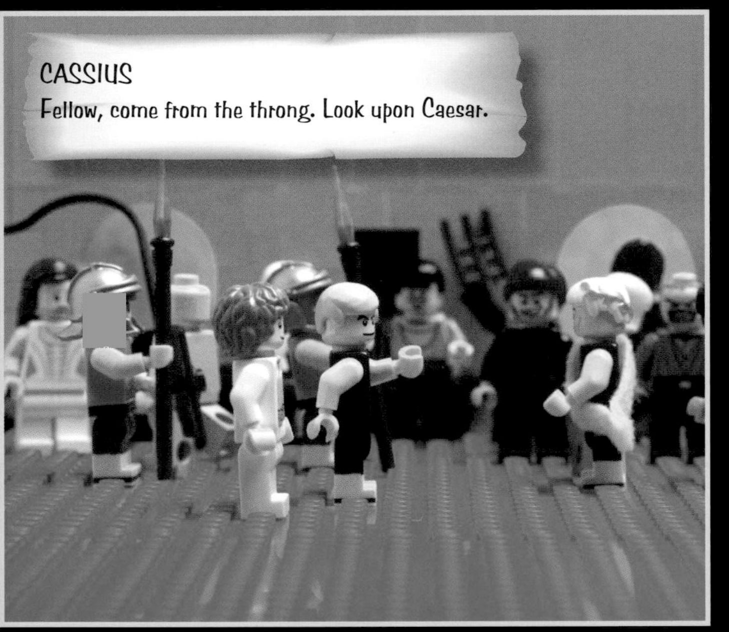
CASSIUS
Fellow, come from the throng. Look upon Caesar.

CAESAR
What say'st thou to me now? Speak once again.

SOOTHSAYER
Beware the ides of March.

CAESAR
He is a dreamer. Let us leave him. Pass.

ACT I. Scene II (80–190).

Caesar and his party continue on to watch the festivities, but Brutus stays behind. Cassius joins him and takes the opportunity to speak with him about Caesar. Shouting in the distance, in the direction that Caesar has gone, interrupts their conversation.

BRUTUS
I would not, Cassius, yet I love him well.
But wherefore do you hold me here so long?
What is it that you would impart to me?
If it be aught toward the general good,
Set honor in one eye and death i'th'other
And I will look on both indifferently;
For let the gods so speed me as I love
The name of honor more than I fear death.

CASSIUS
I know that virtue to be in you, Brutus,
As well as I do know your outward favor.
Well, honor is the subject of my story.
I cannot tell what you and other men
Think of this life; but, for my single self,
I had as lief not be as live to be
In awe of such a thing as I myself.
I was born free as Caesar, so were you;
We both have fed as well, and we can both
Endure the winter's cold as well as he.

CASSIUS (cont.)
For once, upon a raw and gusty day,
The troubled Tiber chafing with her shores,
Caesar said to me, "Dar'st thou, Cassius, now
Leap in with me into this angry flood
And swim to yonder point?" Upon the word,
Accoutred as I was, I plungèd in
And bade him follow; so indeed he did.
The torrent roared, and we did buffet it
With lusty sinews, throwing it aside
And stemming it with hearts of controversy.

CASSIUS (cont.)
But ere we could arrive the point proposed,
Caesar cried, "Help me, Cassius, or I sink!"
Ay, as Aeneas, our great ancestor,
Did from the flames of Troy upon his shoulder
The old Anchises bear, so from the waves of Tiber
Did I the tirèd Caesar.

CASSIUS (cont.)
And this man
Is now become a god, and Cassius is
A wretched creature and must bend his body
If Caesar carelessly but nod on him.

CASSIUS (cont.)
He had a fever when he was in Spain,
And when the fit was on him I did mark
How he did shake. 'Tis true, this god did shake!
His coward lips did from their color fly,
And that same eye whose bend doth awe the world
Did lose his luster. I did hear him groan.
Ay, and that tongue of his that bade the Romans
Mark him and write his speeches in their books,
Alas, it cried, "Give me some drink, Titinius,"
As a sick girl.

BRUTUS
Another general shout!
I do believe that these applauses are
For some new honors that are heaped on Caesar.
CASSIUS
Why, man, he doth bestride the narrow world
like a Colossus, and we petty men
Walk under his huge legs and peep about
To find ourselves dishonorable graves.
Men at some time are masters of their fates.
The fault, dear Brutus, is not in our stars,
But in ourselves, that we are underlings.

CASSIUS (cont.)
"Brutus" and "Caesar." What should be in that "Caesar"?
Why should that name be sounded more than yours?
Write them together, yours is as fair a name;
Sound them, it doth become the mouth as well;
Weigh them, it is as heavy; conjure with 'em,
"Brutus" will start a spirit as soon as "Caesar."
Now, in the names of all the gods at once,
Upon what meat doth this our great Caesar feed
That he is grown so great? Age, thou art shamed!
Rome, thou hast lost the breed of noble bloods!
When went there by an age since the great flood
But it was famed with more than with one man?
When could they say, till now, that talked of Rome,
That her wide walks encompassed but one man?
Now is it Rome indeed, and room enough,
When there is in it but one only man.
O, you and I have heard our fathers say
There was a Brutus once that would have brooked
Th'eternal devil to keep his state in Rome
As easily as a king.

BRUTUS
That you do love me, I am nothing jealous.
What you would work me to, I have some aim.
How I have thought of this and of these times
I shall recount hereafter. For this present,
I would not, so with love I might entreat you,
Be any further moved. What you have said
I will consider; what you have to say
I will with patience hear and find a time
Both meet to hear and answer such high things.
Till then, my noble friend, chew upon this:
Brutus had rather be a villager
Than to repute himself a son of Rome
Under these hard conditions as this time
Is like to lay upon us.

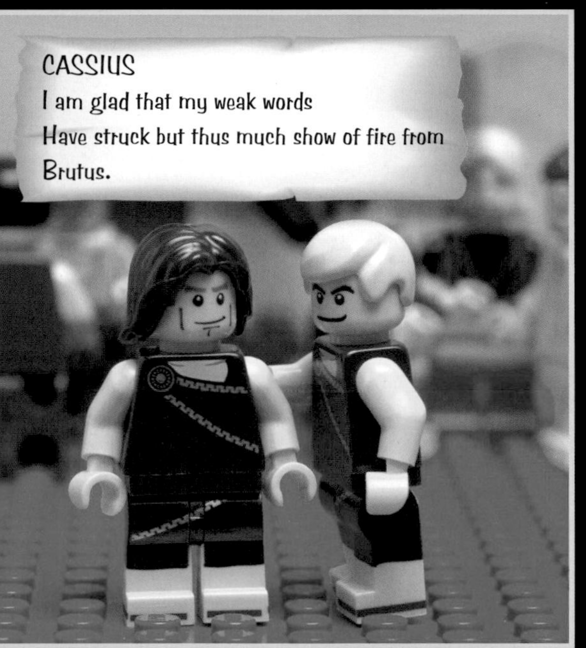

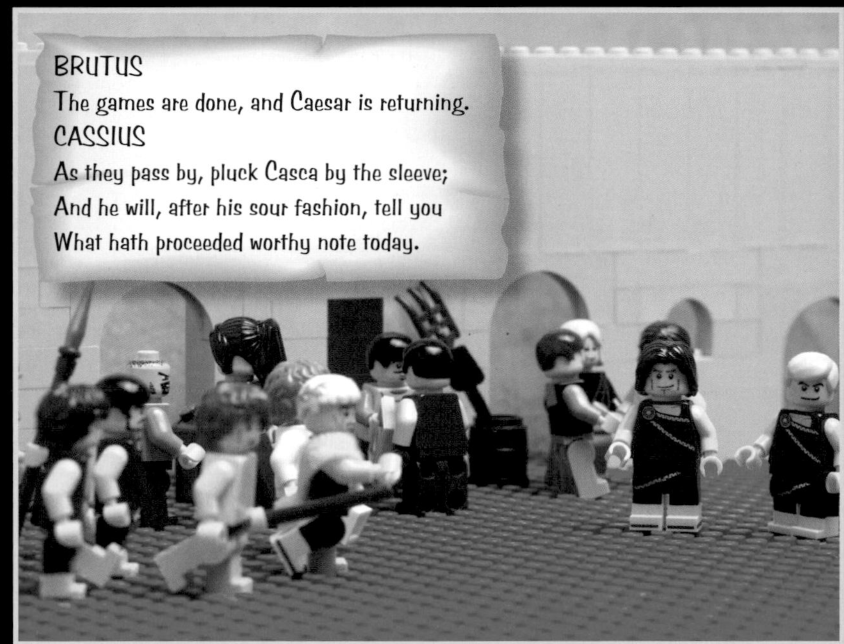

BRUTUS
I will do so. But look you, Cassius,
The angry spot doth glow on Caesar's brow,
And all the rest look like a chidden train.
Calpurnia's cheek is pale, and Cicero
Looks with such ferret and such fiery eyes
As we have seen him in the Capitol,
Being crossed in conference by some senators.
CASSIUS
Casca will tell us what the matter is.

ACT I. Scene II (216–296).

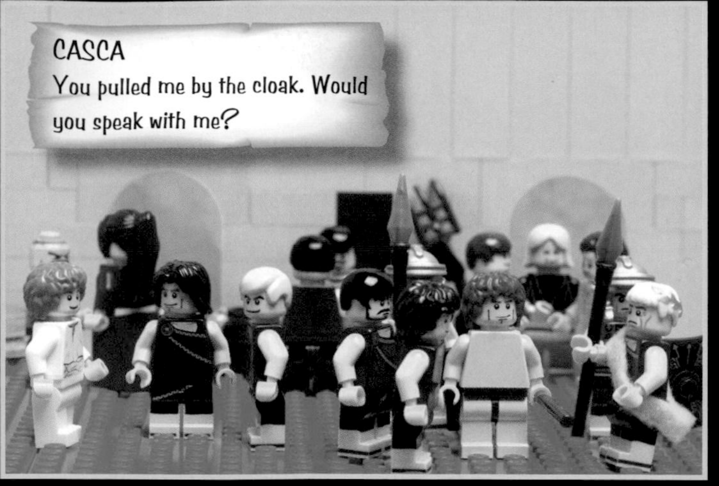

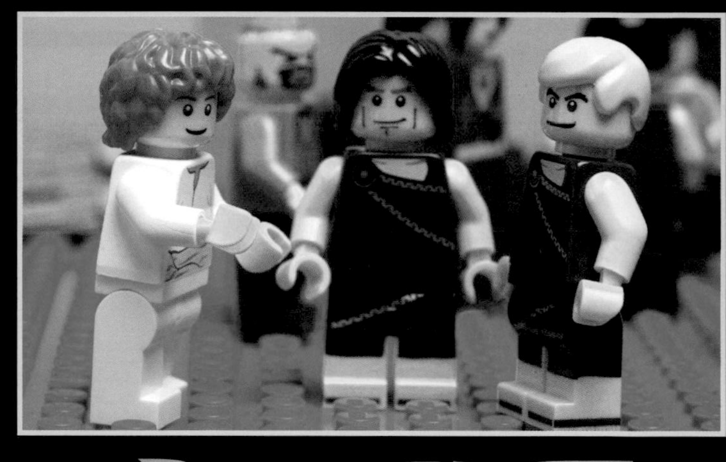

CASCA
Why? You were with him, were you not?
BRUTUS
I should not then ask Casca what had chanced.

CASCA
Why, there was a crown offered him; and, being offered him, he put it by with the back of his hand, thus, and then the people fell a-shouting.
BRUTUS
What was the second noise for?
CASCA
Why, for that too.
CASSIUS
They shouted thrice. What was the last cry for?

CASCA
Why, for that too.
BRUTUS
Was the crown offered him thrice?
CASCA
Ay, marry, was't, and he put it by thrice, every time gentler than other, and at every putting-by mine honest neighbors shouted.
CASSIUS
Who offered him the crown?

CASCA
Why, Antony.
BRUTUS
Tell us the manner of it, gentle Casca.

CASCA
I can as well be hanged as tell the manner of it. It was mere foolery. I did not mark it;

CASCA (cont.)
I saw Mark Antony
offer him a crown—yet, 'twas not a crown neither,
'twas one of these coronets—and, as I told you, he put it by once; but for all that, to my thinking, he would fain have had it. Then he offered it to him again; then he put it by again; but to my thinking he was very loath to lay his fingers off it. And then he offered it the third time.

CASCA (cont.)
He put it the third time by, and, still as he refused it the rabblement
hooted and clapped their chapped hands, and threw up their sweaty nightcaps, and uttered such a deal of stinking breath because Caesar refused the crown that it had almost choked Caesar, for he swooned and fell down at it. And for mine own part I durst not laugh for fear of opening my lips and receiving the bad air.

CASCA

I know not what you mean by that, but I am sure Caesar fell down. If the tag-rag people did not clap him and hiss him, according as he pleased and displeased them, as they use to do the players in the theater, I am no true man.

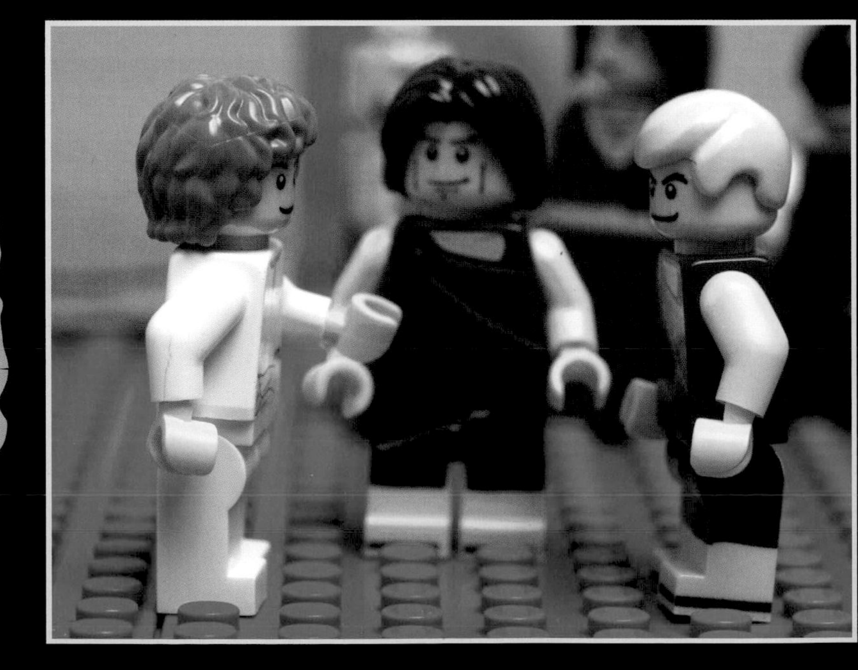

CASCA
Marry, before he fell down, when he perceived the common herd was glad he refused the crown, he plucked me ope his doublet and offered them his throat to cut. An I had been a man of any occupation, if I would not have taken him at a word, I would I might go to hell among the rogues. And so he fell. When he came to himself again, he said if he had done or said anything amiss, he desired Their Worships to think it was his infirmity. Three or four wenches where I stood cried "Alas, good soul!" and forgave him with all their hearts. But there's no heed to be taken of them; if Caesar had stabbed their mothers they would have done no less.

BRUTUS
And after that, he came thus sad away?
CASCA
Ay.
CASSIUS
Did Cicero say anything?
CASCA
Ay, he spoke Greek.
CASSIUS
To what effect?
CASCA
Nay, an I tell you that, I'll ne'er look you i'th' face again. But those that understood him smiled at one another and shook their heads; but, for mine own part, it was Greek to me. I could tell you more news too. Marullus and Flavius, for pulling scarves off Caesar's images, are put to silence. Fare you well. There was more foolery yet, if I could remember it.

ACT I. Scene II (310–324).

CASSIUS
Well, Brutus, thou art noble. Yet I see
Thy honorable metal may be wrought
From that it is disposed. Therefore it is meet
That noble minds keep ever with their likes;
For who so firm that cannot be seduced?
Caesar doth bear me hard, but he loves Brutus.
If I were Brutus now, and he were Cassius,
He should not humor me. I will this night
In several hands in at his windows throw,
As if they came from several citizens,
Writings, all tending to the great opinion
That Rome holds of his name, wherein obscurely
Caesar's ambition shall be glancèd at.
And after this let Caesar seat him sure,
For we will shake him, or worse days endure.

ACT I. Scene III (1–41).

A strange day in Rome is followed by an even stranger night

CICERO
Good even, Casca. Brought you Caesar home?
Why are you breathless? And why stare you so?

CASCA
Are not you moved, when all the sway of earth
Shakes like a thing unfirm? O Cicero,
I have seen tempests when the scolding winds
Have rived the knotty oaks, and I have seen
Th'ambitious ocean swell and rage and foam
To be exalted with the threat'ning clouds;
But never till tonight, never till now,
Did I go through a tempest dropping fire.
Either there is a civil strife in heaven,
Or else the world, too saucy with the gods,
Incenses them to send destruction.
CICERO
Why, saw you anything more wonderful?

CASCA
A common slave—you know him well by sight—
Held up his left hand, which did flame and burn
Like twenty torches joined, and yet his hand,
Not sensible of fire, remained unscorched.

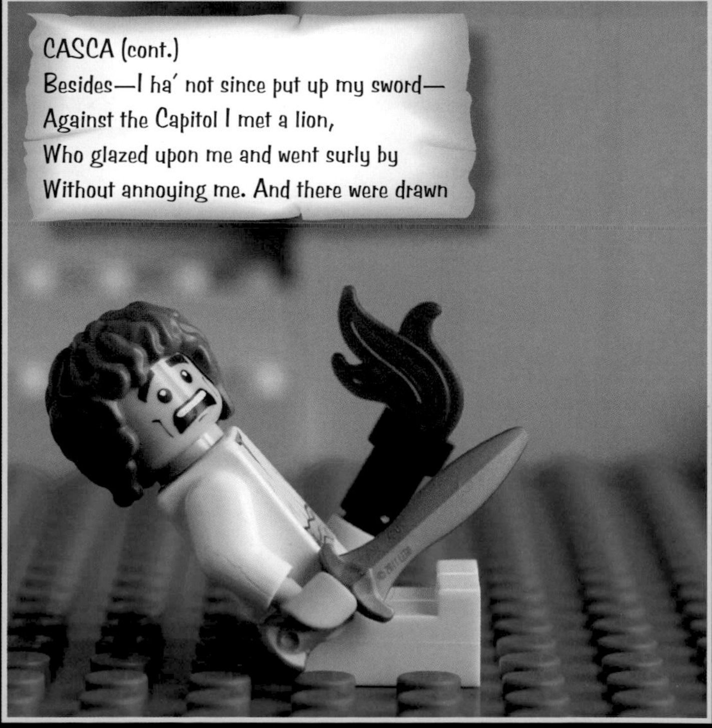
CASCA (cont.)
Besides—I ha' not since put up my sword—
Against the Capitol I met a lion,
Who glazed upon me and went surly by
Without annoying me. And there were drawn

CASCA (cont.)
Upon a heap a hundred ghastly women,
Transformèd with their fear, who swore they saw
Men all in fire walk up and down the streets.
And yesterday the bird of night did sit
Even at noonday upon the marketplace,
Hooting and shrieking. When these prodigies
Do so conjointly meet, let not men say,
"These are their reasons, they are natural,"
For I believe they are portentous things
Unto the climate that they point upon.

CICERO
Good night then, Casca. This disturbèd sky
Is not to walk in.
CASCA
Farewell, Cicero.

ACT II. Scene I (1–76).

J

C

Not all Romans are frightened by the unnatural events of the night. Casca soon comes upon Cassius, who claims it is "a very pleasing night to honest men" (I.iii.44). He soon convinces Casca to join him and his growing band of conspirators. They meet briefly with Cinna in the street, and Cassius enlists his help, instructing him to leave an anonymous note for Brutus encouraging him to act against Caesar, as Cassius has already done. They depart to meet and plot in secret with the other conspirators, under the cover of the strange weather that shakes the streets of Rome.

Meanwhile, Brutus has spent the evening in his garden, deep in thought about what to do about Caesar.

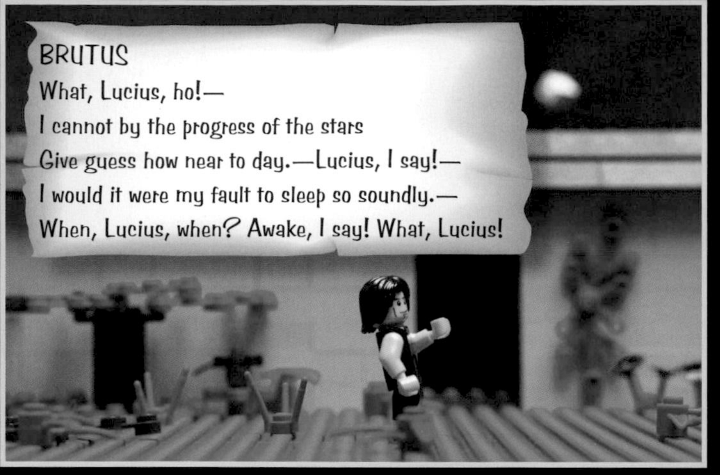

BRUTUS
It must be by his death. And for my part
I know no personal cause to spurn at him,
But for the general. He would be crowned.
How that might change his nature, there's the question.
It is the bright day that brings forth the adder,
And that craves wary walking. Crown him—that—
And then I grant we put a sting in him
That at his will he may do danger with.
Th'abuse of greatness is when it disjoins
Remorse from power. And to speak truth of Caesar,
I have not known when his affections swayed
More than his reason. But 'tis a common proof
That lowliness is young ambition's ladder,
Whereto the climber-upward turns his face;
But when he once attains the upmost round
He then unto the ladder turns his back,
Looks in the clouds, scorning the base degrees
By which he did ascend. So Caesar may.
Then, lest he may, prevent. And since the quarrel
Will bear no color for the thing he is,
Fashion it thus: that what he is, augmented,
Would run to these and these extremities;

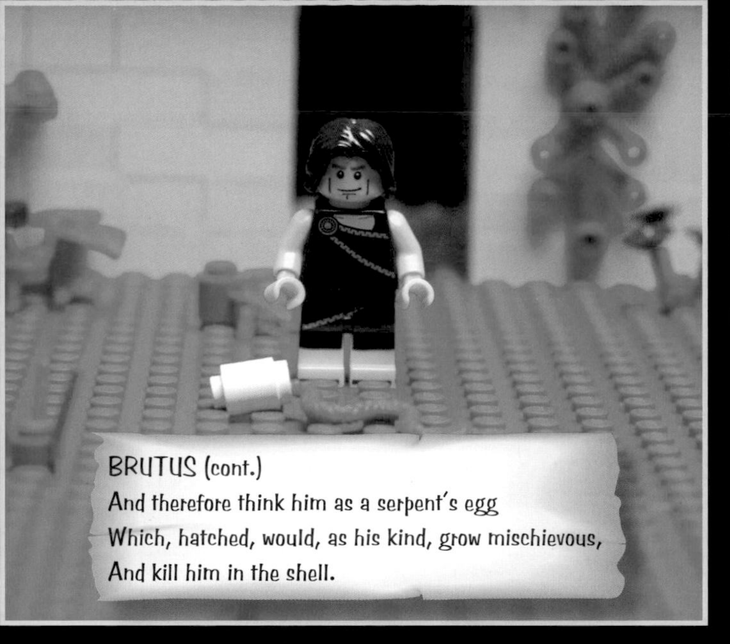

LUCIUS
The taper burneth in your closet, sir.
Searching the window for a flint, I found
This paper, thus sealed up, and I am sure
It did not lie there when I went to bed.

BRUTUS
The exhalations whizzing in the air
Give so much light that I may read by them.
"Brutus, thou sleep'st. Awake and see thyself!
Shall Rome, etc. Speak, strike, redress!"
"Brutus, thou sleep'st. Awake!"
Such instigations have been often dropped
Where I have took them up.
"Shall Rome, etc." Thus must I piece it out:
Shall Rome stand under one man's awe? What Rome?
My ancestors did from the streets of Rome
The Tarquin drive, when he was called a king.
"Speak, strike, redress!" Am I entreated
To speak and strike? O Rome, I make thee promise,
If the redress will follow, thou receivest
Thy full petition at the hand of Brutus!

BRUTUS
'Tis good. Go to the gate; somebody knocks.
Since Cassius first did whet me against Caesar,
I have not slept.
Between the acting of a dreadful thing
And the first motion, all the interim is
Like a phantasma or a hideous dream.
The genius and the mortal instruments
Are then in council; and the state of man,
Like to a little kingdom, suffers then
The nature of an insurrection.
LUCIUS
Sir, 'tis your brother Cassius at the door,
Who doth desire to see you.

BRUTUS
Is he alone?
LUCIUS
No, sir. There are more with him.

BRUTUS
Do you know them?
LUCIUS
No, sir. Their hats are plucked about their ears,
And half their faces buried in their cloaks,
That by no means I may discover them
By any mark of favor.

ACT II. Scene I (112–215).

Brutus invites the conspirators in, and after a few whispered words with Cassius, he calls the men together.

BRUTUS
No, not an oath. If not the face of men,
The sufferance of our souls, the time's abuse—
If these be motives weak, break off betimes,
And every man hence to his idle bed;
So let high-sighted tyranny range on
Till each man drop by lottery. But if these,
As I am sure they do, bear fire enough
To kindle cowards and to steel with valor
The melting spirits of women, then, countrymen,
What need we any spur but our own cause
To prick us to redress? What other bond
Than secret Romans that have spoken the word
And will not palter? And what other oath
Than honesty to honesty engaged
That this shall be or we will fall for it?
Swear priests and cowards and men cautelous,
Old feeble carrions, and such suffering souls
That welcome wrongs; unto bad causes swear
Such creatures as men doubt. But do not stain
The even virtue of our enterprise,
Nor th' insuppressive mettle of our spirits,
To think that or our cause or our performance
Did need an oath, where every drop of blood
That every Roman bears—and nobly bears—
Is guilty of a several bastardy
If he do break the smallest particle
Of any promise that hath passed from him.

CINNA
No, by no means.
METELLUS
Oh, let us have him, for his silver hairs
Will purchase us a good opinion
And buy men's voices to commend our deeds.
It shall be said his judgment ruled our hands;
Our youths and wildness shall no whit appear,
But all be buried in his gravity.

BRUTUS
Oh, name him not. Let us not break with him,
For he will never follow anything
That other men begin.
CASSIUS
Then leave him out.

CASSIUS
Decius, well urged. I think it is not meet
Mark Antony, so well beloved of Caesar,
Should outlive Caesar. We shall find of him
A shrewd contriver; and you know his means,
If he improve them, may well stretch so far
As to annoy us all. Which to prevent,
Let Antony and Caesar fall together.

BRUTUS
Our course will seem too bloody, Caius Cassius,
To cut the head off and then hack the limbs,
Like wrath in death and envy afterwards;
For Antony is but a limb of Caesar.
Let's be sacrificers, but not butchers, Caius.
We all stand up against the spirit of Caesar,
And in the spirit of men there is no blood.
Oh, that we then could come by Caesar's spirit
And not dismember Caesar! But, alas,
Caesar must bleed for it. And, gentle friends,
Let's kill him boldly, but not wrathfully;
Let's carve him as a dish fit for the gods,
Not hew him as a carcass fit for hounds.
And let our hearts, as subtle masters do,
Stir up their servants to an act of rage
And after seem to chide 'em. This shall make
Our purpose necessary, and not envious;
Which so appearing to the common eyes,
We shall be called purgers, not murderers.
And for Mark Antony, think not of him;
For he can do no more than Caesar's arm
When Caesar's head is off.

TREBONIUS
'Tis time to part.
CASSIUS
But it is doubtful yet
Whether Caesar will come forth today or no,
For he is superstitious grown of late,
Quite from the main opinion he held once
Of fantasy, of dreams, and ceremonies.
It may be these apparent prodigies,
The unaccustomed terror of this night,
And the persuasion of his augurers
May hold him from the Capitol today.

DECIUS
Never fear that. If he be so resolved,
I can o'ersway him; for he loves to hear
That unicorns may be betrayed with trees,
And bears with glasses, elephants with holes,
Lions with toils, and men with flatterers.
But when I tell him he hates flatterers,
He says he does, being then most flattered.
Let me work;
For I can give his humor the true bent,
And I will bring him to the Capitol.
CASSIUS
Nay, we will all of us be there to fetch him.
BRUTUS
By the eighth hour. Is that the uttermost?
CINNA
Be that the uttermost, and fail not then.

ACT II. Scene II (1–108).

After the conspirators leave, Brutus's wife, Portia, begs him to tell her what is going on. He promises to confide in her when he has the time, but a latecomer, who wishes to join the conspiracy, interrupts him. They quickly depart to meet with the others, leaving Portia with her questions unanswered.

Caesar's wife has also been disturbed in the night—not by noisy visitors, but by dark and threatening dreams.

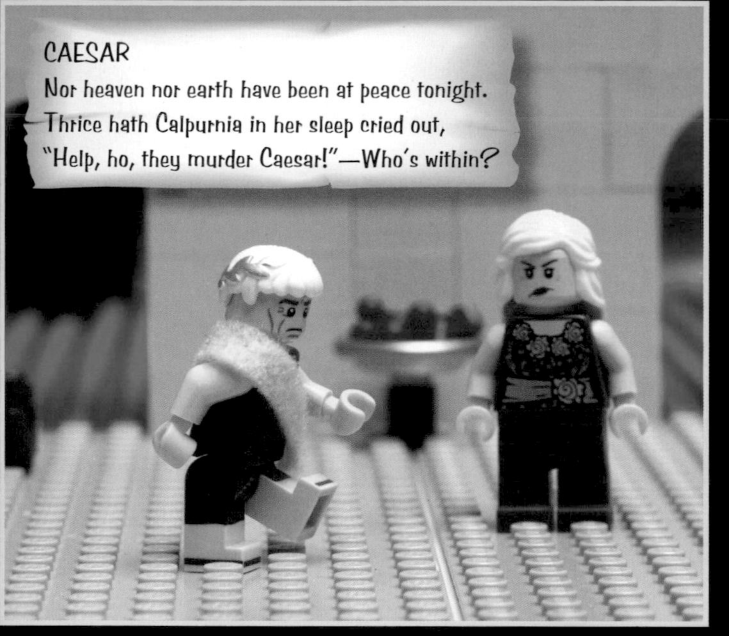
CAESAR
Nor heaven nor earth have been at peace tonight.
Thrice hath Calpurnia in her sleep cried out,
"Help, ho, they murder Caesar!"—Who's within?

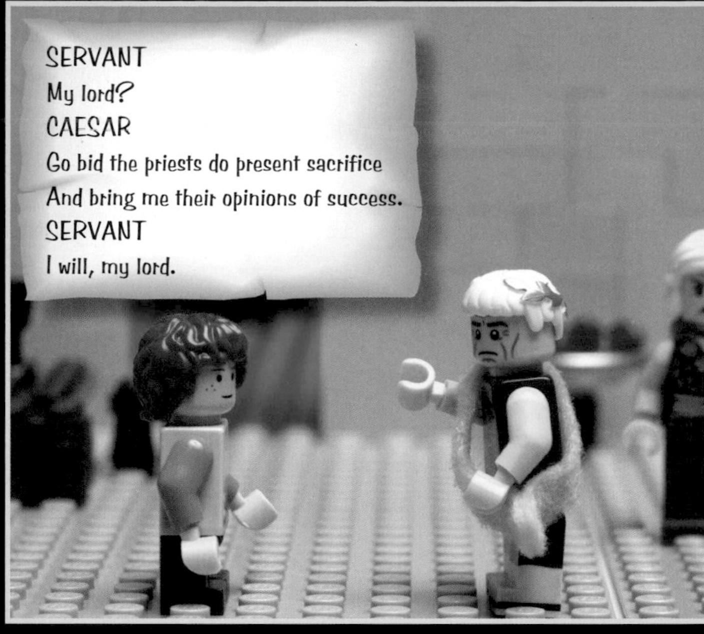
SERVANT
My lord?
CAESAR
Go bid the priests do present sacrifice
And bring me their opinions of success.
SERVANT
I will, my lord.

CALPURNIA
What mean you, Caesar? Think you to walk forth?
You shall not stir out of your house today.

CAESAR
Caesar shall forth. The things that threatened me
Ne'er looked but on my back. When they shall see
The face of Caesar, they are vanishèd.

CALPURNIA
Caesar, I never stood on ceremonies,
Yet now they fright me. There is one within,
Besides the things that we have heard and seen,
Recounts most horrid sights seen by the watch.
A lioness hath whelpèd in the streets,

CALPURNIA (cont.)
And graves have yawned and yielded up their dead.

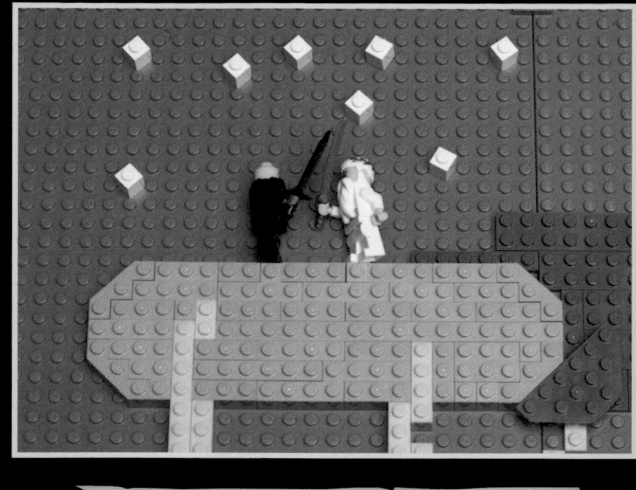
CALPURNIA (cont.)
Fierce fiery warriors fight upon the clouds
In ranks and squadrons and right form of war,
Which drizzled blood upon the Capitol.

The noise of battle hurtled in the air;
Horses did neigh, and dying men did groan,
And ghosts did shriek and squeal about the streets.

CALPURNIA (cont.)
O Caesar! These things are beyond all use,
And I do fear them.

CAESAR
What can be avoided
Whose end is purposed by the mighty gods?
Yet Caesar shall go forth; for these predictions
Are to the world in general as to Caesar.

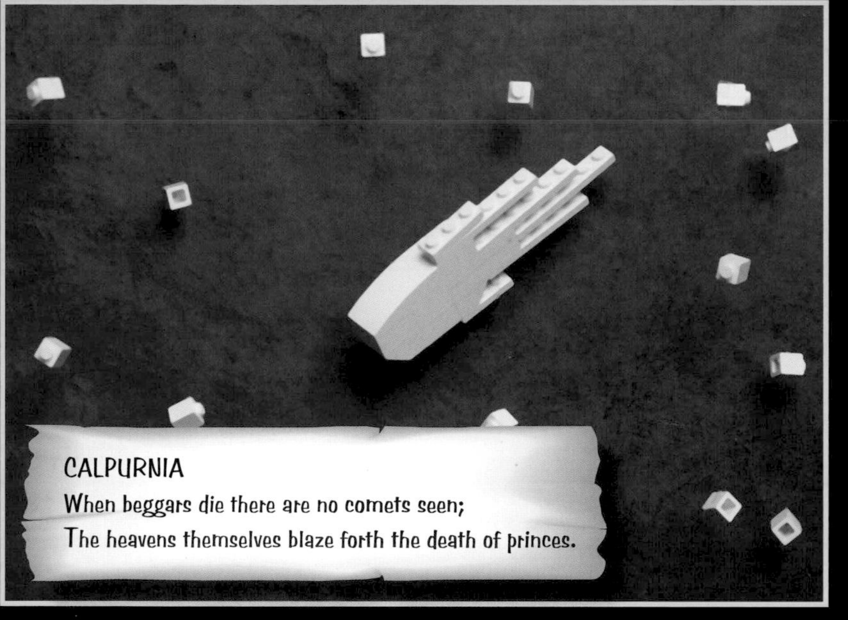
CALPURNIA
When beggars die there are no comets seen;
The heavens themselves blaze forth the death of princes.

CAESAR
Cowards die many times before their deaths;
The valiant never taste of death but once.
Of all the wonders that I yet have heard,
It seems to me most strange that men should fear,
Seeing death, a necessary end,
Will come when it will come.

CAESAR (cont.)
What say the augurers?
SERVANT
They would not have you stir forth today.

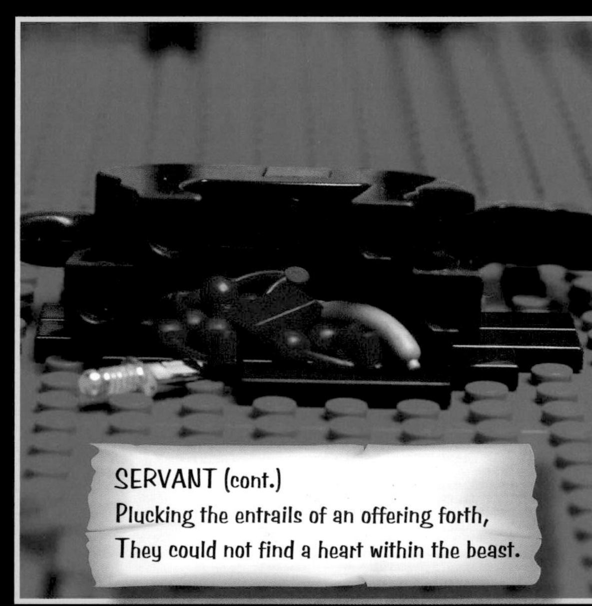
SERVANT (cont.)
Plucking the entrails of an offering forth,
They could not find a heart within the beast.

CAESAR
The gods do this in shame of cowardice.
Caesar should be a beast without a heart
If he should stay at home today for fear.
No, Caesar shall not. Danger knows full well
That Caesar is more dangerous than he.
We are two lions littered in one day,
And I the elder and more terrible;
And Caesar shall go forth.

CALPURNIA
Alas, my lord,
Your wisdom is consumed in confidence.
Do not go forth today! Call it my fear
That keeps you in the house, and not your own.
We'll send Mark Antony to the Senate House,
And he shall say you are not well today.
Let me, upon my knee, prevail in this.

CAESAR
Mark Antony shall say I am not well,
And for thy humor I will stay at home.
Here's Decius Brutus. He shall tell them so.

DECIUS
Most mighty Caesar, let me know some cause,
Lest I be laughed at when I tell them so.

CAESAR
The cause is in my will: I will not come.
That is enough to satisfy the Senate.
But for your private satisfaction,
Because I love you, I will let you know.
Calpurnia here, my wife, stays me at home.

CAESAR (cont.)
She dreamt tonight she saw my statua,
Which like a fountain with an hundred spouts
Did run pure blood; and many lusty Romans
Came smiling and did bathe their hands in it.
And these does she apply for warnings and portents
Of evils imminent, and on her knee
Hath begged that I will stay at home today.

DECIUS BRUTUS
This dream is all amiss interpreted;
It was a vision fair and fortunate.
Your statue spouting blood in many pipes,
In which so many smiling Romans bathed,
Signifies that from you great Rome shall suck
Reviving blood, and that great men shall press
For tinctures, stains, relics, and cognizance.
This by Calpurnia's dream is signified.

CAESAR
And this way have you well expounded it.
DECIUS BRUTUS
I have, when you have heard what I can say:
And know it now. The Senate have concluded
To give this day a crown to mighty Caesar.
If you shall send them word you will not come,
Their minds may change. Besides, it were a mock
Apt to be rendered, for someone to say
"Break up the senate till another time
When Caesar's wife shall meet with better dreams."
If Caesar hide himself, shall they not whisper
"Lo, Caesar is afraid"?
Pardon me, Caesar, for my dear dear love
To your proceeding bids me tell you this,
And reason to my love is liable.

ACT III. Scene I (1–84).

As the conspirators escort the unsuspecting Caesar to the Senate, other forces are in motion to warn Caesar and stop the plot. A man, Artemidorus, has written a letter revealing everything and naming the conspirators. Portia, still uninformed of her husband's plans, questions the soothsayer in the street as he passes by. He tells her he goes to warn Caesar, that he knows of no threat against him yet he fears it is so. Portia realizes what secret business has kept Brutus busy and sends their servant Lucius to the Senate to see how the endeavor has turned out. Meanwhile the conspirators prepare to strike.

CAESAR
The ides of March are come.

SOOTHSAYER
Ay, Caesar, but not gone.

ARTEMIDORUS
Hail, Caesar! Read this schedule.
VENI, VIDI, VICI

DECIUS BRUTUS
Trebonius doth desire you to o'erread,
At your best leisure, this his humble suit.

VENI, VIDI, VICI
ARTEMIDORUS
O Caesar, read mine first, for mine's a suit
That touches Caesar nearer. Read it, great Caesar.
CAESAR
What touches us ourself shall be last served.
ARTEMIDORUS
Delay not, Caesar, read it instantly.

VENI, VIDI, VICI
CAESAR
What, is the fellow mad?
PUBLIUS
Sirrah, give place.
CASSIUS
What, urge you your petitions in the street?
Come to the Capitol.

POPILIUS
I wish your enterprise today may thrive.
CASSIUS
What enterprise, Popilius?
POPILIUS
Fare you well.

BRUTUS
What said Popilius Lena?

CASSIUS
He wished today our enterprise might thrive.
I fear our purpose is discoverèd.

BRUTUS
Look, how he makes to Caesar.
Mark him.

CASSIUS
Casca, be sudden, for we fear prevention.
Brutus, what shall be done? If this be known,
Cassius or Caesar never shall turn back,
For I will slay myself.

BRUTUS
Cassius, be constant.
Popilius Lena speaks not of our purposes;
For, look, he smiles, and Caesar doth not change.

CASSIUS
Trebonius knows his time, for, look you, Brutus,
He draws Mark Antony out of the way.

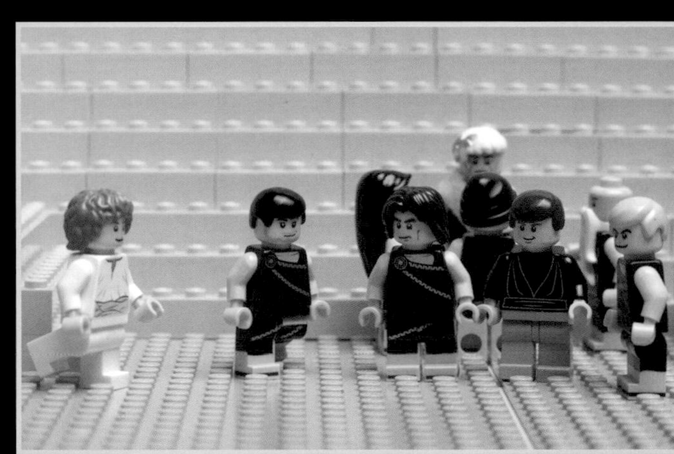
DECIUS BRUTUS
Where is Metellus Cimber? Let him go
And presently prefer his suit to Caesar.
BRUTUS
He is addressed. Press near and second him.

CINNA
Casca, you are the first that rears your hand.

CAESAR
I must prevent thee, Cimber.
These couchings and these lowly courtesies
Might fire the blood of ordinary men,
And turn preordinance and first decree
Into the law of children. Be not fond,
To think that Caesar bears such rebel blood
That will be thaw'd from the true quality
With that which melteth fools; I mean, sweet words,
Low-crookèd curtsies, and base spaniel-fawning.
Thy brother by decree is banished.
If thou dost bend and pray and fawn for him,
I spurn thee like a cur out of my way.
Know, Caesar doth not wrong, nor without cause
Will he be satisfied.

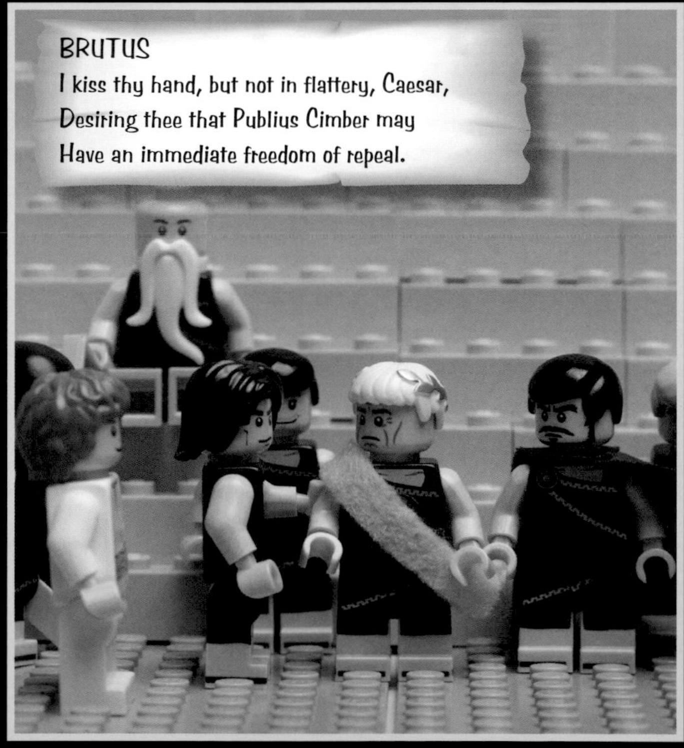

CASSIUS
Pardon, Caesar! Caesar, pardon!
As low as to thy foot doth Cassius fall,
To beg enfranchisement for Publius Cimber.
CAESAR
I could be well moved, if I were as you;
If I could pray to move, prayers would move me.
But I am constant as the northern star,
Of whose true-fixed and resting quality
There is no fellow in the firmament.
The skies are painted with unnumbered sparks;
They are all fire and every one doth shine;
But there's but one in all doth hold his place.
So in the world: 'tis furnished well with men,
And men are flesh and blood, and apprehensive;
Yet in the number I do know but one
That unassailable holds on his rank,
Unshaked of motion. And that I am he,
Let me a little show it even in this:
That I was constant Cimber should be banished,
And constant do remain to keep him so.

CINNA
O Caesar—
CAESAR
Hence! Wilt thou lift up Olympus?
DECIUS BRUTUS
Great Caesar—
CAESAR
Doth not Brutus bootless kneel?

CASCA
Speak hands for me!

CAESAR
Et tu, Brutè? Then fall, Caesar!

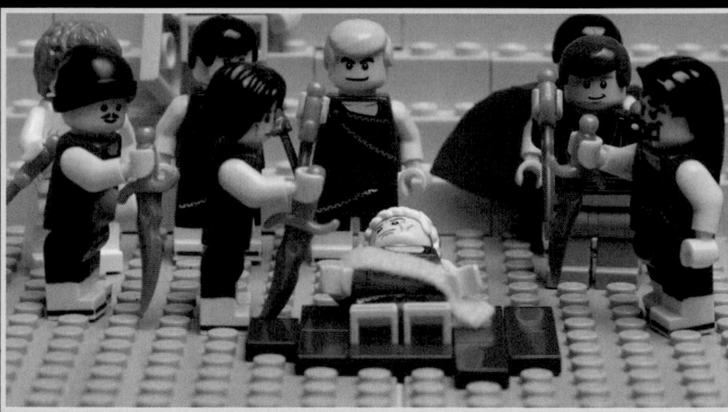

CINNA
Liberty! Freedom! Tyranny is dead!
Run hence, proclaim, cry it about the streets.

CASSIUS
Some to the common pulpits, and cry out
"Liberty, freedom, and enfranchisement!"

BRUTUS
People and senators, be not affrighted.
Fly not; stand still. Ambition's debt is paid.

ACT III. Scene II (1–261).

JC

The deed is done: Caesar is dead. There is a great deal of noise and confusion as some flee in fear and others run to spread the news. At Brutus's suggestion, they then smear their hands and swords with Caesar's blood: They plan, with no little irony, to go out into the streets and proclaim, "Peace, freedom, and liberty!"

Antony, who did not witness the slaying, sends a servant to the conspirators with his message: "Say I love Brutus, and I honor him/Say I feared Caesar, honored him, and loved him" (III.i.129–130). Brutus says they will not harm him, and so he comes to the Senate. He mourns Caesar and begs them to kill him, too. Brutus refuses and insists that once Antony knows the truth, he will agree that Caesar's death was necessary. Antony shakes the bloody hands of all of the conspirators as a show of his friendship, but when he sees the mangled body of Caesar, he is again filled with grief. Brutus grants Antony his wish to speak at Caesar's funeral, against Cassius's advice.

The conspirators depart, and Antony stays to mourn over Caesar's body. He is interrupted by a servant, sent from Caesar's great-nephew, adopted son and heir Octavius Caesar, who has come to Rome at Caesar's invitation. Antony warns that "Here is a mourning Rome, a dangerous Rome,/No Rome of safety for Octavius yet" (III.i.290–291) but says he plans to see how the people will react when he describes the murder in his funeral speech.

PLEBEIANS
We will be satisfied! Let us be satisfied!

BRUTUS
Then follow me, and give me audience, friends.—
Cassius, go you into the other street
And part the numbers.
Those that will hear me speak, let 'em stay here;
Those that will follow Cassius, go with him;
And public reasons shall be renderèd
Of Caesar's death.

FIRST PLEBEIAN
I will hear Brutus speak.
SECOND PLEBEIAN
I will hear Cassius, and compare their reasons
When severally we hear them renderèd.

THIRD PLEBEIAN
The noble Brutus is ascended. Silence!

BRUTUS

Be patient till the last.

Romans, countrymen, and lovers, Hear me for my cause, and be silent that you may hear. Believe me for mine honor, and have respect to mine honor, that you may believe. Censure me in your wisdom, and awake your senses, that you may the better judge. If there be any in this assembly, any dear friend of Caesar's, to him I say that Brutus' love to Caesar was no less than his. If then that friend demand why Brutus rose against Caesar, this is my answer: not that I loved Caesar less, but that I loved Rome more. Had you rather Caesar were living and die all slaves, than that Caesar were dead, to live all free men? As Caesar loved me, I weep for him; as he was fortunate, I rejoice at it; as he was valiant, I honor him: but, as he was ambitious, I slew him. There is tears for his love; joy for his fortune; honor for his valor; and death for his ambition. Who is here so base that would be a bondman? If any, speak, for him have I offended. Who is here so rude that would not be a Roman? If any, speak, for him have I offended. Who is here so vile that will not love his country? If any, speak, for him have I offended. I pause for a reply.

BRUTUS

Then none have I offended. I have done no more to Caesar than you shall do to Brutus. The question of his death is enrolled in the Capitol, his glory not extenuated wherein he was worthy, nor his offences enforced, for which he suffered death.

BRUTUS (cont.)
Here comes his body, mourned by Mark Antony, who, though he had no hand in his death, shall receive the benefit of his dying, a place in the commonwealth, as which of you shall not? With this I depart, that, as I slew my best lover for the good of Rome, I have the same dagger for myself, when it shall please my country to need my death.

FIRST PLEBEIAN
Bring him with triumph home unto his house.
SECOND PLEBEIAN
Give him a statue with his ancestors.
THIRD PLEBEIAN
Let him be Caesar.
FOURTH PLEBEIAN
Caesar's better parts
Shall be crowned in Brutus.
FIRST PLEBEIAN
We'll bring him to his house with shouts and clamors.
BRUTUS
My countrymen—

SECOND PLEBEIAN
Peace, silence! Brutus speaks.
FIRST PLEBEIAN
Peace, ho!
BRUTUS
Good countrymen, let me depart alone,
And, for my sake, stay here with Antony.
Do grace to Caesar's corpse, and grace his speech
Tending to Caesar's glories, which Mark Antony,
By our permission, is allowed to make.
I do entreat you, not a man depart,
Save I alone, till Antony have spoke.

ANTONY
For Brutus' sake I am beholding to you.
FOURTH PLEBEIAN
What does he say of Brutus?
THIRD PLEBEIAN
He says, for Brutus' sake,
He finds himself beholding to us all.
FOURTH PLEBEIAN
'Twere best he speak no harm of Brutus here.
FIRST PLEBEIAN
This Caesar was a tyrant.
THIRD PLEBEIAN
Nay, that's certain.
We are blest that Rome is rid of him.
SECOND PLEBEIAN
Peace! Let us hear what Antony can say.
ANTONY
You gentle Romans—
CITIZENS
Peace, ho! Let us hear him.

ANTONY
Friends, Romans, countrymen, lend me your ears.
I come to bury Caesar, not to praise him.
The evil that men do lives after them;
The good is oft interrèd with their bones.
So let it be with Caesar. The noble Brutus
Hath told you Caesar was ambitious.
If it were so, it was a grievous fault,
And grievously hath Caesar answered it.
Here, under leave of Brutus and the rest—
For Brutus is an honorable man,
So are they all, all honorable men—
Come I to speak in Caesar's funeral.
He was my friend, faithful and just to me;
But Brutus says he was ambitious,
And Brutus is an honorable man.
He hath brought many captives home to Rome,
Whose ransoms did the general coffers fill.
Did this in Caesar seem ambitious?
When that the poor have cried, Caesar hath wept;
Ambition should be made of sterner stuff.
Yet Brutus says he was ambitious,
And Brutus is an honorable man.

ANTONY (cont.)
You all did see that on the Lupercal
I thrice presented him a kingly crown,
Which he did thrice refuse. Was this ambition?
Yet Brutus says he was ambitious,
And sure he is an honorable man.
I speak not to disprove what Brutus spoke,
But here I am to speak what I do know.
You all did love him once, not without cause.
What cause withholds you then to mourn for him?

O judgment! Thou art fled to brutish beasts,
And men have lost their reason. Bear with me;
My heart is in the coffin there with Caesar,
And I must pause till it come back to me.

FIRST PLEBEIAN
Methinks there is much reason in his sayings.
SECOND PLEBEIAN
If thou consider rightly of the matter,
Caesar has had great wrong.
THIRD PLEBEIAN
Has he, masters?
I fear there will a worse come in his place.
FOURTH PLEBEIAN
Marked ye his words? He would not take the crown,
Therefore 'tis certain he was not ambitious.
FIRST PLEBEIAN
If it be found so, some will dear abide it.
SECOND PLEBEIAN
Poor soul, his eyes are red as fire with weeping.
THIRD PLEBEIAN
There's not a nobler man in Rome than Antony.
FOURTH PLEBEIAN
Now mark him. He begins again to speak.

ANTONY
But yesterday the word of Caesar might
Have stood against the world. Now lies he there,
And none so poor to do him reverence.
O masters, if I were disposed to stir
Your hearts and minds to mutiny and rage,
I should do Brutus wrong, and Cassius wrong,
Who, you all know, are honorable men.
I will not do them wrong; I rather choose
To wrong the dead, to wrong myself and you,
Than I will wrong such honorable men.

ANTONY (cont.)
But here's a parchment with the seal of Caesar.
I found it in his closet; 'tis his will.
Let but the commons hear this testament—
Which, pardon me, I do not mean to read—
And they would go and kiss dead Caesar's wounds
And dip their napkins in his sacred blood,
Yea, beg a hair of him for memory,
And dying, mention it within their wills,
Bequeathing it as a rich legacy
Unto their issue.

FOURTH PLEBEIAN
We'll hear the will! Read it, Mark Antony.

ALL
The will, the will! We will hear Caesar's will.
ANTONY
Have patience, gentle friends: I must not read it.
It is not meet you know how Caesar loved you.
You are not wood, you are not stones, but men;
And being men, hearing the will of Caesar,
It will inflame you, it will make you mad.
'Tis good you know not that you are his heirs,
For if you should, O, what would come of it?
FOURTH PLEBEIAN
Read the will! We'll hear it, Antony.
You shall read us the will, Caesar's will.
ANTONY
Will you be patient? Will you stay awhile?
I have o'ershot myself to tell you of it.
I fear I wrong the honorable men
Whose daggers have stabbed Caesar; I do fear it.

FOURTH PLEBEIAN
They were traitors. "Honorable men"!
ALL
The will! The testament!
SECOND PLEBEIAN
They were villains, murderers. The will! Read the will!
ANTONY
You will compel me then to read the will?
Then make a ring about the corpse of Caesar
And let me show you him that made the will.
Shall I descend? And will you give me leave?
ALL
Come down.
SECOND PLEBEIAN
Descend.

THIRD PLEBEIAN
You shall have leave.
FOURTH PLEBEIAN
A ring; stand round.
FIRST PLEBEIAN
Stand from the hearse. Stand from the body.
SECOND PLEBEIAN
Room for Antony, most noble Antony.

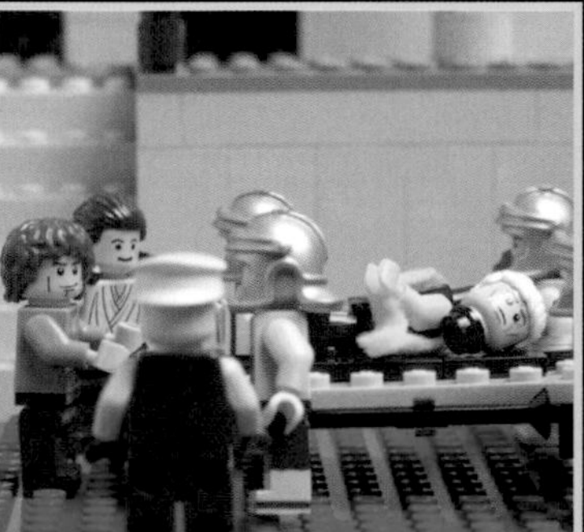

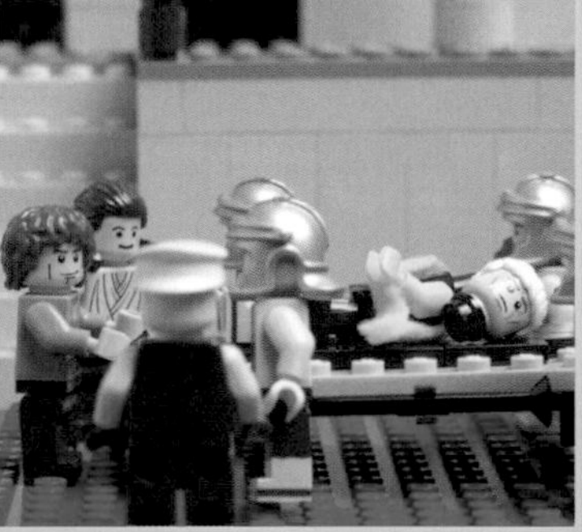

ANTONY
Nay, press not so upon me;
stand farre off.
ALL
Stand back! Room! Bear back!

ANTONY
If you have tears, prepare to shed them now.
You all do know this mantle. I remember
The first time ever Caesar put it on;
'Twas on a summer's evening in his tent,
That day he overcame the Nervii:
Look, in this place ran Cassius' dagger through.
See what a rent the envious Casca made.
Through this the well-belovèd Brutus stabbed,
And as he plucked his cursèd steel away,
Mark how the blood of Caesar followed it,
As rushing out of doors to be resolved
If Brutus so unkindly knocked or no;
For Brutus, as you know, was Caesar's angel.
Judge, O you gods, how dearly Caesar loved him!
This was the most unkindest cut of all;
For when the noble Caesar saw him stab,
Ingratitude, more strong than traitors' arms,
Quite vanquished him. Then burst his mighty heart,
And in his mantle muffling up his face,
Even at the base of Pompey's statue,
Which all the while ran blood, great Caesar fell.
O, what a fall was there, my countrymen!
Then I, and you, and all of us fell down,
Whilst bloody treason flourished over us.
O, now you weep, and I perceive you feel
The dint of pity. These are gracious drops.
Kind souls, what weep you when you but behold
Our Caesar's vesture wounded? Look you here,
Here is himself, marred as you see with traitors.

FIRST PLEBEIAN
O piteous spectacle!
SECOND PLEBEIAN
O noble Caesar!
THIRD PLEBEIAN
O woeful day!
FOURTH PLEBEIAN
O traitors, villains!
FIRST PLEBEIAN
O most bloody sight!
SECOND PLEBEIAN
We will be revenged.

ALL
Revenge! About! Seek! Burn! Fire! Kill! Slay!
Let not a traitor live!
ANTONY
Stay, countrymen.
FIRST PLEBEIAN
Peace there! Hear the noble Antony.
SECOND PLEBEIAN
We'll hear him, we'll follow him, we'll die with him.
ANTONY
Good friends, sweet friends, let me not stir you up
To such a sudden flood of mutiny.
They that have done this deed are honorable.
What private griefs they have, alas, I know not,
That made them do it. They are wise and honorable,
And will no doubt with reasons answer you.
I come not, friends, to steal away your hearts.
I am no orator, as Brutus is,
But, as you know me all, a plain blunt man
That love my friend, and that they know full well
That gave me public leave to speak of him.
For I have neither wit, nor words, nor worth,
Action, nor utterance, nor the power of speech
To stir men's blood. I only speak right on.
I tell you that which you yourselves do know,
Show you sweet Caesar's wounds, poor poor dumb mouths,
And bid them speak for me. But were I Brutus,
And Brutus Antony, there were an Antony
Would ruffle up your spirits and put a tongue
In every wound of Caesar that should move
The stones of Rome to rise and mutiny.

ALL
We'll mutiny.
FIRST PLEBEIAN
We'll burn the house of Brutus.
THIRD PLEBEIAN
Away, then! Come, seek the conspirators.
ANTONY
Yet hear me, countrymen. Yet hear me speak.
ALL
Peace, ho! Hear Antony, most noble Antony!
ANTONY
Why, friends, you go to do you know not what.
Wherein hath Caesar thus deserved your loves?
Alas, you know not. I must tell you then:
You have forgot the will I told you of.
ALL
Most true. The will! Let's stay and hear the will.

ANTONY
Here is the will, and under Caesar's seal.
To every Roman citizen he gives,
To every several man, seventy-five drachmas.
SECOND CITIZEN
Most noble Caesar! We'll revenge his death.
THIRD CITIZEN
O royal Caesar!
ANTONY
Hear me with patience.
ALL
Peace, ho!

FIRST PLEBEIAN
Never, never! Come, away, away!
We'll burn his body in the holy place
And with the brands fire the traitors' houses.
Take up the body.
SECOND PLEBEIAN
Go fetch fire!
THIRD PLEBEIAN
Pluck down benches!
FOURTH PLEBEIAN
Pluck down forms, windows, anything!

ANTONY
Now let it work. Mischief, thou art afoot,
Take thou what course thou wilt!

ACT III. Scene III (1–38).

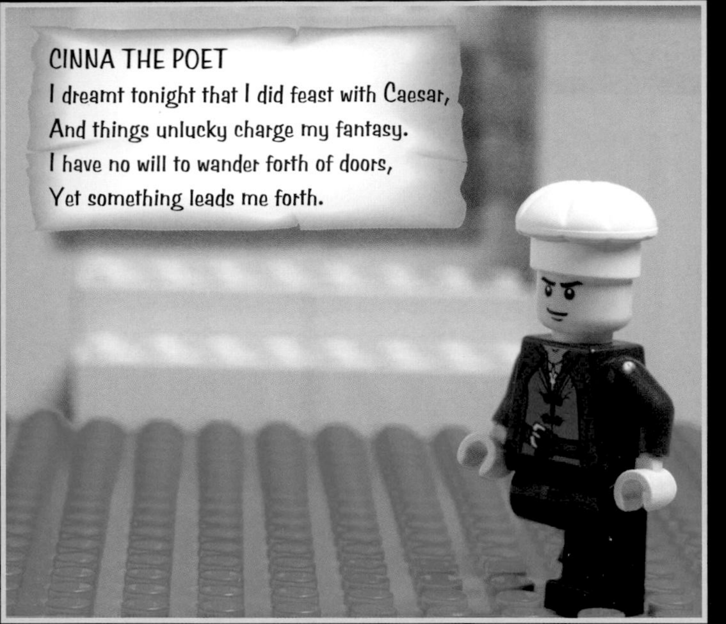

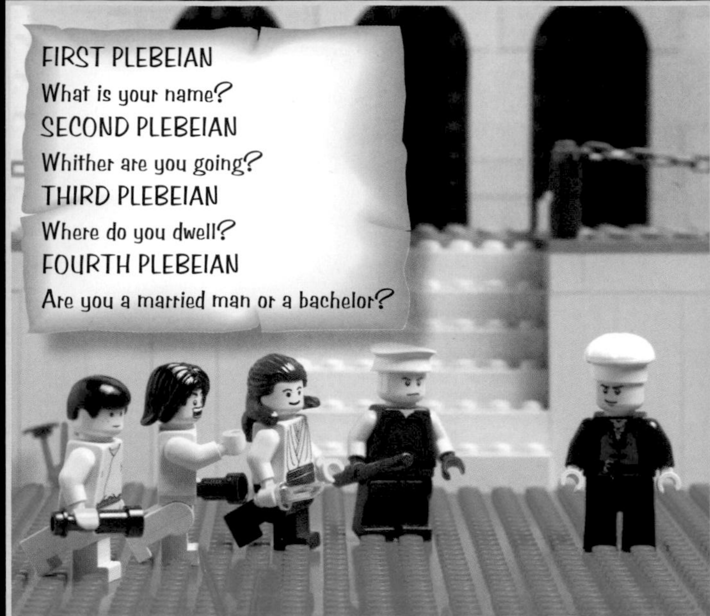

SECOND PLEBEIAN
Answer every man directly.
FIRST PLEBEIAN
Ay, and briefly.
FOURTH PLEBEIAN
Ay, and wisely.
THIRD PLEBEIAN
Ay, and truly, you were best.

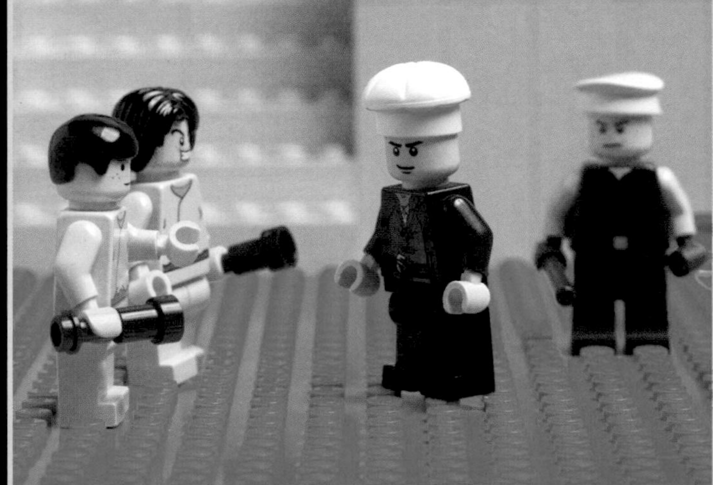

CINNA THE POET
What is my name? Whither am I going? Where do I dwell? Am I a married man or a bachelor? Then to answer every man directly and briefly, wisely and truly: wisely I say, I am a bachelor.
SECOND PLEBEIAN
That's as much as to say they are fools that marry. You'll bear me a bang for that, I fear. Proceed directly.

CINNA THE POET
Directly, I am going to Caesar's funeral.
FIRST PLEBEIAN
As a friend or an enemy?
CINNA THE POET
As a friend.
SECOND PLEBEIAN
That matter is answered directly.

FOURTH PLEBEIAN
For your dwelling—briefly.
CINNA THE POET
Briefly, I dwell by the Capitol.

THIRD PLEBEIAN
Your name, sir, truly.
CINNA THE POET
Truly, my name is Cinna.
FIRST PLEBEIAN
Tear him to pieces! He's a conspirator!

CINNA THE POET
I am Cinna the poet, I am Cinna the poet!
FOURTH PLEBEIAN
Tear him for his bad verses, tear him for his bad verses!

CINNA THE POET
I am not Cinna the conspirator.
FOURTH PLEBEIAN
It is no matter, his name's Cinna. Pluck but his
name out of his heart, and turn him going.

THIRD PLEBEIAN
Tear him, tear him! Come, brands, ho, firebrands!
To Brutus', to Cassius'; burn all! Some to Decius'
house, and some to Casca's; some to Ligarius'. Away, go!

ACT II. Scene III (240–307).

J

C

Brutus, Cassius, and the other conspirators have fled the violence in Rome and have gathered their armies to prepare to meet their enemies on the battlefield. Antony has allied himself with Caesar's loyal follower Lepidus, and his nephew Octavius, to form a triumvirate to rule Rome; they are gathering their own armies to fight the rebels.

The mood is somber and tense in the conspirator's camp: Brutus and Cassius bicker for a time, and they are further moved by sad news: Brutus's wife Portia has taken her own life, and many other friends have had their lives ended by their own hand or at the command of the triumvirate. They hear that Octavius and Antony march with a large army, and they plan their next actions. Brutus, still convinced of the righteousness of their fight, says they should march to meet their enemy at Philippi and attack before the enemy has a chance. Cassius thinks this is unwise, and suggests they make the enemy chase them and tire themselves out before they try to engage in direct combat. But Brutus says, "Our legions are brim full, our cause is ripe./The enemy increaseth every day;/We, at the height, are ready to decline" (IV.iii.214–217). He decides that they should strike now with their armies strong and well-rested, before Antony and Octavius have time to gather even more powerful allies from Rome and the surrounding countryside.

With this decided, Brutus settles down, until a strange visitor interrupts his sleep.

BRUTUS
Farewell, every one.
Give me the gown. Where is thy instrument?
LUCIUS
Here in the tent.
BRUTUS
What, thou speak'st drowsily!
Poor knave, I blame thee not; thou art o'er-watched.
Call Claudius and some other of my men;
I'll have them sleep on cushions in my tent.

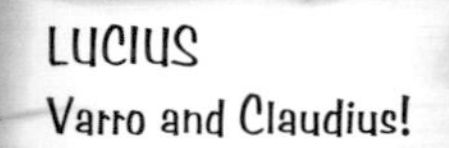

VARRO
Calls my lord?
BRUTUS
I pray you, sirs, lie in my tent and sleep.
It may be I shall raise you by and by
On business to my brother Cassius.
VARRO
So please you, we will stand and watch your pleasure.

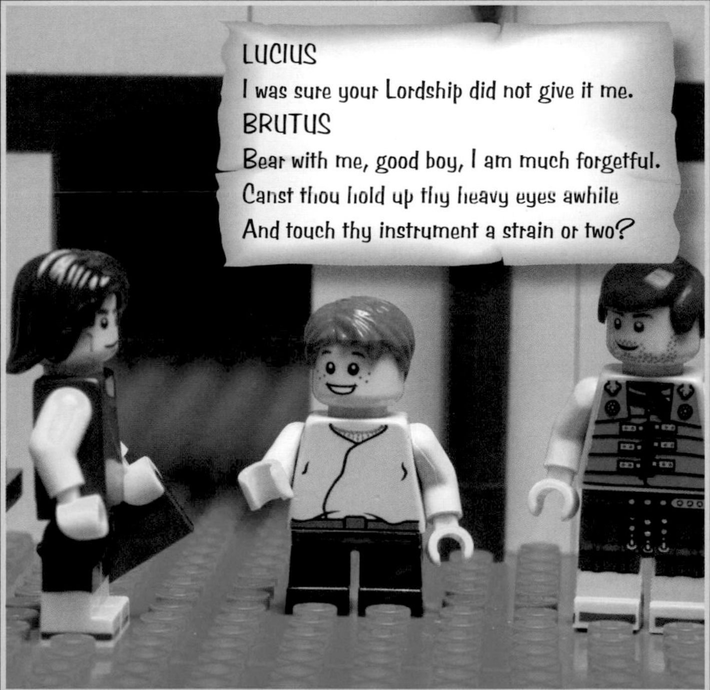

LUCIUS
Ay, my lord, an't please you.
BRUTUS
It does, my boy.
I trouble thee too much, but thou art willing.

LUCIUS
It is my duty, sir.
BRUTUS
I should not urge thy duty past thy might;
I know young bloods look for a time of rest.
LUCIUS
I have slept, my lord, already.

BRUTUS
It was well done, and thou shalt sleep again;
I will not hold thee long. If I do live,
I will be good to thee.
This is a sleepy tune. O murd'rous slumber,
Layest thou thy leaden mace upon my boy,
That plays thee music? Gentle knave, good night;
I will not do thee so much wrong to wake thee.
If thou dost nod, thou break'st thy instrument;
I'll take it from thee. And, good boy, good night.
Let me see, let me see; is not the leaf turned down
Where I left reading? Here it is, I think.

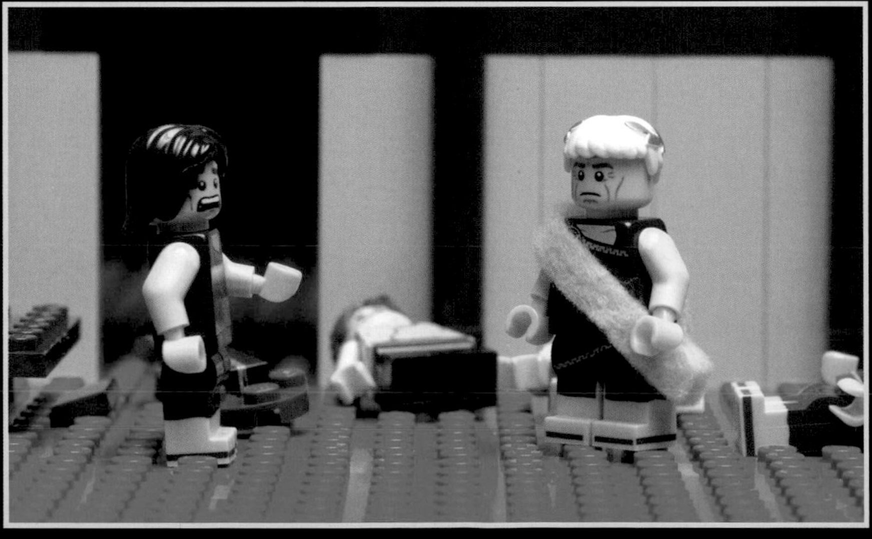

BRUTUS (cont.)
How ill this taper burns! Ha! Who comes here?
I think it is the weakness of mine eyes
That shapes this monstrous apparition.
It comes upon me.—Art thou any thing?
Art thou some god, some angel, or some devil,
That mak'st my blood cold and my hair to stare?
Speak to me what thou art.
GHOST
Thy evil spirit, Brutus.
BRUTUS
Why com'st thou?
GHOST
To tell thee thou shalt see me at Philippi.

LUCIUS
The strings, my lord, are false.
BRUTUS
He thinks he still is at his instrument.—
Lucius, awake!
LUCIUS
My lord?
BRUTUS
Didst thou dream, Lucius, that thou so cried'st out?
LUCIUS
My lord, I do not know that I did cry.
BRUTUS
Yes, that thou didst. Didst thou see anything?
LUCIUS
Nothing, my lord.
BRUTUS
Sleep again, Lucius.

BRUTUS (cont.)
Sirrah Claudius!
Fellow thou, awake!
VARRO
My lord?
CLAUDIUS
My lord?

BRUTUS
Why did you so cry out, sirs, in your sleep?
VARRO CLAUDIUS
Did we, my lord?

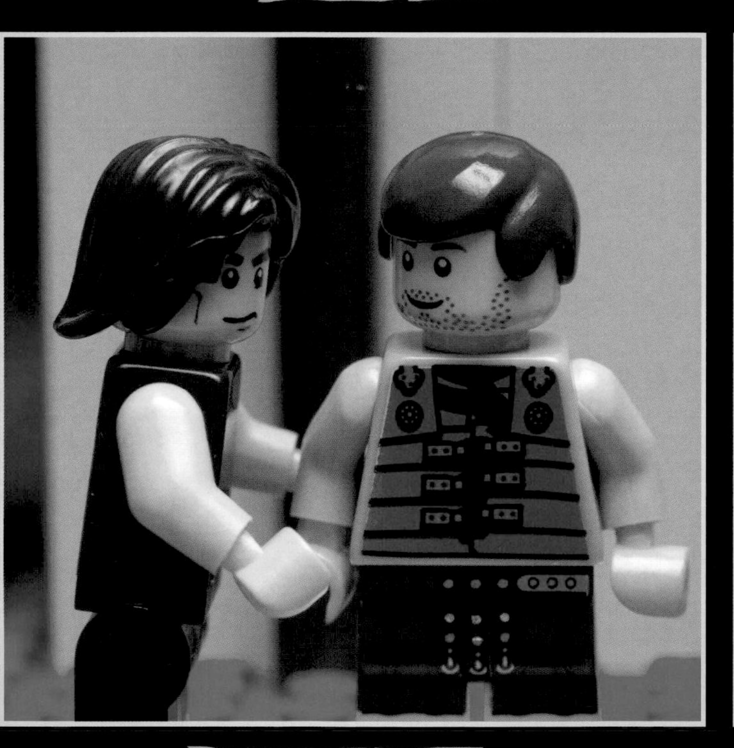

BRUTUS
Ay. Saw you anything?
VARRO
No, my lord, I saw nothing.
CLAUDIUS
Nor I, my lord.

BRUTUS
Go and commend me to my brother Cassius.
Bid him set on his powers betimes before,
And we will follow.
VARRO AND CLAUDIUS
It shall be done, my lord.

ACT V. Scene I (21–66).

The armies meet at Philippi and prepare for battle . . .

BRUTUS
They stand and would have parley.
CASSIUS
Stand fast, Titinius. We must out and talk.

OCTAVIUS
Mark Antony, shall we give sign of battle?
ANTONY
No, Caesar, we will answer on their charge.
Make forth. The generals would have some words.
OCTAVIUS
Stir not until the signal.

BRUTUS
Words before blows. Is it so, countrymen?
OCTAVIUS
Not that we love words better, as you do.
BRUTUS
Good words are better than bad strokes, Octavius.

ANTONY
In your bad strokes, Brutus, you give good words.
Witness the hole you made in Caesar's heart,
Crying "Long live! Hail, Caesar!"

CASSIUS
Antony,
The posture of your blows are yet unknown;
But for your words, they rob the Hybla bees,
And leave them honeyless.
ANTONY
Not stingless too?

BRUTUS
O, yes, and soundless too.
For you have stol'n their buzzing, Antony,
And very wisely threat before you sting.

ANTONY
Villains, you did not so when your vile daggers
Hacked one another in the sides of Caesar.
You showed your teeth like apes, and fawned like hounds,
And bowed like bondmen, kissing Caesar's feet,
Whilst damnèd Casca, like a cur, behind,
Struck Caesar on the neck. O you flatterers!

CASSIUS
Flatterers? Now, Brutus, thank yourself!
This tongue had not offended so today
If Cassius might have ruled.

OCTAVIUS
Come, come, the cause. If arguing make us sweat,
The proof of it will turn to redder drops.
Look, I draw a sword against conspirators.
When think you that the sword goes up again?
Never, till Caesar's three-and-thirty wounds
Be well avenged, or till another Caesar
Have added slaughter to the sword of traitors.

BRUTUS
Caesar, thou canst not die by traitors' hands,
Unless thou bring'st them with thee.
OCTAVIUS
So I hope.
I was not born to die on Brutus' sword.

BRUTUS
O, if thou wert the noblest of thy strain,
Young man, thou couldst not die more honorable.
CASSIUS
A peevish schoolboy, worthless of such honor,
Joined with a masker and a reveler!
ANTONY
Old Cassius still!

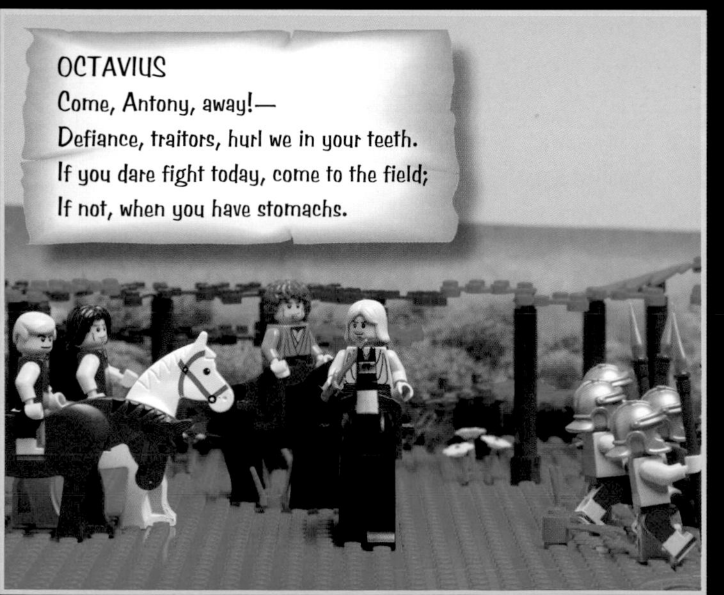

ACT V. Scene II (1–6).

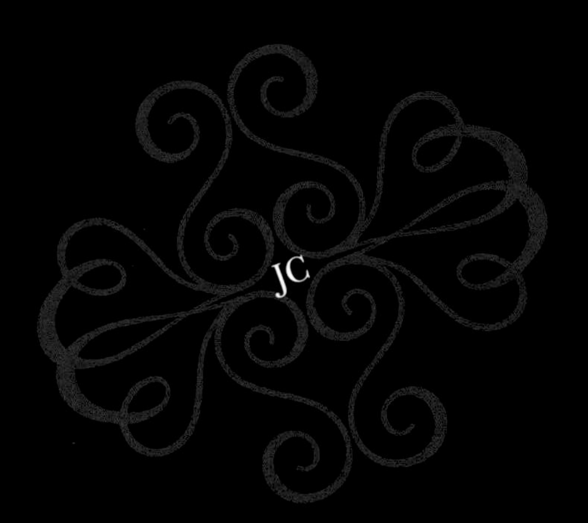

Before they depart to lead their armies in battle, Brutus and Cassius meet once more. Cassius is still reluctant; he clearly expects them to fail, and he declares that he will end his own life before he will be taken captive. Brutus makes no such promises but calls it "cowardly and vile" to end your own life. Brutus is hardly more optimistic than Cassius, as he ends their meeting saying "Oh, that a man might know/The end of this day's business ere it come!/But it sufficeth that the day will end,/And then the end is known" (V.i.124–127).

BRUTUS
Ride, ride, Messala, ride, and give these bills
Unto the legions on the other side.
VENI,
VIDI, VICI

BRUTUS (cont.)
Let them set on at once; for I perceive
But cold demeanor in Octavius' wing,
And sudden push gives them the overthrow.
Ride, ride, Messala! Let them all come down.

ACT V. Scene III (1–110).

CASSIUS
O, look, Titinius, look, the villains fly!
Myself have to mine own turned enemy.
This ensign here of mine was turning back;
I slew the coward and did take it from him.

TITINIUS
O Cassius, Brutus gave the word too early,
Who, having some advantage on Octavius,
Took it too eagerly. His soldiers fell to spoil,
Whilst we by Antony are all enclosed.

PINDARUS
Fly further off, my lord, fly further off!
Mark Antony is in your tents, my lord.
Fly, therefore, noble Cassius, fly far off.

CASSIUS
This hill is far enough. Look, look, Titinius:
Are those my tents where I perceive the fire?

TITINIUS
They are, my lord.

CASSIUS
Titinius, if thou lovest me,
Mount thou my horse, and hide thy spurs in him
Till he have brought thee up to yonder troops
And here again, that I may rest assured
Whether yond troops are friend or enemy.

TITINIUS
I will be here again even with a thought.

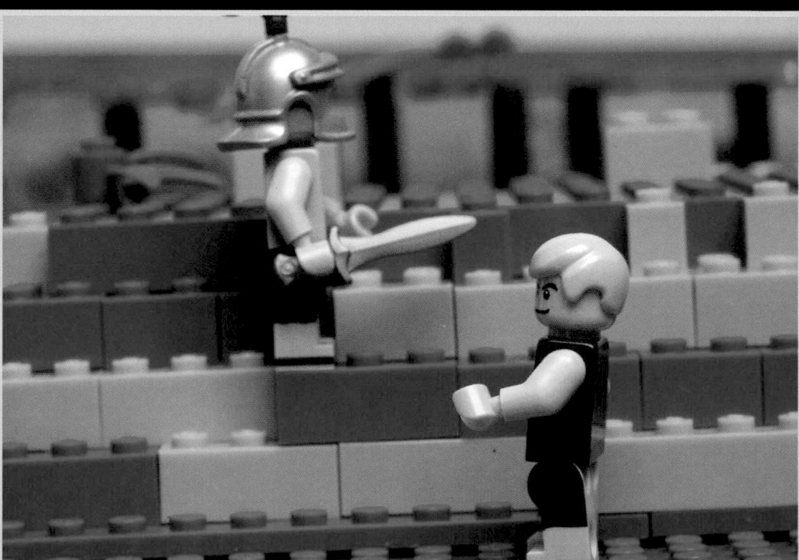

CASSIUS
Go, Pindarus, get higher on that hill.
My sight was ever thick. Regard Titinius,
And tell me what thou not'st about the field.
This day I breathèd first. Time is come round,
And where I did begin, there shall I end.
My life is run his compass.—Sirrah, what news?

PINDARUS
O my lord!
CASSIUS
What news?
PINDARUS
Titinius is enclosèd round about
With horsemen, that make to him on the spur,
Yet he spurs on. Now they are almost on him.
Now, Titinius! Now some light. O, he lights too.
He's ta'en. And, hark! They shout for joy.
CASSIUS
Come down, behold no more.
O, coward that I am, to live so long
To see my best friend ta'en before my face!

CASSIUS (cont.)
Come hither, sirrah.
In Parthia did I take thee prisoner,
And then I swore thee, saving of thy life,
That whatsoever I did bid thee do
Thou shouldst attempt it. Come now, keep thine oath;
Now be a freeman, and with this good sword,
That ran through Caesar's bowels, search this bosom.
Stand not to answer. Here, take thou the hilts,
And, when my face is covered, as 'tis now,
Guide thou the sword.

CASSIUS (cont.)
Caesar, thou art revenged,
Even with the sword that killed thee.

PINDARUS
So, I am free, yet would not so have been,
Durst I have done my will. O Cassius!
Far from this country Pindarus shall run,
Where never Roman shall take note of him.

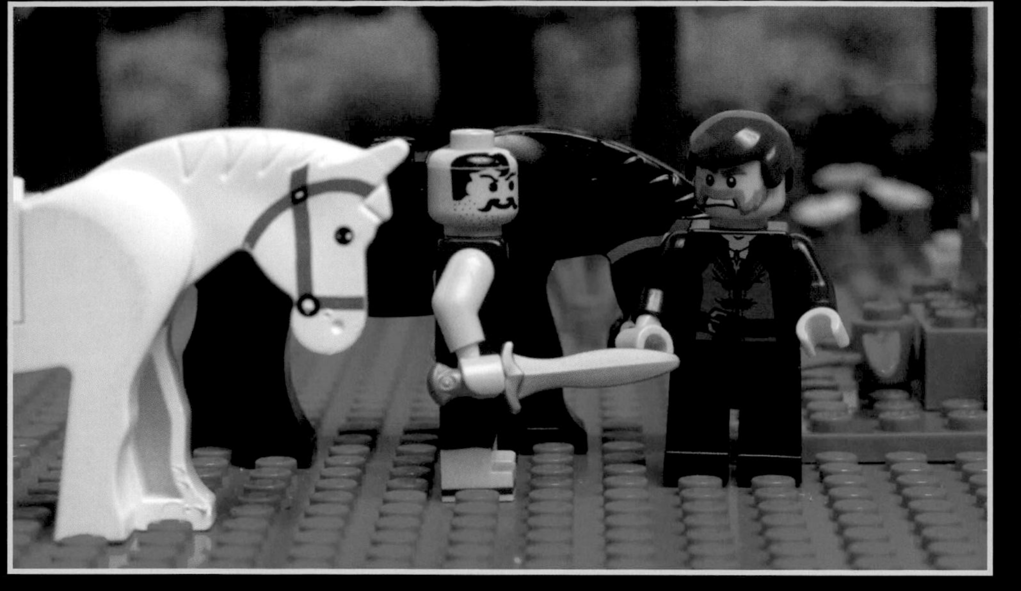

MESSALA
It is but change, Titinius; for Octavius
Is overthrown by noble Brutus' power,
As Cassius' legions are by Antony.
TITINIUS
These tidings will well comfort Cassius.
MESSALA
Where did you leave him?

TITINIUS
All disconsolate,
With Pindarus his bondman, on this hill.
MESSALA
Is not that he that lies upon the ground?

TITINIUS
He lies not like the living. O my heart!
MESSALA
Is not that he?

TITINIUS
No, this was he, Messala,
But Cassius is no more. O setting sun,
As in thy red rays thou dost sink tonight,
So in his red blood Cassius' day is set.
The sun of Rome is set. Our day is gone;
Clouds, dews, and dangers come; our deeds are done!
Mistrust of my success hath done this deed.

MESSALA
Mistrust of good success hath done this deed.
O hateful Error, Melancholy's child,
Why dost thou show to the apt thoughts of men
The things that are not? O Error, soon conceived,
Thou never com'st unto a happy birth,
But kill'st the mother that engendered thee!
TITINIUS
What, Pindarus! Where art thou, Pindarus?

MESSALA
Seek him, Titinius, whilst I go to meet
The noble Brutus, thrusting this report
Into his ears. I may say "thrusting" it,
For piercing steel and darts envenomèd
Shall be as welcome to the ears of Brutus
As tidings of this sight.
TITINIUS
Hie you, Messala,
And I will seek for Pindarus the while.

TITINIUS (cont.)
Why didst thou send me forth, brave Cassius?
Did I not meet thy friends? And did not they
Put on my brows this wreath of victory
And bid me give it thee? Didst thou not hear their shouts?
Alas, thou hast misconstrued everything.
But, hold thee, take this garland on thy brow.
Thy Brutus bid me give it thee, and I
Will do his bidding. Brutus, come apace
And see how I regarded Caius Cassius.
By your leave, gods! This is a Roman's part.
Come, Cassius' sword, and find Titinius' heart.

BRUTUS
Where, where, Messala, doth his body lie?
MESSALA
Lo, yonder, and Titinius mourning it.
BRUTUS
Titinius' face is upward.

CATO
He is slain.
BRUTUS
O Julius Caesar, thou art mighty yet!
Thy spirit walks abroad and turns our swords
In our own proper entrails.
CATO
Brave Titinius!
Look, whe'er he have not crowned dead Cassius!

BRUTUS
Are yet two Romans living such as these?
The last of all the Romans, fare thee well!
It is impossible that ever Rome
Should breed thy fellow. Friends, I owe more tears
To this dead man than you shall see me pay.—
I shall find time, Cassius, I shall find time.—
Come, therefore, and to Thasos send his body.
His funerals shall not be in our camp,
Lest it discomfort us. Lucilius, come,
And come, young Cato, let us to the field.
Labeo and Flavius, set our battles on.
'Tis three o'clock; and, Romans, yet ere night
We shall try fortune in a second fight.

ACT V. Scene V (1–51).

J

C

Cassius is dead, but Brutus and his men fight bravely on. More friends are killed, and others are captured by Antony and Octavius, but Brutus is able to flee, though his enemies follow closely behind and his friends are dead and gone, save a few remaining loyal servants.

BRUTUS
Come, poor remains of friends, rest on this rock.
CLITUS
Statilius showed the torchlight, but, my lord,
He came not back. He is or ta'en or slain.
BRUTUS
Sit thee down, Clitus. Slaying is the word.
It is a deed in fashion. Hark thee, Clitus.

CLITUS
What, I, my lord? No, not for all the world.
BRUTUS
Peace then. No words.
CLITUS
I'll rather kill myself.

CLITUS
O Dardanius!
DARDANIUS
O Clitus!
CLITUS
What ill request did Brutus make to thee?

BRUTUS
Why, this, Volumnius:
The ghost of Caesar hath appeared to me
Two several times by nigh—at Sardis once,
And this last night here in Philippi fields.
I know my hour is come.
VOLUMNIUS
Not so, my lord.
BRUTUS
Nay, I am sure it is, Volumnius.
Thou see'st the world, Volumnius, how it goes;
Our enemies have beat us to the pit.

BRUTUS (cont.)
It is more worthy to leap in ourselves
Than tarry till they push us. Good Volumnius,
Thou know'st that we two went to school together.
Even for that our love of old, I prithee,
Hold thou my sword hilts whilst I run on it.
VOLUMNIUS
That's not an office for a friend, my lord.

CLITUS
Fly, fly, my lord! There is no tarrying here.
BRUTUS
Farewell to you, and you, and you, Volumnius.
Strato, thou hast been all this while asleep;
Farewell to thee too, Strato. Countrymen,
My heart doth joy that yet in all my life
I found no man but he was true to me.
I shall have glory by this losing day
More than Octavius and Mark Antony
By this vile conquest shall attain unto.
So fare you well at once, for Brutus' tongue
Hath almost ended his life's history.
Night hangs upon mine eyes; my bones would rest,
That have but labored to attain this hour.
CLITUS
Fly, my lord, fly.
BRUTUS
Hence, I will follow.

BRUTUS (cont.)
I prithee, Strato, stay thou by thy lord.
Thou art a fellow of a good respect;
Thy life hath had some smatch of honor in it.
Hold then my sword, and turn away thy face,
While I do run upon it. Wilt thou, Strato?

STRATO
Give me your hand first. Fare you well, my lord.
BRUTUS
Farewell, good Strato.
Caesar, now be still.
I killed not thee with half so good a will.

ACT V. Scene V (68–81).

The enemy arrives at Brutus's camp too late to find him alive. The battle is ended but much has been lost. Antony takes a moment to speak over Brutus's body.

ANTONY
This was the noblest Roman of them all.
All the conspirators save only he
Did that they did in envy of great Caesar;
He only in a general honest thought
And common good to all made one of them.
His life was gentle, and the elements
So mixed in him that Nature might stand up
And say to all the world, "This was a man!"

OCTAVIUS
According to his virtue let us use him,
With all respect and rites of burial.
Within my tent his bones tonight shall lie,
Most like a soldier, ordered honorably.
So call the field to rest, and let's away
To part the glories of this happy day.

About the Authors

Members of the Hollan Publishing team, John McCann, Monica Sweeney, and Becky Thomas all collaborated to make *Brick Shakespeare* possible.

John McCann, Brick Engineer: John designed, constructed, and photographed the brick scenes. A New England native, John has over two decades of experience playing with LEGO bricks. He enjoys relaxing lakeside and can solve a Rubik's Cube in three days flat. John has a BS in Biomedical Engineering from the University of Hartford and is currently pursuing his Masters. This is his first book.

Monica Sweeney, Shakespeare Wrangler: Monica selected and interpreted Shakespeare scenes for construction and wrote corresponding narratives. Monica loves all things related to Spain and Chaucer, and has yet to say no to a mini powdered doughnut. She graduated with honors in English from the University of Massachusetts–Amherst. Monica and Becky have written several bestselling works together.

Becky Thomas, Shakespeare Wrangler: Becky selected and interpreted Shakespeare scenes for construction and wrote corresponding narratives. In her spare time, she enjoys breaking the bindings of all books Jane Austen, playing video games, and trying out new recipes. She lives with her husband, Patrick, and her cat, Leo. She graduated with honors in English from the University of Massachusetts–Amherst.

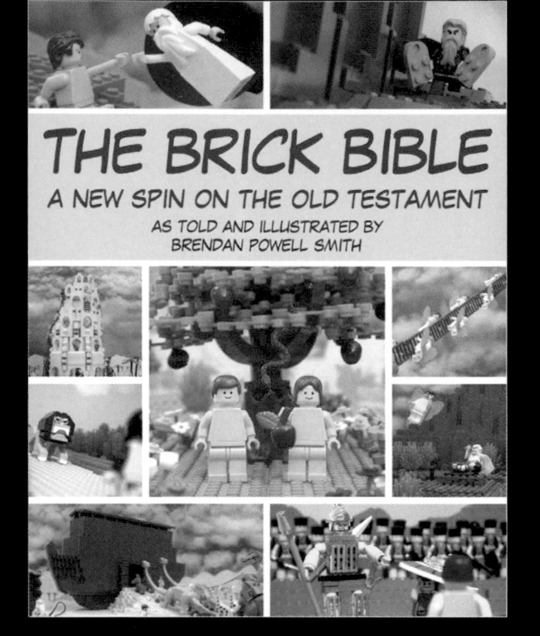

The Brick Bible

A New Spin on the Old Testament

by Brendan Powell Smith

Brendan Powell Smith has spent the last decade creating nearly 5,000 scenes from the bible—with Legos. His wonderfully original sets are featured on his website, Bricktestament.com, but for the first time, 1,500 photographs of these creative designs—depicting the Old Testament from Earth's creation to the Books of Kings—are brought together in book format. The Holy Bible is complex; sometimes dark, and other times joyous, and Smith's masterful work is a far cry from what a small child might build. The beauty of *The Brick Bible* is that everyone, from the devout to nonbelievers, will find something breathtaking, fascinating, or entertaining within this collection. Smith's subtle touch brings out the nuances of each scene and makes you reconsider the way you look at LEGOs—it's something that needs to be seen to be believed.

ALSO AVAILABLE

The Christmas Story

The Brick Bible for Kids

by Brendan Powell Smith

Santa, sleigh bells, mistletoe, reindeer, and presents: these are the tell-tale signs of Christmas. But for Christians, December 25 is also the time to celebrate the birth of Jesus, and what better way to introduce your kids to the story of the Savior's birth than through LEGO!

Every year, children of all ages revisit the scene in Bethlehem with Joseph, Mary, the three wise men, the angels and shepherds, and the baby Jesus, swaddled and lying in a manger. Kids will love seeing the story of Christmas played out using their favorite toys. Brendan Powell Smith, author of The Brick Bible for Kids series—beginning with *Noah's Ark*—creates a magical "brick" world around the simplified text of the Immaculate Conception, the census, the guiding star high above Bethlehem, and the promise one little baby brings to the Christians of the world. This important Christmas story is sure to be the perfect holiday gift and a book for families to cherish for years to come.

$12.95 Hardcover • ISBN 978-1-62087-173-7

ALSO AVAILABLE

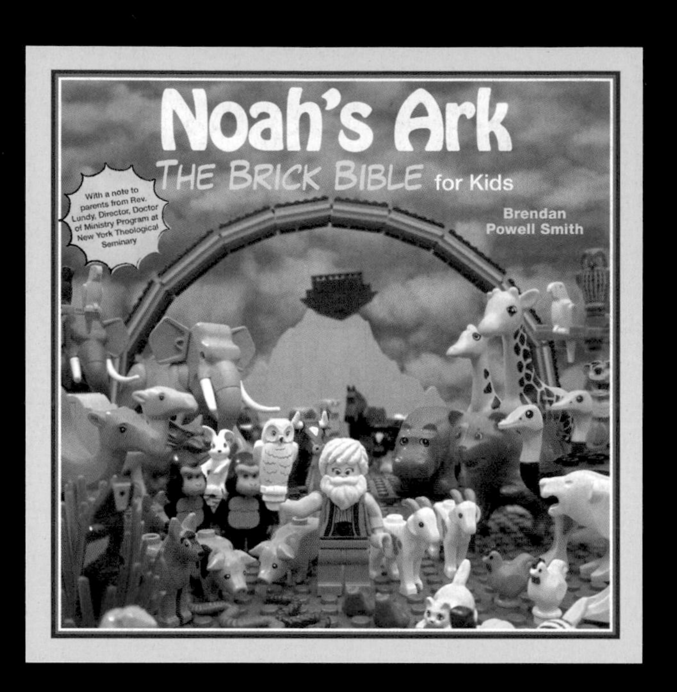

Noah's Ark

The Brick Bible for Kids

by Brendan Powell Smith

The story of Noah and his ark full of two of every animal on Earth has been a favorite Bible story of children for years. And now, for the first time, *Noah's Ark* is brought to life through LEGOs!

Kids will love seeing the world's flood and God's subsequent covenant with Noah to never destroy mankind again played out using their favorite toys. Brendan Powell Smith, creator of bricktestament.com and author of *The Brick Bible*, creates a magical "brick" world around the simplified text of the story of Noah, the flood, a wooden ark full of animals, and the promise of a rainbow. A story with a powerful message of forgiveness and love, this is the perfect gift for children.

$12.95 Hardcover • ISBN 978-1-61608-737-1

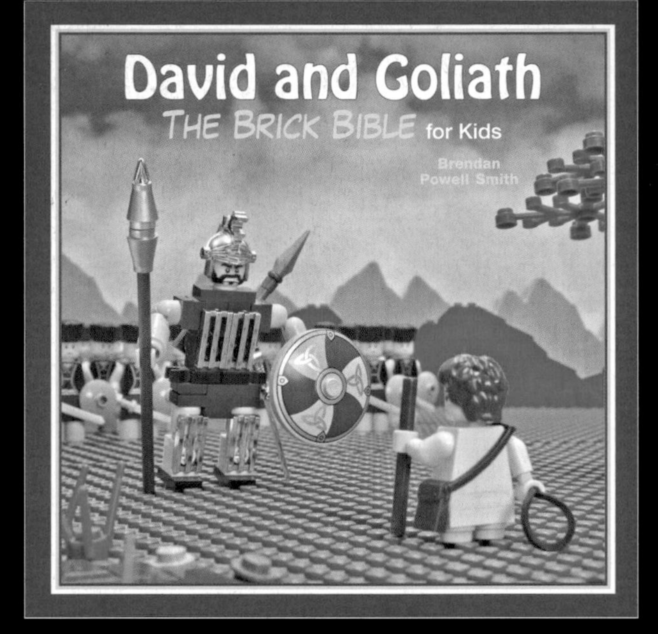

David and Goliath

The Brick Bible for Kids

by Brendan Powell Smith

The Philistine army has gathered for a vicious war against King Saul and the Israelites. With great suspense, a Philistine giant named Goliath boldly approaches the Israelites presenting a challenge: Defeat him and the Philistines will forever be their slaves; but if the Israelites lose, then they must become slaves to the Philistines. But who would want to defy such a giant, wearing only the finest armor and carrying the sharpest spear?

Nearby, a young boy named David is told to bring food to his older brothers in the army. When he arrives, he hears of Goliath's challenge. He offers to face the giant by himself. Goliath is convinced this must be some joke. But don't underestimate young David! Enjoy reading one of the Bible's best stories illustrated in LEGO as a family.

ALSO AVAILABLE

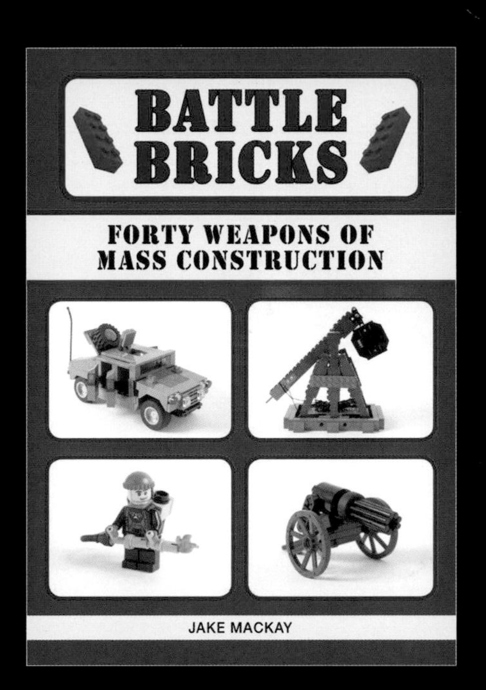

Battle Bricks

Forty Weapons of Mass Construction

by Jack Mackay

LEGO is fun. So are toy weapons. The only thing more fun is LEGO toy weapons! A compilation of badass brick weapons—some that actually even work—this book is designed for the adult brick enthusiast. Each project is original (i.e., not from a LEGO kit) and is accompanied by how-to schematics and full-color original photographs of the finished object. Dangerous and exciting projects include:

- Tomahawk
- Broadsword
- Claymore (two-handed sword)
- Ninja throwing star
- M1911 pistol
- Siege tower
- Gatling gun
- MK2 grenade
- Scythed chariot
- Paris gun
- Flamethrower
- And many more!

Hobbyists love to make weapons, and this book goes far beyond the kits that are available to showcase forty projects for amazing weapons. The projects range from medieval to modern, from small hand grenades to an actual working guillotine to an assault amphibious vehicle. *Battle Bricks* will keep adults occupied for hours and is the perfect book for the adult brick enthusiast, weapons hobbyist, or all-around badass!

$17.95 Paperback • ISBN 978-1-62636-304-5